THE MIDDLE OF NOWHERE

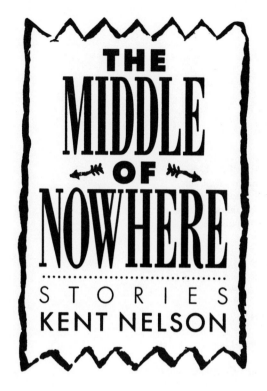

THE MIDDLE OF NOWHERE

STORIES

KENT NELSON

PEREGRINE SMITH BOOKS

SALT LAKE CITY

First edition

92 91 5 4 3 2 1

This is a Peregrine Smith Book, published by
Gibbs Smith, Publisher
 P.O. Box 667
Layton, UT 84041

Design by Galie Jean-Louis
Cover illustration by Pete Spino
Manufactured in the United States of America

Library of Congress Cataloging-in-Publication Data
Nelson, Kent, 1943-
        The middle of nowhere / Kent Nelson.
        p.   cm.
        ISBN 0-87905-393-3
        I. Title.
PS3564.E467M53   1991
813'.54—dc20k   91-8693
                                                    CIP

To Dylan and Taylor

Acknowledgments

The author is grateful to the following publications in which these stories originally appeared: *Agni Review:* "The Tarpon Bet"; *Boulevard:* "Yellow Flowers"; *Denver Quarterly:* "Spirits of Animals"; *Grand Street:* "The Middle of Nowhere"; *The Southern Review:* "Discoveries," "Learning to Dream," and "A Country of My Own Making"; *Southwest Review:* "The Mine from Nicaragua"; *The Virginia Quarterly Review:* "Invisible Life" and "The Trogon Dish." "Absences" was selected for the Pen Syndicated Fiction project.

Contents

THE MIDDLE OF NOWHERE

This happened just after I'd dropped out of high school, when I was seventeen and living with my father. We had this trailer out southwest of Tucson about twenty-three miles, right at the edge of what was then called the Papago Reservation, at the end of a dirt road which petered out into the Baboquivari Mountains. Across to the east you could see the Sierritas, which were a low rim of jagged hills, and to the south there was not much of anything except saguaros and greasewood and mesquite and the highway which ran from Robles Junction to Sasabe on the Mexican border.

Our trailer sat on a hill above two sand gullies. The previous occupants had seen fit to throw their trash into the steeper ravine, but the other one was a nice broad wash, rocky in places, with good cover for deer in the thickets of paloverde and ironwood. There were a couple of other trailers back down toward the highway, their TV antennas and satellite dishes the main evidence that someone else lived out there. Now and then you could hear a dog barking at coyotes at night.

By this time in my life I'd pretty much seen everything. I don't mean I had anything figured cold or that I possessed some ultimate knowledge. Pretty much the opposite was true. I mean, nothing surprised me anymore. When I was nine and ten I lived with my mother in Phoenix, and she had done about everything I could imagine. She drank and went on benders, leaving me in the apartment for two or three days at a time. And it was a crummy building. People got beaten up there, and I watched one man carried out on a stretcher.

My mother had boyfriends, too. When a man stayed over, I slept on the sofa instead of in the one bed my mother and I shared, and I could hear through the thin walls my mother's calling out a stranger's name. When the man liked me, it was all right, but when he didn't, which was more usual, I got shipped down on the Greyhound to my father.

I didn't mind it in Tucson. My father had a house in the barrio then, and there were lots of people moving around the streets at all hours. I liked to watch them doing their deals and loving up and just walking around. I liked the sirens and the shouts in Spanish and the music.

Sometimes I stayed a few days, sometimes a few weeks. But always a time came to go back.

"You sure you want to go?" my father used to ask.

"Why wouldn't I?"

"Your mother's not very well," he said. "She's fragile."

"I can take care of her."

The truth was I didn't know whether I wanted to go back. I didn't much like the apartment on the eighth floor or my mother's boyfriends. My father's girlfriends were nicer to me. But I kept thinking of my mother's sad face and how much she wanted to be happy.

So it went that way for a long time, back and forth between Phoenix and Tucson. I tried to get my mother to take better care of herself—to go to sleep earlier so she could get to her job, which was in a plant nursery over in Mesa, to eat better, and not to drink so much. She did all right for a while, until she met this man named Ray, who started her on pills. Ray moved in, and off I went to Tucson, thinking I'd stay for good.

My father and I got along pretty well. He was a spindly man, wiry, very good-looking in a rough way. He had good hands and a sleek brown mustache, and he was a smooth talker. Over against him, I was softer like my mother, with a disposition more inclined to observation. We weren't close, though, in the sense of camaraderie or talking things out. Maybe he felt guilty about leaving.

Anyway, we didn't discuss things much, so there were spaces around us unfilled, like something way late at night left unsaid.

I spent a whole school year when I was sixteen with my father and only saw my mother once. That was in the fall when she got sick and went to the hospital, and she called for me.

I guess I knew she was dying because I asked her questions I had never thought of before—what she used to be like when she was a girl in California, about her parents I'd never met (they owned a small artichoke farm), what she had hoped for in her life. She couldn't speak very well. By then she was sleeping most of the time, and she'd wake up only for brief glimpses of me. She'd start describing a place she remembered or a special day, and then she'd drift off into a terrible stillness.

When she died, I was left hanging.

After that I decided not to go back to school. I hadn't been a bad student or a troublemaker. I just hadn't done anything. I wrote my homework, but couldn't turn it in, and even when I knew an answer in class, I'd sit with my head down on the desk. The teachers talked to me; they sent me to counselors. Why wouldn't I try? Why not cooperate? They even got my one friend, George White Foot, a half-breed Apache, to speak to me. But finally they gave up and let me seep down into groundwater.

About this time my father got hold of the trailer. He had been evicted from his house, which was going to be torn down to make room for a renewal project, but I suspected he had other reasons for wanting to be out of town. He liked women. He had a way with them, too, but unlike my mother, he wanted the relationships to be simple.

My mother had been in love with every man she had ever met. But my father liked things uncomplicated, and one way to keep them that way was to live out in a trailer in the middle of nowhere.

So pretty much I stayed out at the trailer for the next year. My father might have made me get a job, but in a way I had the upper hand there. My mother had left me a few thousand dollars, and I was able to pay my share of rent and food. Now and then I'd go into Tucson to the library or a movie, but mostly I stayed home, as if I were waiting for something to happen. I didn't know what. It wasn't waiting exactly, either. It was passing time. It was as if everything up to then had been a test of endurance, and I had to recover from it. I needed to rest.

I spent some time watching the cars float along the highway

in the distance, imagining who was in them and what future they were heading toward. I could see pickup trucks coming from Mexico, red sedans, half-tons, vans. At night the headlights skimmed through the darkness like comets.

For a month I exhumed the trash in the ravine and tried to piece together the lives of the people who'd lived there before. I couldn't come up with much except they were poor, and someone had done a good trade with whoever sold Jim Beam.

But mostly I took target practice with the .22 and I read. I read everything I could get my hands on. My father brought me books and magazines whenever he happened to think of me—from the 7-11, from someone's house where he was repairing an air conditioner or a washing machine, from a girlfriend's apartment, sometimes even from the book mobile parked in the mall where his appliance repair company had its dispatch office. He never asked me what I liked. His idea was that in the general variety he'd hit on something that would move me off high center. He gave me manuals about engines, a history of Vietnam, a book on oil painting, porn magazines, English novels. I imagined him standing in front of a library shelf or a magazine rack wondering what he should take home to a son that he didn't have the slightest notion about.

But I knew him. His whole life was women. He met women in bars or on the job or at diners, supermarkets, offices, even at the bookmobile. He had a gift for it, a genius. Educated or uneducated; black, white, Hispanic; tall or short: he could have charmed the underwear off a nun. But there weren't many nuns who made the long drive to the trailer.

He had a system worked out. He'd bring a woman for a night and take her back to Tucson in the morning. It'd be dark when they'd get to the trailer—a turn at Robles Junction, head west on gravel, keep left when the road forked, and so on. The woman would ride blindfolded, so to speak. There was no telephone, either, so she couldn't ever call.

Sometimes he'd bring someone home on a Friday night, and she'd stay until Monday. I dreaded those weekends because my father worked Saturdays half-days, and often overtime, and he'd leave the woman, whoever she was, with me. On such occasions the woman usually slept late. One slept all day without stirring, and I was certain she was dead; another one, when she woke up late and looked out the window, thought she'd been sent to hell.

But the worst thing was there were no introductions. Sometimes my father hadn't even told the woman I was there, and more than once a woman I'd never seen before came naked from my father's bedroom and, when she saw me, started screaming. After a few times, I made it a habit on Saturday mornings to take target practice with the .22 from the kitchen window.

Even that wasn't enough every time. I had the idea my father asked some of his one-nighters to flirt with me, but it was a suspicion I never proved.

One rainy Saturday afternoon, for example, I was reading in the living room, listening occasionally to the barrage on the tin roof. My father was late. Out the window little waterfalls collected from nowhere and rushed into the gullies. The sandwash was a torrent. Then this woman, whose name was Jake, came to the window. Maybe she was watching for my father; maybe she thought he'd never get there in the storm. Maybe she was bored. Anyway, she turned to me and said, "Steve, do you want to make love?"

"Who-what?"

"Don't you think I'm pretty?"

Jake was pretty. She had a smooth oval face and dark eyes and nice high breasts which stood out under my father's shirt she had on. "I think you're very pretty."

"Well then?"

"You're my father's girl."

She made a face that was supposed to show hurt or maybe defiance, but which made her look spoiled. "I'm not anybody's girl," she said.

I won't say I wasn't tempted. Under ordinary circumstances I wouldn't have cared whose girl she was, but these were not ordinary circumstances. I wanted to kiss her and slap her both. I wanted to shake her. What did she mean offering herself like that? But I didn't say anything.

She came over and put her hand on my arm, and I felt a terrible dark chill run through me like a sliver of cold steel. In that instant I knew what torture my mother must have suffered to be so helpless in desire. But the rain stopped abruptly. The drumming on the roof ebbed to a hum, and not far down the gravel road, the headlights of my father's truck delved through the steam rising from the hot earth.

• • •

One woman stayed nearly a month. Her name was Esther, and she'd just been divorced from a doctor in Tucson and was waiting to hear about a nursing job in Los Angeles. She didn't have a place to stay, so my father said what-the-hell, and she came to the trailer.

She was not so pretty as most of the women my father had. She had curly hair and a broad face and rather sad blue eyes which looked right at you, which I liked. We used to drink beer together in the afternoons and play gin rummy at the kitchen table. She never asked about my father as some of the women did. Instead she asked about my mother: what was she like, what did she do, where was she? Why did she and my father get divorced?

I was usually a little drunk, and trying to answer was like exploring a region of myself I'd never encountered. I went down one wrong path after another, found dead ends, labyrinths. If I forced words too quickly, I missed details; if I labored too long, I became lost in a confusion of images. At the same time as it was hopeless to answer, I understood it was important to try. No matter what fleeting impression I gave, no matter how mystified I felt, I needed to know who my mother was to know who I was.

Esther didn't hurry me. She'd listen and fetch new beers. She was as solid as I was shaky. Her own divorce, she said, made her tougher, and she knew what she wanted. I admired her patience, and I remember it seemed hopeful to me at the time that someone could choose to change her life, get on a bus one day, and do it.

After Esther left for L.A., there was a month or so when my father didn't bring anyone home. During this stretch, George White Foot showed up one day with a bottle of tequila, which we took down into the sandwash, along with the .22. George told me he'd run into my father in a bar, and my father said I was anxious for company.

George had quit school, too. He was bagging groceries at the Safeway and thinking of going over to Safford to work in the copper mine. "You want to go?" he asked. "I got Apaches who can get you in."

"I'm not done here yet," I said.

George nodded and gulped the tequila. "What are you doing out here?"

"Taking notes."

He laughed and drank some more. "Taking notes on what?"

I didn't have an answer. I thought I was taking notes. I sighted the rifle and picked off a cholla blossom. "I bet I can outshoot you," I said. "I'll stand and you can shoot prone. A dollar a target."

"You have to drink some tequila," he said.

I drank some tequila, and George picked the targets, and I beat him five times in a row.

"Where'd you get the name White Foot?" I asked.

"Where'd you get the name Steve?"

He sat down in the sand and skewered the bottle down and took off his tennis shoes and socks. One of his feet was brown like his arms, but the other was albinistic—almost totally white up to the ankle.

I took off my boots and my socks. "I got two of them."

We laughed and drank more tequila, and he called me Steve White Feet. "I'll bet the five dollars I owe you, you can't give me the right question to the answer 'sis-boom-bah.'"

I pretended to think for a minute, but nothing came to mind. "I don't know."

"Guess."

I didn't want to guess. I was getting drunk and it struck me that George shouldn't go to work in the copper mine in Safford. It made me sad. "Don't go, George," I said.

He stared at me. He was drunker than I was. "Don't you want to know the question?" he asked.

"I want to know every question."

"An exploding sheep."

He laughed, but it wasn't funny. We put on our shoes again, finished the bottle of tequila, and staggered up the sandwash to hunt rabbits. By then the rabbits were safe.

TWO

It was late fall when something changed. The long-day heat was out of the rocks, and I had found a ledge behind an outcropping where I could sit and read and see nothing except the blue Sierritas and farther away the Las Guijas Hills and the Santa Ritas. Now and then through my binoculars I'd watch a hawk drifting on the updrafts which poured from the ravines.

One evening my father came home early with a stack of books from the bookmobile and some groceries. He actually sat down in the living room with me.

"I'm going to stay in town for a couple of days," he said.

THE MIDDLE OF NOWHERE

"Oh, yeah? What's her name?"

"Don't be that way."

"What way? I just asked what her name was."

"Goldie."

My father didn't often stay in town, but I didn't think much of it at the time. It didn't matter to me one way or the other. He didn't tell me the details, and I didn't ask.

"You be okay?"

"Sure," I said. "Thanks for the books."

A couple of days later I was on the ledge, when I heard the horn of my father's truck. I scrambled up to the ridge where I could see down to the trailer. In the circle of my binoculars, I made out my father standing on the porch beside a short-haired, dark-haired woman. He was waving for me to come down.

I figured this was Goldie, though I'd imagined her as a blond. She looked tall from a distance, as tall as my father anyway, who was six feet. She wore fancy sandals, and he had on cowboy boots. She looked like some kind of real-estate person, dressed in a gray business suit, or maybe a social worker, and for a moment I wondered whether my father had some deal going, some scam. A piece of sunlight flashed from one of her earrings.

I climbed down into the sandwash and halfway up the hill. My father and the woman appeared at the lip of the trail above me. I paused in a tangle of cholla and ocotillo and looked up. The woman's hair, which I'd thought was short, was pushed up on top of her head in a twist. The gray business suit was a sweater and slacks. I guessed she was about thirty, maybe a little older.

What impressed me most, though, was not the way she looked; it was the way my father looked. He kept motioning for me to hurry, and he had a grin on his face that seemed to say he had this secret he couldn't wait to tell me. He must have won the lottery, I thought, the way he was grinning.

"Steve," he said. "Come up here. This is Goldie. Goldie, this is my boy, Steve."

I climbed the last few yards, and Goldie took a step forward and put out her hand. I took her hand, felt the smooth palm. "You don't look like a Goldie," I said.

She squeezed my hand and smiled. "You don't look like a boy."

When I heard her voice, I knew she wasn't the lottery representative or a real-estate lady or like any of the other women who'd ever been to the trailer. Her voice slid over words with a lilting inflection like water over slickrock.

"She's Irish," my father said. "I met her on a job at her uncle's place out Gates Pass. We've been up at the Grand Canyon for a couple of days."

"Your father rescued me," Goldie said. She gave a small, sweet laugh.

"I thought, if she wants, she might as well stay out here a while," my father said. "What do you think, Steve?"

He'd never asked me before what I thought. "Sounds all right to me," I said. "If she wants."

Right away it was strained. Goldie liked privacy, and in a trailer privacy's as scarce a commodity as snow in hell. From back to front there was a bedroom, a hallway up one wall which joined the bathroom and a second small bedroom where I slept. The kitchen opened into the living room. Whenever Goldie wanted to use the bathroom, she knocked to make certain it was empty. And when she walked around the house, she had on at least a robe. In some ways it would have been easier having around a woman who didn't mind being seen half-undressed, even a flaunter, than one who was so prissy about things.

She also changed the hours of our days. My father didn't go drink in bars anymore, which was his usual habit after work. When Esther was there for that month, my father took her to bed as soon as he got home, but with Goldie it was more civilized. When my father tried to talk her into going to bed, she'd laugh and say in a voice both teasing and gentle, "You're nothing but a bloody Englishman."

Goldie wanted to learn to cook—not necessarily fancy things, but meals more substantial than hamburgers. She was anxious to try rabbit and venison and rattlesnake, and she liked Mexican food—burritos, jalapeño omelettes, enchiladas—which my father and I were pretty good at. So the three of us ate dinners at a normal hour. She called me Stephen, and I called her Blackie, and we talked about whatever happened to strike Goldie's fancy.

I could take the knocking on the bathroom door and the robe and the family dinners, but I chafed under Goldie's idea that the day started at five A.M. I liked to stay up late and read and then sleep in the next morning. So to hear Goldie making coffee in the dark drove me crazy. The kettle whistled, and she clanked silverware and unscrewed the jar of instant and got out the milk. Then the front door opened and closed. I'd lie there as the gray light seeped through the window, angry, unable to sleep. What was she doing outside? And how long was my father going to let this last?

Once I got up to see what she did at that hour. I expected to see her taking a walk down the road, or maybe doing calisthenics in the yard, or praying—something like that. But when I opened the door, Goldie was sitting on the porch steps bundled up in a wool coat against the chill of the desert. Her coffee was steaming into the air.

"What the hell are you doing?" I asked.

"Sometimes I miss Ireland," was all she said.

For the first several weeks, she went into town with my father in the mornings. She borrowed his truck and toured the countryside—the Desert Museum, the mission of San Xavier, the university, the Pima Air Museum. She ranged as far as Phoenix and Nogales, and even drove by herself through the Papago Reservation to Puerto Peñasco on the Gulf of California.

She asked me to go with her once. It was on one of those stormy days when low-flying clouds banked into the Baboquivaris and slipped over into the basin. I couldn't go up to my ledge, so I said all right, I'd go. She wanted to go into the Catalinas to the top of Mount Lemmon. So that's what we did. The road started in ocotillo and saguaro along Tanque Verde Drive and wound up into oaks and sycamores. A warm misty rain was falling. But when we got higher into the pines it was snowing. I'd seen snow before, but I'd only been in it once, up in Flagstaff when I was about nine. My mother had gone up there to surprise a man—just the kind of scene my father hated. This man had told her he owned a sporting goods store, and we went to every store in Flagstaff before we found him. It turned out he was a salesman, and he obviously wasn't expecting my mother. She sent me outside to play, and it was snowing on the streets. I remember how dirty the snow seemed, mashed down by tires and turning the buildings gray.

But at the top of Mount Lemmon the snow was clean. The pale trees were ghostly as the air, and even the road was white and unmarked.

"You should see the snow fall into the sea," Goldie said.

"I've never seen the sea."

"Oh, you must, Stephen. I live in Donaghadee, which is a fishing village near Belfast, and to watch the snow settle over the boats in the harbor and sweep across the gray water . . . it's lovely really."

The snow was beautiful then, too, coming down through the huge ponderosas. We came out of the trees into a clearing where the whole world looked white.

"Stop," Goldie said.

I pulled over, though there were no other cars. Goldie got out and ran into the meadow full of snow. It was so white you couldn't tell where the hills were or how far the meadow extended into the whiteness. I didn't know what she was doing. She looked so frail, running like that into the wide expanse of nothing. It was eerie to see her fading behind the white sheen, as if the air were a deep hole and would swallow her.

I rolled down the window and called to her, but she didn't stop running.

Two months went by, right into December, and Goldie was still there. She had stopped going into town with my father. I guess she'd seen as many museums and churches as anyone could stand.

So she stayed at the trailer with me. Not that I found that a problem: by then I was used to the way she did things. When she got dressed, I stayed out of her way, and I developed a grudging respect for her five A.M. coffee. Sometimes I got up and watched the sunrise with her, and we all had breakfast together like ordinary people.

After my father went off to work, Goldie and I sorted out the day. Sometimes we hunted the wash for rabbits or quail, and Goldie got so she could shoot a bird in the head from twenty-five yards. I showed her how to hold the dead bird tightly and break the skin at the breastbone so the skin and feathers peeled back like a jacket. We cleaned the quail and soaked them in salt water and made stuffing with bread and spices.

More often we just scouted the terrain. Goldie liked the desert. Ireland was cool and wet, the antithesis of the Southwest, and she was fascinated how the ocotillo rolled its leaves in the dryness and the saguaros stored tons of water. We looked for animals—coatis, javelinas, snakes. She saw animals more quickly than I, maybe because the land was new to her. She picked out a stock-still deer on the hillside, an eagle sitting on rocks with a rock background.

"Do you think we could see a mountain lion?" she asked.

"Not in daytime."

"I'd like awfully to see one."

"They're here," I said, "but they hunt at night."

That evening she begged my father to take her to look for a mountain lion.

"A puma, hah!" my father said. "We wouldn't have the chance of a pimp at St. Peter's to see a mountain lion."

"We could drive the back roads," Goldie said. "Don't they hunt at night?"

"No thanks," my father said. He pinched her arm and smiled patiently, and every night for two weeks after that, they drove the back roads over in the Papago Reservation.

Something changed during these excursions. When they returned late at night my father looked haggard and drawn, and he'd sit down and have a stiff shot of rye whiskey. He wasn't angry or short with me or with Goldie. He'd talk normally, but I could tell the trip had exhausted him in a way that was beyond just the driving. At first I thought it was burning the candle late and early. My father wasn't used to staying up till midnight and waking up at five. But it was more than that.

The next night, just as they were about to leave, I asked whether I could go along. "Do you mind?" I asked Goldie.

"You don't want to go," my father said.

"Why don't I?"

"You don't."

He wouldn't give a reason, and Goldie didn't mind, so I went. She sat between us in the front seat, and nothing much happened on the paved road over to the reservation. Then, when we turned off, Goldie sat forward. She braced her hands on the dash, pressed her face close to the windshield. We proceeded slowly, thirty miles an hour or so, the speed at which Goldie said she could see best. The headlights jerked over mesquite and saguaro and cholla, and sometimes we ran without a bend in the track for ten miles or more toward villages whose names were no names—Vamori, Idak, Gu Oidak.

All the while Goldie talked. The silhouette of her glassy forehead and her arced nose and her mouth blurred against the splayed light that moved in front of the truck, but she spoke without pause, in that lilting voice. She recounted incidents from her childhood in Donaghadee. Her father was a fisherman, her mother a baker. They had a small house, old it was, she said, down at the rocks. She had got a stipend to study in Dublin, the first of her family to go away to school. They had all been fishermen laboring over nets and boats. . . .

———

And I gradually began to feel the cloudy days over the sea, and to see the long, sloping green farms bordered by gray stone walls. And I felt my father sink down gently behind the wheel.

We saw kangaroo rats, badgers, snakes, deer. Once a coyote crossed the track in front of the lights. But there were no mountain lions.

Not long after that, my father stopped taking Goldie on those late rides. He said it was the expense of the gas, and finding a mountain lion was against all odds. But I understood it was something else which troubled him. He had come up against a problem he'd never faced before, which was what to do next. He liked Goldie. She was the first woman he'd cared about since my mother, or maybe ever, but she was a strain on him, too. Normally he was the one in control, the person to say what happened, but with Goldie he found himself the one holding on. At dinner he'd stare at her, not listening to her talk, but looking at her as if he were trying to figure out something. From what I could tell, Goldie was satisfied with her life. She had no plans to leave. But the idea of her leaving was always there in the air like a hawk circling, throwing its shadow across the ground.

It was about this time, too, that I went to see George White Foot. He was on the last half hour of his shift at the Safeway over on Speedway, and when I first got a glimpse of him—black hair in a ponytail, tall, slouched over the end of one of the check-out stands, he looked as though he were moving in slow motion.

"Hey, George," I said.

"If it isn't Steve White Feet," he said. "What you got, man?"

His eyes were glazed, and I could tell he was operating on batteries. "I was going to buy a six-pack," I said. "What kind do you like?"

"Any kind."

I bought a double-pack of Miller and waited in the truck. When George finished, we drove out Tanque Verde. All along the highway huge divots had been scoured in the saguaro and greasewood for new houses. While one crew scraped the hillside, another was erecting frames for the families that would settle there. I wondered where the water would come from.

But George wasn't paying attention to the houses. He was swilling beer and staring through the neon lights. "I'm going to

Safford next week," he said. "Are you done out there yet with your old man?"

"Not yet."

"Shit," George said in a disgusted voice. Then he softened. "It's not bad pay. The union takes an interest."

"I'm not a copper miner," I said.

"Neither am I."

I imagined the daylight breaking across the huge orange copper pit, and men filing one at a time through a metal gate. All day they would chew the earth to pieces with huge machines, then go home and come back the next day. At the end of the week, they'd have money.

"You got to do something, Steve," George said.

He looked at me, but his eyes were blank. "Give yourself a break," I told him. "You don't have to go."

"A break? Like you? Give myself a break like you? At least I see my chances when they come at me. I got to jump."

"Jump where?"

"Fuck you," George said. He turned away and swigged the beer. He was afraid, that was all. But he wasn't afraid of Safford. He was afraid of the same thing I was: that dark land up ahead beyond the headlights where the highway went on into nothing.

In January my father became more distant, as if he were edging away from us. I didn't notice it at first because it was a gradual shift, and day to day things didn't change much. He was often late for dinner—that's what I remember—and I began to wonder whether he was working late or going drinking or what.

One night Goldie and I had prepared a rabbit with gravy and rice and a nice salad. She'd dressed up for the occasion in a Mexican skirt and blouse she'd bought in Nogales as a souvenir, and she'd fixed her hair with turquoise pins. She'd put on perfume, too, which she seldom wore.

We were drinking Coors to tide us over, watching out the kitchen window at the gray dusk sliding down from the mountains. I was conscious how soft her skin looked above the scalloped neckline of her blouse, how her bare neck curved so delicately from her rounded shoulders. Her cheeks were flushed from the beer and from the heat of the rabbit's cooking.

"Where is he, do you think?" she asked.

"Looking for mountain lions," I said.

She smiled but did not look at me. "They must be in caves all through these hills."

I nodded. The land out the window had faded. The Sierritas were lavender and blue, ebbing toward black, and in the yard the arc light had come on.

"You'd look for a mountain lion for me, wouldn't you, Stephen?"

"I would," I said.

She laughed and stood up and twirled around in the small space of the kitchen. Then she stopped and looked back out the window. "Do you know what he's really doing?"

"No."

"You do."

"He's looking for a place in town," I said.

Goldie seemed surprised. "What place?"

"Somewhere better than the trailer. He wants it for you."

We were silent for a long time, and the small space tightened up. Goldie didn't move from the window.

"Are you going to stay with him?" I asked.

That was the only time Goldie didn't say anything. She looked around at me with an expression so pained I couldn't move.

"Let's drink," she said finally. "The Irish are famous for drinking."

She got out the whiskey bottle from under the sink and poured two big glasses and gave me one. Then she went into the living room.

A moment later, I heard the door open and close, and the trailer was silent.

That was when I knew how my mother had lived through all those years. I felt at that moment the weight of that emptiness of love, that terrible absence which wanted filling. Momentum: it was like wind seeking and seeking. Even when it was invisible it was there, driving forward, unable to be calm. I held my breath for a minute.

Then I went outside and stood on the landing. Goldie was in the yard, illuminated by the arc light, holding her glass of whiskey above her head. She swirled through the light, lifting her skirt with one hand and twirling like a dancer across the gravel. She paused once and drank, and then continued dancing toward the rim of the trail into the sandwash.

"Stephen," she said. "Come on."

She didn't wait for me, but her voice carried through the stillness. Then suddenly she was gone over the edge onto the trail into the ravine.

I glanced down the dirt road toward the highway hoping to see the headlights of my father's truck sweeping up among the saguaros. But there was nothing but the vacant dark highway and the barely perceptible ridge of hills.

I followed Goldie, not knowing what else to do. By the time I reached the sandy wash, she had started upstream. Her dark tracks curved through the sand and around the first bend. I called to her and heard my own voice echo against the rocks.

I knew she was waiting for me. I walked slowly, feeling my steps yield in the soft sand.

She was there, around that first outcropping of rocks. Her white blouse was vivid in the air. She had taken the turquoise pins from her hair, and it fell across her shoulder like black feathers.

I stopped and waited.

"Come here, Stephen," she said.

I went closer.

"Smell my hair." She bent her head so that her black hair cascaded into her hand, and she held it up to me.

I breathed in. She pushed her hair into my face, across my cheek. Her hair smelled of apricot.

"Smell here," she said. "What does my skin smell like?" She pulled her blouse down over one shoulder.

"Cholla blossoms."

"Close your eyes."

I closed my eyes.

"Tight," she said.

I kept my eyes tightly closed, feeling my heart beat different colors behind the lids. The breeze smoothed across my damp forehead. In the thicket not far away, thrashers and quail were settling in. I heard the swishing of Goldie's skirt, the movement of cloth, the sigh she made when the cool air touched her skin.

In the early morning, while my father and Goldie were still sleeping, I packed the few things I had and coasted the truck out of the yard. About a mile down, I abandoned the truck where the sand gully intersected the gravel. It would take my father a while to understand, then at least an hour to reach the truck. I walked from there to the Sasabe road, and sometime toward dawn got a ride north from a Mexican businessman. A Papago took me west on the main road to Sells, and by evening I was in Blythe, California.

I was going somewhere where it snowed into the sea—Northern California or maybe Oregon. I wasn't certain of anything. It was the beginning for me of a sadness which, I suppose, had to come to me sometime, an aching that lasted for years.

THE TROGON DISH

"It's hand-painted," Martha said. "Look, Aiken."

Aiken took the dish, but barely turned it in his hand. "Everything is hand-painted," he said. "God, it's hot." He wiped the sweat from his forehead with his hand and wiped the hand on his trousers. They had come to the mountains because it was so hot on the coast, but they'd gained nothing.

"Look at it, please. It's lovely."

"I thought you weren't feeling so well," he said.

"Can't you look?"

He examined the piece. It was a shallow bowl the size of a small dinner plate, with a swirl of light blue and black around the edge. In the center, amidst a design of dark green leaves, was a trogon with a vivid red breast, green wings, and a coppery tail.

"How much is it?" he asked. "Ask her the price." He motioned toward the shopkeeper who sat with her eyes closed, fanning herself.

"¿Cuanto cuesta?" Martha asked, taking the dish from Aiken and holding it up.

The woman opened her eyes, but that was the only change in her face. "Ochenta."

"Offer her thirty," Aiken said.

"You offer her thirty."

"Thirty," Aiken said to the shopkeeper. Then he asked Martha, "What's the word for thirty?"

"Treinta."

"Treinta," Aiken said, flashing his fingers. "Treinta pesos." He looked at Martha. "It's probably worth twenty. Thirty's generous."

"You and generous," Martha said, "never the twain shall meet."

The shopkeeper shut her eyes and went on fanning herself.

The idea had been to stay on the Pacific coast of Mexico. It was the trip they'd talked of for years before Aiken retired. They'd buy a camper van and get out of Denver. He was not about to sit through old age in a house on Bellaire playing solitaire and listening to game shows on television. He didn't want to play golf or garden or glue together the accumulated fragments of broken furniture, or find some other hobby. He wanted to travel. He wanted to pull the camper onto a stretch of deserted beach and live from the land—gather bananas and papayas, shoot jungle fowl, and fish in the sea.

Back in Denver the names of the regions meant nothing to him. Michoacan, Oaxaca. He couldn't pronounce them. It made no difference whether they were Mexican names or Indian, whether they were the words for mountains or towns or tribes. Cerro Teotepec, Chilapa de Alvarez, Sierra Madre del Sur. They were all mysteries to be solved later.

They bought a used VW camper the year before he turned sixty-two. Martha had refreshed her Spanish in a night course, and he had fitted out the van with everything he could think of—two extra water containers, a rock screen for the windshield, two spare tires. He bought an exhaustive set of maps and an arsenal of insect repellents, sunscreens, and prescription remedies for stomach disorders, diarrhea, and insomnia.

Then one night as he was kneeling over the maps, studying the route he had long ago marked in red pen, he looked up at Martha. "Maybe we should make reservations in a hotel."

"What for?"

"A room. I mean just for a few nights."

"If you want."

"I don't want. I thought after all the driving we'll be tired, and until we know our way around . . ."

"You read the newspaper," Martha said.

"Of course I did. What do you think about that incident?"

"I think that sort of thing could happen anywhere."

"It didn't happen anywhere. They were banditos. It happened to three Americans right on the road we're going to drive."

Martha smiled. "So if you'd feel better, call for a room. It might be our last vacation."

He hadn't called. They'd driven interstate all the way to Nogales, and then south through Guaymas, Mazatlán, and Manzanillo. Nothing had happened except they'd had to pay off children who washed their car without being asked.

Zihuatanejo was the fishing village he'd dreamed of, but Ixtapa, just down the beach, was jammed with luxury hotels. Martha wanted to sightsee; she wanted boat rides and bus tours and shopping. "We're here," she said. "We might as well enjoy ourselves."

"I guess it depends what you enjoy," Aiken said.

Even so, it would have been a place to stay on if he'd been able to sleep. He thought he could accustom himself to fishing and swimming, but at night he sweated the sheets wet. Chickens and donkeys cried out all night long. Even when the sea breeze came through the wide-open pop-top of the camper, he kept imagining people lurking around the camper, robbers shooting out his tires. The pills helped a little, but in the mornings he felt wrung out, as if he'd had bad dreams he couldn't remember.

The mountains would be cooler. If it were cooler, he could sleep. But in the mountains Martha got sick. One day after lunch she'd felt dizzy and nauseous, and they'd stopped in a place called Huetamo, which had a hotel.

The town was a rough collection of buildings and shacks on a hillside facing west, poor as other towns. The white church that fronted the plaza had two bells in the steeple, and a few crude shops were scattered among the debris. There was no doctor.

Martha took some medicine they'd brought and slept. She felt better, then worse again, then better. They went out one afternoon to walk and had found the trogon dish they'd argued about. Martha had been willing to pay seventy pesos for it. Aiken wrested it from her, set it back on the counter, and said he wouldn't be cheated.

On the way back to the hotel, Martha walked behind him in strained silence. Now and then she stopped to catch her breath or simply to rest, but he knew she was angry at him.

"Would you like a drink?" he asked.

"No, thank you."

"A beer might make your stomach feel better."

"It's not my stomach."

"It's damn hot."

"It's not the heat, either."

Nothing in the street moved. The sun had passed its zenith, but the heat still radiated from the beige walls of the houses, from the adobe walls. Turkeys and chickens crouched in the slivers of shadows, and dogs slept under the rusted cars parked at random. They passed a spigot which dripped a small wet circle on the ground.

"We could sit under a tree," Aiken said, pointing to a stone where a single tree cast a dappled shadow. "Or in the square."

"I don't want to sit. I want to lie down."

Everything seemed to Aiken as if in a dream: the roadway, the stone walls, the houses of clay and cement, even the dusty leaves of the tree.

Just then, in front of them, three men emerged from an open doorway in an alley. One shoved another as if a joke were being told, and the third man made a remark at which the other two laughed.

"What are they saying?" Aiken asked. "Are they talking about us?"

"I don't know."

"But you understand . . ."

"They're Indians," Martha said, as if he ought to know at least that much.

The three men stumbled across the street and got into a rattletrap Ford whose exhaust pipe was wired to the back bumper. The driver revved the engine and the car bolted into the dusty alley.

Immediately a dog began yelping.

Aiken stopped, and Martha came up and held his arm. The dog lay on its side, screeching and pawing the ground. The car stopped, and the Indians got out. A crowd gathered quickly from the nearby square—Indians, Mexicans, children from the houses. The dust which the car had raised settled over the dog.

No one said anything; no one moved to help the animal.

"Why doesn't someone do something?" Aiken asked. "Can't you ask?"

Martha spoke to the man beside her, and the man replied in a hushed, rapid voice.

"What'd he say?" Aiken whispered.

"He said, 'The dog has had enough trouble already today.'"

"For God's sake, what does that mean?" Aiken's voice rose against the quiet.

The animal calmed down a little, as if he were becoming inured to pain. After a few minutes the crowd dissipated. The Indians got back into their car and drove away. People moved off. Two Mexicans who had come from the plaza picked up the dog and laid him in a patch of shade which jutted into the alley.

Martha gathered Aiken's arm. "Please, let's go back to the hotel."

"And leave him?"

"What can you do?" Martha asked. "And I'm tired, Aiken. If there's no doctor here, there'll be no vet."

But Aiken moved closer. The dog's ribs were outlined through its mangy black-and-white fur. That wasn't unusual. Most of the dogs they'd seen were hungry. Yet clearly this dog's legs were broken.

A few children edged nearer, too. Aiken flicked his hand at them. "Go away. Away. Vamos."

"Please," Martha said.

Aiken looked around. The sun caught Martha's shiny forehead, and he had a glimpse of her suddenly as old. She seemed tired, worn, far away from him, like their house on Bellaire and his job at the office. "You go ahead," he said. "I'll be along."

She paused as though she were gauging something invisible, and then she went on into the square. Her step away from him was slow and methodical. At the small of her back was a dark, spreading spot of perspiration.

Aiken kneeled and extended his hand to let the dog smell him. But the dog was panting, dripping saliva into the dust. It couldn't lift its head.

Water, Aiken thought. The dog needed water. He stood up and peered into one of the empty doorways. No one. In another he found an old man sitting in half-darkness. He was dressed in white and seemed to be praying, pressing his hands together over and over.

"Señor?"

The man pressed his hands together but did not speak.

Aiken backed away and into the street. He retraced the way he and Martha had come, past the spigot where the water dripped, past a doorway with a red curtain over it, and through an intersection of unnamed alleys. In a few minutes he had found the house where the woman sold the ceramic dishes.

The same woman was there, rolling meat in flour, and he had to wait, money in hand.

At the hotel Aiken went straight to the room. Martha was lying with her eyes closed on the bed, the ceiling fan whirring above her, and the windows open. The curtains wafted in the moving air.

Martha did not turn her head.

"I gave the dog some water," he said, "but he's still in pain."

She didn't answer him.

"How do you feel?"

"Better. I want to go home."

"Home?"

"To Denver. Home."

"We can't go home." He looked through the curtains where red and purple bougainvillea framed the town and the tan and yellow hills beyond.

"We can do whatever we choose, can't we?"

"After all this time?" He sat down on the bed. "I know this isn't the place we want to be, but we'll go up higher into the mountains. It'll be cooler yet, and we'll find . . ." He hesitated, not really hearing his own voice. He opened the drawer in the table beside the bed and took out the bottle of sleeping pills.

"What are you going to do?" Martha asked.

"Give these to the dog."

There was a long silence. Martha still lay on her back, watching, it seemed, the whirling fan on the ceiling.

"Aiken?"

"What?"

"Do you love me still?"

"Of course I love you."

"Don't go out."

He didn't answer.

"Let someone else worry about the dog."

He was surprised at the resolute tone of her voice, as if she were telling him what to do, as if staying in the room were a special thing he might do for her. "Don't you have any sympathy?" he asked.

She turned from the fan toward him. "I do, yes," she said. "Yes, I do."

He looked away. The sun came through the window with a clear, urgent light.

Outside the hotel he turned left toward the plaza. Leaves fluttered in a gust of warm air, puffing dust in billows. Heavy, high-burgeoning cumulus clouds rose in the north beyond the church—rain, he hoped. A car rolled past through the square, honking its horn for no reason Aiken could glean. The honking changed tone as the car went around the corner and moved away.

A small girl asked him for money, but Aiken pushed past her and continued across the plaza to the open market. He bought a slab of meat and held out more than enough pesos in his open palm.

When he got back to the alley, the dog had raised its head and was drinking from the trogon dish. A bone poked now through the skin of its hind leg. Blood was clotted around the wound. Flies swarmed around the dog's eyes.

Aiken lay the paper with the steak in it on the ground, and with his pocketknife, cut the slab in half. He took out the sleeping pills and poured a pile of them onto each piece of meat. Then he folded the meat carefully into tight rolls and offered them to the dog. The dog gulped the food down.

A bar in the plaza was the closest place to drink, besides the hotel, but Aiken walked three extra blocks to a cantina on the outskirts of town, where Martha wouldn't look for him. It wasn't that he wanted to hide. He wanted peace was all. From the dusty terrace he could look out over the plowed fields along the mesa and farther up to the edge of the jungle, which rose into the higher mountains.

He ordered a Corona, drank it quickly, and had another.

He did not understand Martha. Just when he was beginning to feel at ease in the country, she wanted to go home. He had worked all his life for this time with her—it was more than a vacation, it was a new beginning—and she wanted to go back! Go back to what? To the little circles they ran in? To the smog and the traffic? Of course he'd been worried about being on the road. But he'd overcome those fears. And she wanted to leave!

He drank the second beer as quickly as the first—against the heat, he said to himself—and resolved to make the third one last. He could take his time until dinner. Martha could rest. They'd have a good meal in the hotel and sleep well, and in the morning maybe she'd have changed her mind again, and they could start out fresh into the mountains.

He was drunk by late afternoon when the shadows came into the square. Sunlight illuminated the church wall, pinked it slightly, and fell into the open doorways of the shops and houses. The shadow of the fountain was skewed, thirty feet long, and the trees on the ground were ragged black splotches.

Aiken walked the perimeter, touching the adobe buildings with his outstretched hand to measure his posture. He skipped doorways, now and then teetered away from the hard, dusty clay walls. A crowd had gathered near the fountain. Two children had climbed into the lower branches of a nearby tree to see over the men and women who were laughing at something in the middle of the ring.

It was still hot, and the beer made him sweat. He wasn't interested in a cockfight or a carnival act—whatever the focus was of the crowd. But then the milling people shifted a little, and he caught a glimpse through the knots of people. It was the dog, lurching and stumbling this way and that, as if it had been struck by a bullet but would not fall. Whenever it took a clumsy step, the crowd hooted and clapped.

Aiken ran over and pushed through the startled people. "Idiots!" he screamed at them. "Fools! Get away!"

The people drew back. He caught the dog in his arms, and the people retreated from him further, back to their houses, into the side streets. The two children scrambled out of the tree and ran.

He carried the animal back to its place in the alley. The narrow street was gray now, sunless. But heat still flowed from the walls, from the dry ground. He lay the dog on the same doorstep.

Now what could he do? The pills had only given it courage—walking on its broken legs. Now it would only be a matter of time before the effect of the pills wore off, and the dog would be worse than before. Who knew what new damage it had done to itself performing before the crowd?

Perhaps he could buy cyanide. In Mexico almost anything was sold over-the-counter, but would they have cyanide here? Anyway, it was late; the shops were closed. It wasn't a tourist town.

He filled the trogon dish at the spigot and hurried back, afraid the dog would move again.

When Aiken returned, someone else was standing over the animal. From a distance he could tell it was the old man he had seen before in the house pressing his hands together. He was dressed in white and wore a beat-up straw hat which darkened his face.

The man was smoking a cigarette rolled from a scrap of newspaper, and he took a puff and pressed his hands together, mouthing through the smoke words which Aiken couldn't grasp.

Aiken put down the dish, but the dog didn't drink.

Indian, Aiken thought. He felt drawn to the old man's calm. Yet that calm was unsettling, too. The man's skin was seared by years of sun, and he was dirty and smelled of smoke and sweat. But he nodded intently, as if he understood the necessity of doing something about the dog's pain.

He puffed on his cigarette and squinted through the smoke. He spoke again, words which were incomprehensible. Aiken nodded. Then the man smiled and bent down. He lifted his white trouser leg and drew out from his boot a long-bladed knife.

For an instant Aiken thought the man might attack him, and he fell back a few steps into the alley. But quickly he realized the mistake. The man grinned again, gray teeth ragged in his mouth. He motioned at the dog and offered the knife to Aiken.

Aiken felt dizzy. "No," he said, holding up his hand. "You."

The man held the knife out farther.

The dog was breathing erratically, its moans punctuating the hot silence. Whenever the dog squirmed, a low whine caught in its throat.

This was a different thing, Aiken realized, a fear he had never thought of, though it had been there inside him his whole life. He gazed at the Indian for a long moment, an impasse, but he could not take the knife.

Finally the old man motioned him toward the doorway, and he himself backed away and disappeared into the darkness.

Aiken followed.

The dark air in the room was cooler, absent the day's long

strafing of sunlight. Aiken entered cautiously, his eyes unaccustomed to the dimness. A scent of cedar smoke hung in the air from a dead fire.

No one else was there but the old man, who stood in the center of the small space, still speaking softly, pointing with the knife at something on the wall. Aiken moved closer into the poor light.

On the wall was the carving of a dog, roughly hewn from a piece of wood, a crude dog with sticklike legs and bulging eyes. In the corner, by a pallet on the floor, was another carving, a different dog, with a candle burning beneath it. The man kept speaking, but Aiken could not make out any words. The carving in the corner was nothing like the mongrel in the street, but an immense dog adorned with beads, painted in gold.

The man stopped speaking, and in the silence the living dog yelped and whined. The old man held the knife out to Aiken.

"I understand," Aiken said. He took the knife and went outside into the alley.

The dog was frothing at the mouth. Every breath wheezed like a sigh escaping from the bottom of pain. Aiken felt the terrible tightness in his own eyes, though he was not crying. He kneeled and, in his blindness, knocked the trogon dish, spilling the water. He grasped the dog's nose firmly so it could not bark or snap at him and pulled its head back into his lap.

The knife was sharp. He cut through the fur and skin under the neck, peeled away a layer of gristle and skin, and slit the main artery in the dog's neck. Blood spurted over his hands and onto his trousers at the thigh. He made certain the wound was lasting.

Then he stood up and let the knife fall from his fingers.

Martha found him in the plaza by the empty fountain. He was sitting on the ground with his back against the broken tiles, looking up at the stars which flooded the sky.

"Aiken?" she called to him. "Aiken."

He didn't answer, but watched her come toward him hesitantly, as she might have approached someone whom she barely recognized. Behind her the lights of the hotel shone across the corner of the square. Now and then a voice interrupted the silence, but the town, for the most part, lay sleeping.

"When you didn't come back, I got worried," she said. "Where have you been?"

"Here."

"You must be tired."

"No, I'm not tired." He tried to see her face, but it was veiled in shadow, concealed by the soft air. "I don't think I'll ever be tired again."

"What happened to the dog?"

"Dead," he said softly.

"That's what you wanted, isn't it?"

He nodded. A meteor sped across the heavens, and he breathed a draught of cool air which slid from the hills. "Do you remember why we came here?" he asked.

"You said it would be cooler."

"To sleep, yes." He paused. "But sometimes in a great while, maybe once in your lifetime—once—you get a chance. . . ." He stopped because he knew he could not explain it.

Sitting had made his muscles stiff, fragile, and he got up slowly from the ground. Martha helped him.

"Come with me," he said. He started across the plaza toward the alley.

"You're not going to show me that animal?"

"No," he said. "No, the old Indian took the dog. But I've forgotten something."

She followed him to the edge of the plaza, but he went into the alley alone. The alley was darker now, and only a glint of light reflected from a car window across the narrow street. The scent of flowers came to him on the stirred air.

The dog was gone, as he knew it would be, but the trogon dish, that luminous circle, was still on the old man's doorsill. Aiken picked it up, tilted the dish into the dim light, saw for a brief instant the resplendent bird. He brushed the dust from the dish with his hand. Then, with this gift, he went back to where Martha was waiting for him in the light at the edge of the plaza.

LEARNING TO DREAM

Rose envied Henry's dreaming, even when he thrashed in bed. "What is it?" she asked. "I'm right here. What's wrong?"

Henry didn't wake, and in the cool nightglow from the street—was it moonlight? she wondered—she watched him twitch and jerk. He unbuttoned one button of his pajama tops and brushed his mustache carefully with the back of his hand.

"What is it?" she asked. She turned on the bedlamp.

Henry opened his eyes, stunned by the light. "What is what?"

"What were you dreaming?"

"Oh, Rose, please. Not again."

"I want to know. You unbuttoned one button of your pajamas. Why did you do that?"

"Not now," he said. He buttoned the button and rolled over. "It won't help you, Rose. Believe me."

In a minute Henry was asleep again. Rose turned off the light and lay back, wondering how the mind ordered the body in sleep. What made Henry think he was somewhere else? Of course Rose knew it wasn't willful behavior. No one could dictate the form or substance of dreams or how they would end. That was what Henry said. She couldn't will herself into dreaming. But she still felt as though she were missing some part of herself—a hand, or an eye, or the sense of smell.

Even Kelly dreamed. Rose sometimes kept the neighbor girl on weekends when her mother wanted to see a new boyfriend, and one night Kelly had wakened and called out "No! No!" so loudly Rose was certain the girl was being murdered. Rose had rushed into the living room and had found Kelly sitting bolt upright on the sofa, still asleep, and Rose had held her just as she would have held her own child and sang soothing songs to her until the dream went away.

Rose would have even been glad to have that kind of nightmare. She wanted to sigh in her sleep, or see colors, or talk to people she had not thought about in years.

In the morning Henry claimed he had forgotten everything. "What difference does it make?" he asked. "Now is now."

"I want to learn," Rose said.

"There's nothing *to* learn. You either dream or you don't. Let's have breakfast. And turn on the news, will you? I want to see what's happened in the cab strike."

She turned on the television and went into the bathroom to roll her hair. Mr. Trevino at her office always teased her if she didn't make an effort with her appearance, and she stood away from the mirror and looked at herself. She still had a slight figure, girlish almost, and though there were crow's-feet beginning around her eyes, the skin of her forehead was smooth and her mouth was taut. Henry was right, she thought. Every psyche manufactured its own latticework, as Henry called it, and she couldn't learn to dream from someone else. Dreams weren't transferable. She couldn't borrow them or rent them or buy them in a store.

Henry said she didn't dream because she worried too much what Mr. Trevino thought and about Kelly's troubles with her mother, or else she felt guilty.

"Guilty about what?" Rose had asked.

"You tell *me*."

She hadn't argued with him. Henry was nicer if she didn't argue. But she hadn't felt guilty about anything.

"Those damn cabbies," Henry said from the other room. "If they were my students, they'd keep driving. How am I supposed to get to work?"

Rose leaned from the bathroom with her hair rolled in hot

curlers. "You could walk," she said. "That's what the rest of us do."

It was only October, but one cold snap had killed the leaves, and right on cue, Henry had got out his winter overcoat and his pipe. From then on, Rose knew, he would not often go out, except when his duties as dean of the college demanded it. This was his reading phase, and he sat evenings under his gooseneck lamp leafing through biographies and plays and Rose did not know what all. His hair grew longer and pushed over his collar, and he wore sweaters every evening. And because it was darker earlier, he went to bed at nine-thirty, whether she went or not.

The truth was, Rose had had trouble sleeping lately. She didn't know the cause of her insomnia. She just felt a density about herself, as if every day she had picked up a small pebble, and finally she had become too heavy to move.

She stayed up late, long after Henry had gone to bed, reading magazines and tabloids to make herself tired. The stories she read were about daring rescues or killer tornadoes or sensational love affairs. In one, a man had flown a homemade glider across the border of Czechoslovakia to escape with his family to the West (though one child had been killed), and in another, a young woman in Indiana had braved a raging fire to save a retarded boy's life. Rose cried for half an hour imagining the joy and gratitude the boy's mother must have felt.

After reading these stories, though, Rose was more wide awake than ever.

Once, in desperation, she went to a psychiatrist without telling Henry. "I can't sleep," she said, "and if I can't sleep, I can't dream."

The doctor raised his white eyebrows. "Are you afraid to dream? Is that it?"

"I'm not afraid," Rose said. "I want to. I've never had a dream."

"You've never dreamed?"

"No."

"And you think it's time?"

"I'm not getting younger," Rose said. The man's eyebrows made her nervous, the way he raised them and lowered them.

"I suspect you don't want to sleep because you think time will pass," the doctor said. "The body shrinks and shrivels even at night. It's a natural phenomenon."

"What?" asked Rose. "Do I look so old?"

"If you'd like, we could examine this fear of yours. We could embark on a therapy to unravel . . ."

Rose stood up and touched her temple. "Isn't that strange?" she asked vaguely. "No. No, thank you. I believe I'm all right."

One evening not long after that, while the cab strike was in its third week, Rose prevailed on Henry to go to *Cousin, Cousine,* which was playing again at the theater down the street. They went early so Henry could browse in the bookstore nearby.

Rose had never liked going to bookstores with Henry. He melted into the pages of fiction or philosophy, and she felt as though she didn't exist at all. So that evening she walked on ahead to look in the shop windows for a new purse which she'd needed for months. The old one had holes in the bottom, and she'd already tied up the straps twice with twine. Leather purses were expensive, and Henry would complain, so she'd hidden away a few dollars each week from her salary so she could buy what she wanted.

She didn't find anything she liked, and when Henry did not come along after her, she was afraid they'd be late for the movie. She found him still in the bookstore, immersed in psychology.

"What time is it?" he asked.

"A quarter to seven."

"What's the hurry? They always show previews."

"I like the previews."

"Go ahead then," he said. "I'll be there."

Rose knew what that meant, so she drifted over into the children's alcove. Kelly always needed a new book. Kelly had learned to read at age four, and she had a photographic memory, too. She'd once entertained the neighbors—even Henry—by reciting by heart a whole book on dinosaurs, complete with dramatic gestures of battles and the exact pronunciation of ichthyosaurus and triceratops and Tyrannosaurus rex. But now that Kelly was in junior high and her parents were divorced, no one except Rose thought she was special anymore.

Rose picked out a book with a rave blurb on the back—a story of a Vietnamese orphan adopted by American parents—and went to find Henry, who was now in the new fiction section. "Just a minute," he said. "I'm almost ready."

Rose dabbled over the decorator books, leafing through

Lansdowne's *Birds of the Northern Forest*—such warblers!—and an elaborate Southern cookbook which featured not only the recipes for shrimp creole and crab bisque, but also photographs of the lovely, oak-lined driveways of the plantations where such delicacies were served. She longed for the South, where women were either cool as a breeze or crazy.

Then she glanced at *The Art of the Prado,* which Henry would have liked. He was always talking music or art with his friends at the college. The little Velasquez girls were so shiny and prim, but Rose could not help feeling a remoteness about them. The pictures made the subjects seem inert and distant and small, as though they were twice removed from where she was.

Rose was about to close the book when another picture, not a Velasquez, caught her eye. A shiver passed through her as she gazed at it, and the hair on her arm actually prickled. Some soldiers in a town square were firing their rifles at other men at very close range, and the terrified and helpless expressions of the victims were illuminated by stark lantern light. One man's arms were raised above his head as if he were both begging for mercy and wondering in his darkest soul how the shooters could be so cruel.

She slapped the book closed so loudly that Henry, who had come up beside her, jumped.

"Come on," he said. "We'll be late."

She was still trembling when she got to the cashier's desk, where she laid Kelly's book on the Updike novel Henry had picked out.

"Is it the girl's birthday again?" he asked.

"It's an un-birthday present," Rose said. She looked at Henry. "What's the occasion for your book?"

The movie was in French with subtitles. Two relatives, a man and a woman, each married to a different philandering spouse, had fallen in love with one another, and the new liaison was permeated by such infectious happiness that it flowed over like a brimming spring. The affair was even flaunted at a family reunion in front of children and old people and, of course, the other spouses. The whole mood of the movie was joy.

"That was absurd," Henry said, when they walked out after the show. "No one in his right mind would behave that way."

Rose was not certain what he meant by 'that way'—whether he thought love could not take such a delightful form, or whether no one would be so brazen about it as the lovers in the movie. She did not ask what he meant. Instead she said, "Let's take a cab home."

"A cab?" Henry asked. "And support those crooks?"

"The drivers do risk their lives," said Rose, "especially at night."

And off Henry went into paroxysms of outrage. He rehashed the issues and explained why the cabbies should be tarred and feathered. Rose nodded and nodded, thinking how wonderful it must have been for the woman in the movie to have had the most personal and emotional parts of her life so unashamedly in the open.

Later that night Henry watched the news in bed. Rose rarely paid attention to the news, and she was not interested in what Bush said or how Congress was going to bail out savings and loans or in the riots in Eastern Europe. That night, though—such a strange thing!—there was a story about a robbery in Paris. Two men had overpowered a museum guard at the Louvre and had scooped up from an exhibition case a series of etchings by Francisco Goya. While the newsman explained the robbery, one of the etchings appeared on the screen—a wolf writing out a legacy of war to the gathered churchmen and peasants. Rose felt the same remarkable shiver run through her as she'd felt in the bookstore, and she picked up the remote control and snapped off the set.

"Hey," Henry said, "what are you doing?"

"I want you to hold me."

"After the news. I'll be glad to." He took the tuner and turned on the set again.

After a few minutes, during the weather, he slid down in the bed and pressed his head against her shoulder. Rose pushed him away gently. "I'm all right now," she said. "Really."

Rose had promised Kelly she'd have lunch with her on Thursday at the junior high school. Mr. Trevino complained about Rose's leaving early, but Rose pointed out she had rarely missed a day's work and her desk was clean. "It'll give you time to make more work for me," she said, and off she went.

An icy wind blew down the avenue, and Rose pulled her coat tightly around her throat. She braved the cold cheerfully, though, because that morning she had read about a man whose car had plunged off a bridge into a frigid river near Milwaukee. He was underwater for thirty-eight minutes before divers had reached him, but the miracle was he was alive. The cold water had so numbed his heart and blood that doctors were able to revive him.

It was cold now, but maybe by Saturday it would warm up again. Saturday Rose had planned to take Kelly to Central Park and to the Museum of Natural History, and afterward they'd have lunch and shop for a purse. Rose needed a purse, and on her way to the school, she glanced idly into shop windows. But the only place she stopped was at the window of the print-and-frame shop.

The paintings on display represented, she supposed, some school of art which Henry would have known about, but she could not make sense of the various lines and splotches. Still, she went in.

The gallery was a warm, thin room, long front to back, and painted an austere white. A man called to her from the back of the gallery. "Hey, there," he said, and he came forward across the wooden floor.

"Oh," Rose said, "I didn't know anyone was here."

"Were you looking for something in particular?" the man asked.

"I was looking for a print by a painter named Goya."

"Goya?" The man smiled suddenly. "I'm sorry. People seldom ask for Goya these days."

Rose did not understand why the heat in the room rushed through her. She heard a faint ringing, more like a vibration than a sound, and she felt perspiration bead on her forehead.

The man seemed not to notice. "You might try at the Met," he said.

Rose nodded weakly. She rushed out the door, and the strange vibration vanished into the soothing, cold wind.

Kelly was waiting beside the double door into the cafeteria, and Rose gave her a big hug. Usually Kelly's smile was electric, but that day she looked pained. "I have some bad news," she said.

"I hope not *too* bad."

"Mom says I have to go with her to Montauk on Saturday. I can't go to the museum."

"Oh," Rose said, "well, we can go another time. You should do what your mother says."

They gathered their trays and silverware and moved along the lunch line. The morose women behind the counter in their dirty aprons and white caps spooned out chili and boiled carrots from huge steamer trays.

"I'd rather go with you, Aunt Rose," Kelly said. "Couldn't you talk to my mom?"

But Rose was watching the counter women. Normally she sympathized with them—You poor things! was what she usually thought—but today she was angry at them. Why are you doing that job if you don't like it, she wondered. Why don't you find other work that will make you happy?

"Aunt Rose, are you listening?"

"I'd rather have you go with me, too," Rose said.

As soon as she said the words, Rose knew she'd lied. It wasn't a lie she meant to tell. She *had* wanted Kelly to come with her to the museum and to shop for a purse. But the moment the words were in the air, the wanting ceased. Such a twist! Something uttered with a pure motive turned out to be a lie!

"Oh, I nearly forgot," Rose said. "I have a present for you. Let's open it at the table."

They got dessert, a piece of peach pie stuck to a dish, and Rose followed Kelly to the table, where they set down their trays. Rose opened her ragged purse and took out the book.

"Aunt Rose, why do you give me presents?"

"To please you," Rose said. "I hope you like it."

"Not to compensate?"

"To compensate for what?"

"Because you feel sorry for me."

"I don't feel sorry for you," Rose said. "There are millions of children whose parents don't live together anymore."

"Or because you want me to like you."

"Kelly!"

"Well, Mom thinks it's kind of weird."

Rose felt suddenly lightheaded and confused. Around her the boys were shouting at each other and the girls chattered away. All those children! She held her hand to her forehead.

Then just as quickly her mind cleared. The children were so spirited! How she longed for that energy. Her mind danced away on the children's laughter and from Kelly's urgent touch on her arm.

On Saturday morning Rose was up early. She went to the bathroom and showered and came out with a towel wrapped around her.

"Where can you possibly be going at this hour?" Henry asked, rolling up onto one elbow in the bed. "It's my day off."

"I can't sleep," Rose said. "I'm going shopping. You can stay in bed as long as you like after I leave."

"Shopping for what?"

"A purse." She picked up the old one from the chair, and thrust it toward Henry as if he had accused her of a crime and she had to defend herself. "Look, the zipper is broken. The seams are torn. I lose my pencils and my change through the holes in the bottom. Maybe you can get along for centuries with a floppy old wallet, but I need a new purse." She paused, surprised at the intensity of her own voice. Henry was awake now. "And it's my day off, too. I'm going to Bloomingdale's."

She took a cab uptown, though she knew Henry would disapprove of consorting with an enemy. "Seventy-fifth Street," she said. She felt giddy. The cab sailed past Bloomingdale's and on up Lexington. When she got out at Seventy-fifth, she tipped the cab driver five dollars. "I'm glad you won the strike," she said.

She walked over to the park, hoping the fresh air would calm her. But if anything, walking made her more excited. The park was lovely at that hour. The trees were past their color, but she liked sienna and tan, and the air had in it a crisp smell of dew and sweet grass. There were almost no people. She strolled briskly along the path, marveling at the fog which seeped up from the pond. She had never seen a place so perfect—the pond, the bridge, the orange-brown leaves still on the trees.

Then all of a sudden she felt guilty for not going to Bloomingdale's. Or maybe it was remorse for not having talked to Kelly's mother so Kelly could have come. Or should she have invited Henry? He might have wanted to go to the Met. But he would have explained to her every painting—why people were arranged in this position or that, how the colors were organized. She shouldn't feel guilty, she said to herself. It wasn't her fault Kelly couldn't come. And she didn't want a lesson from Henry. She hadn't kept anything from him, either, not really. She was going to Bloomingdale's later. All she wanted was to see one painting by Goya. There was nothing wrong with that.

The anteroom of the Met was like a tomb, and Rose had to take a few deep breaths to muster the courage to ask about the Spanish artists. The Goyas—there were several—were on the second floor in the André Meyer Collection. She sorted out from the floor plan where she was and where she had to go—left through the Greek and Roman sculpture, then past the cafeteria, and to the left up the stairs. As she walked through the statues of naked men and women, she kept telling herself how silly she was being. She knew nothing about Goya. She hadn't ever read anything about him or seen his work. All she knew was that he must have had immense, dark dreams.

The first painting she saw was a swarm of reds, tans, blues, blacks—colors she knew were his. It was not savage or cruel as she had expected, but was, rather, a frenzy of energy. A village crowd surrounded two adjoining bullrings, and in one of the rings a matador was preparing to kill a bull. The matador didn't move, but Rose felt as if he had.

She was about to lift her hand to touch the canvas, when out of the corner of her eye she saw a museum guard gazing in her direction. She turned away, feeling so weak she could barely stand.

Then she caught sight of another painting more stunning than the bullfight. It had to be one of his. Two women in lace shawls and greenish-white dresses were posing coquettishly on a balcony. The women's skin was so light, the dresses intricately woven. She floated toward the painting. In the background were two men covetous of the women, talking to one another. She could almost hear them. Rose, unable to breathe, eased herself down on the bench in the middle of the room.

The guard came toward her, and she lowered her head, listening to his footsteps on the wooden floor. His drab black shoes and light blue trouser cuffs passed before her eyes. His steps slowed. She would scream, she thought, if the man touched her.

"Miss?" His voice was so soft she looked up. He had reddish hair and blue eyes. "Are you not feeling well?" he asked. "Would you like me to call someone?"

She smiled wistfully. Whom would he call? she wondered. The police? Henry? Goya? "Isn't that odd?" she said.

Her dizziness cleared, and she stood up. She had never felt more vibrant than at that moment. She sensed the blood pulsing through her arteries into her arms and through the capillaries into her fingertips. She could *feel* it. She smiled again at the guard, took a last glance at the two women on the balcony, and walked out of the room.

That night Rose woke in the darkness and opened her eyes. Her hands were shaking, and her heart was racing madly. What had made her wake if not a dream? She turned over and shook Henry.

"What now?" Henry asked.

"I had a dream."

Henry turned on the light on his side of the bed and looked at the clock. "Three-fifteen in the morning, October twenty-fifth, no twenty-sixth, in the thirty-fourth year in the life of Rose Grimball. Hallelujah."

"I mean it," she said. "I had a dream."

"What did you dream about?"

"I don't know."

"Jesus Christ, Rose."

"It's still a dream, isn't it, if you can't remember?"

"I suppose it is," Henry said, slumping back into the bed. "Why don't you go back to sleep and try again?" He turned off the light.

"I think I will."

She rolled onto her side away from him, but she kept her eyes open, smiling to herself at the wondrous thing that had happened. Isn't that marvelous? she thought to herself, and she knew she was approaching a misty world in which were concealed shapes and things more bizarre and enchanting than she had ever imagined.

TWO

That winter, two evenings a week, Rose attended classes to learn sign language, and on Saturdays she worked with deaf children at the Community Center. Henry did not mind her new avocation because he stayed in and read. He was glad of the quiet.

"Are you back?" he asked one afternoon, glancing up from his book when Rose came in. He was listening to violins and sitting in the easy chair.

Rose stamped the snow from her boots and brushed the snow from her coat.

"Cold out?"

Rose gazed into the mirror at her red forehead and cheeks. She made signs to Henry with her hands.

"All right, Rose," he said.

Rose hung her coat in the closet and went to the kitchen to heat some milk. She brought a cup of hot chocolate to the living room and stood at the window and watched the snow. The street was misted and pale, and traffic was sparse.

Henry leaned forward and put down his book on the coffee table. "I've been wanting to talk to you, Rose."

She shook her head as though she couldn't hear.

"Rose, please. Don't think I haven't noticed how strangely you've been acting."

She made signs at him with her hands.

"Will you please talk? You're not deaf and dumb."

Henry's voice seemed to come to her from a great distance, though he was just across the room. "I want to go to Spain," she said.

"Spain?" He sank back into the chair. "Spain!"

"Spain."

"Where did you get that idea? I didn't know you were interested in Spain."

"I am now."

"With what money? How would we pay for it?"

"I've saved a thousand dollars. I was going to buy a purse with it, but I changed my mind."

"A thousand dollars for a purse?"

"It's my money," Rose said. "I want to go alone."

"Rose, what is wrong with you?"

Rose shook her head and made signs at him with her hands.

It had been their first real argument in eight years of marriage. Henry's position was that they had both worked and contributed, so the money was as much his as hers. Rose countered that he spent their money on books and concerts and never gave credence to anything she wanted.

"Like what?" he asked. "You don't like concerts."

"Like the purse."

"You never bought the purse."

"Exactly. But I had to hide the money for it."

"So you want to hide things?"

"You hide things," she said. "You hide being afraid."

"I'm not afraid."

"I always thought you were smart and brave, but the truth is you don't want to take risks. The cabbies take risks."

"I'm not a cabbie."

"You said you didn't want children because it was immoral to raise them in the city. But that's a lie. You don't want interference."

"We couldn't afford children with your hoarding all the money. . . ." Henry stopped abruptly. "You know I'd love to go to Spain to visit Madrid and El Escorial and Toledo. What have I done that you don't want me to go?"

"Nothing."

She had kept silent after that, and Henry had gone to bed hurt and angry. Rose had stayed up. She straightened the magazines on the coffee table, watched the snow fall and fall over the street, and when Henry was asleep, finally, she felt safe. She went to the walk-in closet and took out a folded piece of paper. She knew each of Goya's posters by heart now, each person and scene, each nuance of color and detail. Pepito made her weep. He looked so much like a soldier, but he was too young to grasp that a soldier's life was killing. *The Madhouse* and *The Inquisition* were both so dark and frightening that Rose could not help shuddering. She knew Goya was deaf, and those paintings were his world.

That night, though, she chose *The Majas on the Balcony* from the museum collection. She spread the poster out, pinned it to the inside of the door, then stepped back one step. The women's eyes were so alluring, the tint of their skins—the creams and yellows—so soft. Rose could feel their hearts beating just as her own. The *majos* lurked in the shadows should the *majas* ever falter in their game.

After a few minutes Rose took down the poster, folded it again, and replaced it in its hiding place. She snapped off the light and emerged into the cooler air of the living room, relishing like a scent of flowers the momentary flirtation she had had. A dark owl swept through the room, and she laughed. She had seen the owl before and was not afraid. Wolves and bats, too, were as familiar to her as the olive trees and the bleached yellow hills that rose in the distance. A man's face, shrouded by a dark hat, loomed in the air. That odd hat! The man was curious about her and eager. She had seen him in the infirmary and once at a ball, where he had tried to coax her away from the dance floor. He gestured to her with his delicate hands, begged her to come to him, a little closer. Sit down beside me, he seemed to say. He was the deaf one, and he followed her everywhere.

Rose would not go. No, first he had to introduce himself properly before she consented to sit with him. He had to come out from the shadow. She spoke to him in sign language. Yes, she said, she might in time consent to his embrace, but there was no hurry.

Every morning Rose did calisthenics. She stretched, did windmills, ran in place. She had never done exercises before, and at first she felt slow and cumbersome, but each day the awkwardness diminished and she felt more agile, more accustomed to the new pace of breathing. The tightness went from her body.

At the office she had never been more attentive to work. She solved problems before Mr. Trevino saw them coming. She reminded him of calls he'd forgotten to make, suggested rearranging displays, reorganized the inventory. Nothing was beyond her alert eye.

One day Mr. Trevino called her into his office. "Rose," he asked, "how long have you worked here? Sit down, please."

She remained standing at the door. "Nine years, almost ten."

"I've been noticing how well you've been doing lately, how efficient you are." Mr. Trevino smiled at her.

Rose blushed.

"I want to give you more voice around here, more responsibility, perhaps in accounting."

"No, thank you," Rose said.

"It would mean a good increase in salary," Mr. Trevino went on. "Perhaps some travel. . . ."

"I'd rather stay where I am," Rose said. "I like going home at five. I have a busy life beyond work. Thank you, though. It's just that there are so many things to do."

Saturdays Rose went to the YWCA to run on the track. Afterward she met Kelly at Brigham's to catch up on Kelly's week at school. At Rose's urging, Kelly had started learning sign language, too, and as they ate ice cream, they practiced on one another. Kelly was delighted when other people thought they actually were deaf.

"You are very pretty today," Kelly said, flashing signs at Rose.

"Thank you."

"It's the new eyes."

Rose nodded and lowered her eyelids, showing the blue wash. She had made her face up with pale shades of red on her cheeks and coral on her lips.

"What does Henry say about it?" Kelly asked aloud.

Rose was surprised to hear Kelly's voice. "He doesn't know."

"You did it last week, too."

"He would think I was stupid," Rose said.

Kelly laughed, but stopped quickly. They went back to their sign language, fooling people in the cafeteria and on the sidewalk on their way to the Community Center.

The rest of the morning they worked with the deaf children, talking or playing or helping them build with blocks or Legos. Rose never ceased wondering at how the time flew. But sometimes she felt sad for the children. That morning, for instance, she watched a little girl walking a wooden goose. The goose's legs were attached by puppet strings, and the girl made it step, clop, clop, clop, along the floor. But somehow the goose's legs became tangled. The little girl tried to separate the strings, but couldn't, and tears bubbled up. How awful, Rose thought, to feel the tears streaming down your cheeks without being able to hear yourself cry.

At three o'clock the deaf children got onto their bus to go back to their school, and Rose always missed them when they went. She walked with Kelly up the block to the corner.

"Aren't you going home?" Kelly asked, when Rose stopped.

"No."

"Can I go with you? Where are you going?"

"I have to meet someone," Rose said, as though she were telling a secret.

"Who?"

Rose smiled. "Not Henry," she said. "I'm going to the museum."

"You went to the museum last weekend, too," Kelly said. Then Kelly's expression changed, as if she'd had a terrifying thought. "Are you seeing someone else, Aunt Rose? Are you in love with someone not Henry?"

On the uptown bus Rose opened her old purse and looked at herself in the mirror on the inside flap. She was certain the exercising had tightened the skin of her face. She ran a brush through her hair, which was longer now and rinsed darker. She put on a touch more eye shadow.

She was familiar now with the museum. She bore left in the big entrance hall, followed the corridor through the Greek and Roman sculpture, and proceeded to the bathroom near the cafeteria. There she tucked in her blouse and straightened her skirt and gave herself a final glance, with the vague disquiet that her lips were too pink. Then she went out and climbed the stairs to the André Meyer gallery.

At the doorway she hesitated and calmed herself with two deep breaths.

"So this is where you go," Henry said.

Rose turned and saw Henry coming up the stairs behind her. "What are you doing here?"

"The question is the reverse. What are *you* doing here?"

"You have no right to follow me."

Henry reached the landing and looked into the gallery. "This is where you meet him?"

"No."

"No? How unobservant do you think I am?" He ticked off the evidence on his fingers. "You never bought a purse. You start exercising. You want to take a vacation alone in Spain. You go to these classes." He looked at her. "And the make-up! My God."

For a moment Rose did not know what to say. What did he mean by these indictments? Then a coolness descended upon her just as though she had stepped out of the hot sun into the shade of an olive tree. Henry knew nothing. "Why are you stopping me now?" Rose asked. "Why not wait for proof?"

Henry looked confused.

"What time is it?" Rose asked. "It's almost four. If I were to meet someone here, as you say, it would be at four o'clock, wouldn't it? I'm dressed up. I should go."

"Rose, listen to me."

"You listen. I'm going to sit on that bench in the middle of the room. That's a likely place, isn't it? If someone is meeting me, you can watch. Now that you've followed me. . . ."

"I don't want to watch, Rose."

She didn't argue. She walked into the gallery and sat down facing Goya's portrait of the child, *Don Manuel Osorio Manrique de Zuniga*. The boy's hair was long and dark, and his lips were as red as the suit he wore. A wide white satin sash was tied at his waist on his left side, and the collar of his suit was white lace. The white satin slippers on his feet and the elegant clothes made him appear uncomfortable, as though he were unhappy with the moment. And yet, what a beautiful child! His cheeks were so pure, and the dark eyes so sharp and innocent! In his hands he held a leash tethered to a magpie on the ground. In the darkness behind—Goya was such a master of foreboding—three cats leered at the magpie as if ready to leap on the bird as soon as the child ceased his vigilance.

Rose felt guilty, yes, but her guilt was a manifestation of health, not of sickness. She was overjoyed that her own small existence was so blessed. She, of course, dreamed of Goya. She had not yet succumbed to him, but the anticipation made the enchantment more unbearable and sweet. The natural evolution would make her yield. He asked nothing of her, and she could give and give as much as she liked.

Henry watched her, half-hidden at the door. She nodded to him furtively and turned one corner of her mouth in an ambiguous smile. She made signs to him with her hands.

THE SPIRITS OF ANIMALS

The next day we were going bow hunting for antelope in the dry plateau west of Del Norte, and that Friday Wayne Carson and Jorge Martinez, two friends of mine from high school, drove over from Alamosa. Wayne had been pretty crazy for a couple of weeks because his wife Carol had run off to Pueblo with a steelworker. He'd broken up a bar and bashed in the windshield of a Mercedes, and his probation officer was threatening to send him back to county jail. Jorge thought Wayne could get interested in killing something, so we were going to spend the night in my trailer and get up before dawn on Saturday, which was opening day.

That evening we organized our gear—oiled the eccentric wheels on the compounds, tightened and waxed the bowstrings, filed the broadheads to razor sharp. Our camouflage was laid out. Wayne and Jorge had already picked up sandwiches from the Safeway. In the morning we'd make a thermos of coffee and be gone.

We were sitting around, and Jorge suggested we go into town. "Make some laughs," he said. "Have a couple of cold ones."

"There are cold ones in the fridge," I said.

"But in there no women." Jorge smiled. "You want to sit

around this dump all your life, man?"

He was right, the place wasn't very clean. There were books and magazines scattered all over, dirty clothes in the corner, dishes on the counter. There was never much reason to straighten up. When I got home from the dam construction site, I'd drink a couple of beers and doze and read.

"Do us all good, man," Jorge said. "Wayne needs to hear some music."

We took Wayne's truck. I figured we'd stay an hour or two, maybe watch the last few innings of the Cubs game on cable and be back by eleven. I knew how Jorge's excursions for women usually went.

It was a cool night with a breeze off the mountains. Jorge kept the window open, and we could smell the smoke from the Yellowstone fire in Wyoming five hundred miles to the north. That's what people said it was, though it was hard to imagine smoke's traveling so far. Smoke drifted through the headlights and made the town of Del Norte look far away, as if we were seeing it through gauze.

If it had been deer season, the town would have been jammed with hunters; but it wasn't deer season. It was late August and another Friday night. The ranchers and farmers had come in, along with the dam workers. The Elks were having a dance, but a live band was playing at the Sidewinder, so we went there.

We settled into a booth and ordered pitchers. Wayne asked for a round of tequila shots. That was the first bad sign. When Wayne was on edge, he gave his money away, but there was no pleasure in it. You didn't know how or why, but you owed him, and when he would collect was anybody's guess.

We drank our beers and tequilas and listened to the music—a band called Super Iguana—and between sets we talked. Jorge was a pipe fitter for a natural gas company, married with three children, though that didn't slow him any. And he could tell a good story. He told one about a left-handed woman giving a blow-job that made me laugh. I swear Jorge could make a nun forget about God. But he couldn't reach Wayne.

Around ten a few women came in from the Elks' dance. They didn't belong in the Sidewinder. They had on brightly colored dresses and jewelry and had their hair done up. There were maybe eight or ten of them—pretty women not from Del Norte. Jorge went over to the bar, and in a few minutes he'd brought two of them over to the booth.

"This here's Wayne," Jorge said to them. "He's a ranch foreman over in Alamosa. And this other one is Jimmy, who knows just about everything there is about construction. Jimmy's smart, too. He was fourth in our class."

"Fourth *boy*," I said. "And we had a small class."

"Jimmy Buffett," the one in the dark red dress said. "You look like Jimmy Buffett."

"This is Ruth," Jorge said, "and Ruth's friend."

Ruth had short, blondish hair and a lopsided smile that was more hard than friendly. "There wasn't any music at the Elks," she said. "Not so you could dance. We came here with a church group."

"Why don't you girls sit down?" Jorge said. "Slide over there, Wayne."

Wayne moved to the corner, but he didn't look too happy about it. Ruth slid in, and then Jorge, and the other woman sat next to me, not too close.

She was prettier than Ruth, I thought—dark hair nearly black, a round face, brown eyes—and quiet. When I asked her name, she said Cacky. That was all. She looked part Hispanic, which wasn't unusual around Del Norte, but there was something uncommon about her eyes. They were too dark, or maybe angry for a cause—something that made her appeal to me. She had on a tan dress and three bracelets on one wrist.

The bar gained momentum with the arrival of the women. People danced and moved around. Wayne ordered another round of tequilas.

The women had never drunk tequila before, but they seemed eager to learn. At least Ruth did.

"The best way to drink tequila," Jorge said, "is without using your hands." He picked up his glass in his teeth and snapped his head back. Ruth did the same, though she coughed and laughed, and dropped the glass on the table when it was empty.

Jorge, the gentleman, gave her some beer.

Cacky wouldn't talk much. She sipped her drink and stared at the dance floor. I could tell Wayne bothered her. She didn't like it when he spilled some beer and we had to sop it with napkins. Then he glowered from the corner. His head nodded, and just when it seemed he would pass out, he woke up again to see what he'd missed.

But Cacky made no move to leave or to find anyone else.

Neither did she move any closer.

"So what do you do?" I asked. "I heard Ruth say you two were from Monte Vista."

"I'm from Arizona."

"But live in Monte Vista."

"We work for the wildlife service. We count cranes."

"Cranes that fly?"

Cacky nodded. "Sandhills and whoopers. We're doing a migration census."

"And where do the cranes come from?"

"Idaho, Montana, Alberta. It's a little early still, but they'll start to move pretty soon."

Jorge and Ruth got up to dance. I looked at my watch.

"You have somewhere to be?" Cacky asked.

I nodded. "Hunting." I looked at Wayne, who had his head on the table. "We have to be out early morning, first light."

"Hunting birds?"

"Antelope."

Cacky's eyes brightened. "I know antelope," she said.

Jorge and Ruth came back locked arm in arm.

"It's almost eleven," I said. "We should get Wayne home."

"That's Wayne's way of having a good time," Jorge said. "We can't go yet."

"Maybe we should move the party," Ruth said. "Do you all have a place to go?"

Jorge looked at me. "We do, don't we, Jimmy?"

The next thing I knew we were hoisting Wayne into the truck. He was a big man, six two, and already with a gut. We propped him against the window on the shotgun.

Jorge and Ruth climbed into the bed of the truck, where they settled in among the sacks of feed and the toolboxes Wayne carried loose. Cacky had no choice but to get into the front seat between Wayne and me. She never once said she didn't want to go.

We started up the highway, crossed the irrigation canal, and turned northwest onto the gravel. Ruth and Cacky had left their car at the church in Monte Vista, seventeen miles the other direction, which raised in my mind the problem of how they would get home. But events moved along without regard to tomorrow. The line of willows along the canal diverged from us, and in a few minutes we were out into the blank darkness with the headlights funneling into smoke. I imagined flames leaping through brush and tons of ash pouring into the clear sky up in Wyoming.

Now and then I glanced over at Wayne passed out against the window. But I saw Cacky. She was staring ahead at the road, but not seeing it, the way I sometimes stared at the walls of my trailer, or at a line on a page without reading it. It wasn't the liquor. She had nursed her one tequila and had drunk only half a beer. I wondered what she meant to have happen, why she'd let Ruth talk her into coming.

The truck shimmied, as if it were bearing through a gust of wind, and I let up on the gas. A toolbox clanked in back. Cacky looked around, and in the rearview, I saw Jorge bare-assed on his knees. Ruth had her dress up around her waist, one leg over a sack of feed, and her arms wrapped around Jorge's back.

Cacky didn't say anything. Jorge and Ruth stopped after a few minutes, and the ride smoothed out again. Gravel skittered under the tires. In the far distance up ahead, the pole light above the trailer winked out of the smoky sky.

"What do you know about antelope?" I asked finally.

I could feel her smile, felt her look at me, though I couldn't see her face in the shadow. "I know they're dust devils," she said. "Whirlwinds and spirits, and their horns are made of silver."

TWO

It was still dark when we got up the next morning. Jorge and Ruth had taken my bed, so Cacky and I ended up in the living room—she on the sofa the last few hours and I on the floor. I woke Jorge, who was groggy from booze, and let Ruth sleep.

Wayne came in from the truck. Cacky had on Jorge's jeans and my camouflage jacket. "What the fuck is she doing?" Wayne asked.

"Going with us," I said.

"In dancing shoes?"

"She can drive the Jeep back from Devil's Quarry," I said. "We won't have to backtrack in the truck."

Wayne didn't like it, didn't like anything he wasn't in on. He got his gear and went out to the truck to wait for Jorge.

Jorge took his time. He put on his camouflage—two shades of brown and tan, no green—and brushed his face with charcoal. He had a bite to eat. I knew the wait out in the cold truck wasn't helping Wayne's mood.

Cacky and I led in the Jeep because I knew the country better than Wayne. We headed northwest, past the arc light at Achesons' feed pens and then back out into the darkness along the dry bed of Old Woman Creek.

The night before still addled me. I remembered Jorge and Ruth leaning against each other like two dazed fighters while I tried to unlock the door. It was chilly, and Cacky shivered beside me on the porch. Inside, the living room was as we'd left it, with our gear all over. I moved a bow and bow quiver from the sofa so people could sit down. But Jorge took Ruth down the hall to the bedroom.

Cacky stayed by the door. "You hunt with bows?" she asked.

That had been a revelation to her. She'd wanted to know all about it—how the compound bows worked, how we tracked game, where we went. It wasn't that we took the hunting that seriously, I told her. We shot a deer once in a while, but none of us had ever got an antelope.

She lifted one of the bows, felt its weight, the tension of the string. She had strong shoulders, and she could draw a compound easily. "Do you have an extra one?" she asked. "Can I go with you?"

"I have an old recurve," I said and managed a smile. "You want to go dressed like that?"

"I could borrow some clothes."

Cacky laid the bow down gently. I had no particular objection to her going. There was no reason a woman couldn't cover as much territory as a man. But I shook my head. "Wayne would be pissed," I said.

"Do you listen all the time to Wayne?"

I didn't answer. I was tired, too tired to think about it. That was when Cacky came over to where I was. She unzipped the back of her dress and slid her arms from the sleeves. "Please," she said. "I'll be quiet." She let the dress fall.

It was eerie driving the Jeep in the dark through terrain I knew well. It was a bleak country, dry as dust, a land of hogbacks rising from the earth like the backs of dinosaurs, and mesas that broke off into a series of barren ravines that petered out into sage flats. The Jeep had only one good headlight, and we couldn't see much— just gray sage at the sides of the road and now and then an outcropping of rock that loomed up like a shadow against the stars.

A quarter mile past the feedlot, the stench dissipated and the road disintegrated, too. In the rearview Wayne's headlights jumped and shifted as the truck tires hit rocks. He had stayed back a ways because of the dust, and now, when the terrain got steeper, he dropped back even farther.

Wayne had always had a streaky temper. I remembered once he hit his wife with a horseshoe because she'd said "fuck you" to him, and another time in a bar, he'd belted someone over whose quarter was up next for eight-ball. It didn't matter to Wayne what was right. The time I remembered best was in the state football playoffs. Wayne had kicked a field goal, and Alamosa was up 10–7 in the fourth quarter against Pueblo South. South was driving, but we had them fourth down and three on our 27-yard-line. They ran a sweep. I came up from linebacker and tackled their halfback for a loss, but Wayne, trailing the play, piled on and broke the ballcarrier's leg. With the penalty, South got first down on our 12, and we lost 14–10. That was how Wayne did things.

We traversed the flank of an invisible hill, then crested onto the plateau on a narrow, pockmarked track wide enough only for a single car. Cacky and I didn't speak. It was as though our fatigue was so pervasive that nothing made sense right then. Two people—total strangers—met in a bar and then, through flukey circumstances, ended up making love on the floor. Now we were careening over potholes and rocks on our way to hunt antelope. It seemed preposterous. Yet to me it had some meaning beyond fatigue, beyond mere coincidence. I wanted it to.

We stopped at the turnoff for the natural arch and waited for Jorge and Wayne. There was no sign for the arch. It was a place the locals knew, with just a trail leading north into the dark hills. This was where we left the truck.

Our plan was to take the Jeep another three miles cross-country. We'd drop Wayne off at the head of a wide ravine we called The Scoop, and then Jorge on the sandflats lower down. I'd drive the Jeep to Devil's Quarry and walk back over the hogbacks and the sage plateau, pushing the antelope ahead toward the two of them. It was a strategy that seemed logical but had never worked.

"So where are your friends?" Cacky asked. "I thought they were supposed to station themselves before it got light."

"They're coming," I said. I poured coffee from the thermos

and leaned against the front bumper. Light was beginning to seep up over the river and the hills.

Finally Wayne's headlights appeared at the lip of the mesa and sprayed out into the piñons on the upslope. He pulled up in a sweep of rising dust. When the dust settled, Wayne and Jorge got out.

"Jorge got sick," Wayne said. "The weak little shit."

"Too much love," said Jorge. He smiled and went off into the sage and threw up again.

Then Wayne climbed into the front seat of the Jeep where Cacky had been. Cacky and Jorge got in back, and we drove east on the level contour through the smoky dawn.

The mood was somber from hangovers and fatigue, or maybe from some unspoken anger. Except for Cacky. She wanted to know more about the bows, what the arrows were made of, why the strings had silencers on them. "Have you scouted this place?" she asked. "How do you know there are antelope here?"

"Jimmy comes up here all the time," Jorge said. "He brings his girlfriends."

"So you know there are antelope?"

I nodded. "Lots of antelope," I said, "but none with silver horns."

Wayne got out at the headwall of The Scoop. In other years we'd had a ceremonial shot of bourbon for luck, though it had never brought us any, but this time no one mentioned it. Wayne grabbed his bow and the back quiver he liked with six razorheads in it. Before I'd even thought about the bourbon, he was striding away down the hill. He didn't turn or wave.

"That Wayne," Jorge said. "No wonder his wife left him."

Cacky climbed up front again, and we kept on east, skirting the ravine and picking our way through piñons and junipers on the other side. The headlight ricocheted through the trees and out into the plateau.

Then we were into the sage. The brush crackled under the Jeep. The sage smell rose around us like mist. We bounced over the anthills and prairie dog mounds and clumps of buffalo grass. I stopped on the edge of the sand wash and let Jorge out.

Jorge didn't look so good. He was sweating and shaking.

"Sure you're okay?" I asked.

I held out my hand, and he slid his palm across mine. Then he snugged on his camouflage cap and smiled. "You drive them to me, and I'll pick them off."

Cacky and I went on. By then it was nearly full light, and I snapped off the headlight. We rode, listening to the revving engine and the scraping of the sage. In about half a mile I pointed to a collection of boulders ahead of us. "That's Devil's Quarry," I said. "You think you can find your way back in the Jeep?"

"Follow the Jeep tracks," Cacky said. "But I'm going with you. I want to try the bow."

"Okay," I said. "For a while."

We came over a low hogback and down into a stretch of hills and gullies barren of trees. At Devil's Quarry I stopped and let the engine die. For a minute we listened to the breeze slide through the rocks. The sun was rising now into thin smoke. It was quiet, cold.

I leaned across the seat and kissed Cacky on the lips. She didn't object, but she didn't help, either. She kept her eyes open. Then after a moment she broke away. "I thought we were hunting antelope," she said. She cracked open the side door and climbed out.

The breeze up from the river was cool, and I buttoned my jacket. I broke off a branch of sagebrush and rubbed the sage into my palms and across my face and shoulders.

"Cover the scent," I said.

Cacky did the same.

I strung up my old 45-pound recurve for her—a fiberglass model I'd shot a deer with once over by Antonito. A recurve didn't take so much experience as a compound, but it took more strength to pull. The bow still had a bowsight on it, which was useful, and I'd sighted it in last week in case my compound broke down.

Cacky had a good instinct with a bow. I gave her three broadheads with damaged feathers to shoot at an anthill, and she barely missed with the first two and drove the third center left.

"How're your feet?" I asked.

"Cold."

"You'll warm up when we walk. When we get to the fenceline, we'll stay along it. Antelope don't go over fences. They go through them, but they need an angle. We'll try to keep them parallel."

We descended along the general edge of the trees to our right, through piñons and scrub oak. Now and then Cacky stopped to get her bearings or to look at some track of an animal, and once at a bluebird perched in the sage. But mostly we kept moving. We skirted the trees and angled across the low hogbacks. On the flats Cacky walked fine, but in the boulders her shoes slipped, and I had to help her.

When we emerged from the boulders, I scanned the wide sweep of the plateau with the binoculars. After a minute, I handed the glasses to Cacky. There was a small herd of antelope grazing in a swale ahead of us maybe three-quarters of a mile—half a dozen of them, pale tan and white.

"What should we do?" Cacky whispered.

"They haven't caught wind of us yet," I said. "We'll stalk them."

The breeze was tricky, coming uphill. We needed to get lower to have a good bead on them. There were five does and a pretty nice buck. I motioned Cacky to head out to the left and circle. I'd wait and then go to the right. The idea was to get close for a shot, or, if they bolted, to push them toward Jorge or farther up the ravine to Wayne.

"Go gently," I said to Cacky, pushing down the air with my hands.

It was a slow dance. Cacky picked her way downhill through the sagebrush, which billowed around her knees like clouds. I followed the same path on the hill, as if connected to her by mirror image. There was no real cover. I stood still when Cacky advanced. Then she would duck down while I took a few careful steps. She moved away and diminished until she was a speck against the backdrop of gray-green cottonwoods far past her at the river.

It was impossible to guess what the antelope would do. I'd seen them hold still when I approached into a headwind and carried no weapon, and I'd seen them run when a car backfired two miles away. That morning they stayed put. Maybe the Yellowstone fire had scrambled their senses. Maybe the buck was lazy or sick. But we were able to sneak in as close as I'd ever been to an antelope.

At a hundred yards I took an arrow from my bow quiver and nocked it on the string. Any moment I expected the buck to snort and take off. At sixty yards I knelt down and took aim. The buck was facing away from me, and I didn't like rear shots, so I waited a second for him to turn. The sun glanced from the aluminum arrow. I squinted past my bow hand, closing out everything except a spot on the buck's pale shoulder.

Then Cacky clapped her hands.

I was as startled as the antelope, but they were quicker. They leaped forward and were at full speed by the second or third step. I let the arrow fly more from instinct than aim, and it sailed wildly over the buck's white rear end.

I looked over at Cacky, who was standing with her hands on her hips watching the antelope bound away through the sage. "Aren't they beautiful?" she called out. "It would be a shame to kill the spirit of an animal."

THREE

There was no sense crying. I started down the slope toward Achesons' fenceline—a mile-long stretch of barbed wire and cedar posts that cut the plateau off from the crusty alkali flats below. I was hoping to keep the antelope on the fence until it jagged back to the right about where Jorge was.

I walked fast, more from frustration than any idea of catching the antelope. I shouldn't have brought Cacky, should never have got mixed up with her. It had been my first good chance in four years to shoot an antelope. Wayne and Jorge and I had spent days waiting and stalking, sweating and freezing, camouflaged, scented up with sage or apple or dung. Antelope were the hardest animals to hunt because of the open terrain, and there I was finally with a fair chance, a real chance, and Cacky had spooked them.

I looked back once to see where she'd gone, but she wasn't headed toward the Jeep where I thought she'd go. She was in the trees at the lower end of the hogback, having trouble with her shoes. Or maybe she'd brushed a prickly pear. She was bent over as if she were pulling cactus spines from her ankle.

I didn't care about Cacky. A quarter mile farther on I reached the jog in the fence, held up there, and scanned for Jorge. He was asleep on a ledge just above the sandflats in the shade of a rock.

Through the muddled glass he looked peaceful, more peaceful than I ever was, a man without worry. He had a wife and family and a Catholic God to forgive his sins. He obviously hadn't seen the antelope.

I yelled to him, and he stood up on the ledge and waved. I motioned for him to meet me at the other side of the wash.

I liked the wash. Every time it rained, the sand smoothed out and you could read the signs of what animals had passed there. But it hadn't rained in a while. Tracks were scattered all over—the cloven hoofprints of deer and antelope, the padded marks of rabbits and coyotes. In the middle of the wash I found the dry carcass of a fawn maybe caught by a flashflood and washed down from the canyon.

The sun was up now and warm, and sweat rolled under my jacket. Jorge joined me on the far side near a stunted pine tree that had somehow taken root in the sand.

"There were six of them," I said. "We pushed them to you."

"I was ready," Jorge said, "but they were pretty far away."

"I saw how ready you were."

Jorge smiled. "You scared them with your yelling." He nudged me with a pint of Yukon Jack. "Where's Cacky?" he asked.

"Up top." I took a swallow of the whisky and felt the burn.

"She working on over?"

I shrugged and drank another hit. Up the hill the air was oddly translucent, like looking through quartz.

"How was she?" Jorge asked.

"Who?"

"Who do you think?"

I gathered what he meant. "It didn't happen," I said. "We went to sleep is all."

Jorge took back the bottle, drank, wiped his mouth on his sleeve. "She's Indian. You know that? That's what Ruth said."

"What kind of Indian?"

Jorge stared at me. "Shit, man, I don't know. What difference does it make?"

It seemed it ought to make a difference. Everything should make a difference one way or another. It must have made a difference to Cacky, which explained some things.

Jorge capped the bottle and put it back into his pocket. "Let's get an antelope and go home," he said. "Ruth's waiting."

The hard ground on the west side of the wash yielded no tracks. It was anybody's guess where the antelope had gone, so Jorge and I split up. He took the lower route, out and around, and I went higher along the mesa. I climbed to the ledge where Jorge had been sleeping and worked my way below the trees. I couldn't see Cacky. She must have been above me in the trees or over one of the hogbacks between where I was and The Scoop.

I wondered now about her, why she'd wanted to hunt, or as

it was, not hunt, how she'd grown up. In Arizona there were Navajos, Hopis, Pimas, and several groups of Apaches. My guess was she was Apache, a warrior.

From up in the hills I could see the smoke ribbon the sky above the whole valley all the way to Alamosa. It was no clean view I was used to—high clouds, clear distant peaks. That morning the only landmark visible was the natural arch, a curving bow silhouetted in a whitish sky.

I stood for a long time watching because that's what I did in my life.

Then Cacky called.

My first thought was that she had an antelope down, but that was absurd. If she wouldn't let me shoot one, she wouldn't shoot one herself. Or would she? I came off the treeline full tilt.

I ran awkwardly, keeping the bow and the arrows tucked in my bow quiver tight against my body. I two-stepped into a swale and up a grassy embankment, dodging sagebrush. I felt my legs soften.

At the edge of The Scoop, I clambered up a rocky outcropping where I could see down and across. My whole body was shaking, and my breath was gone. Cacky was on the hillside on the far side of the ravine, and she had the recurve drawn on Wayne.

Wayne was on the same contour twenty feet from Cacky, one leg lower down the slope than the other. He had stripped off his camouflage and was shirtless, still holding his bow at his side. At his feet with an arrow in its shoulder was a dead coyote.

Wayne saw me and lifted his head, but he didn't make any sudden move. "Tell her to ease off," Wayne said. "Do something."

I didn't know what I could do. I glanced around for Jorge, but he hadn't appeared yet at the bottom of the ravine. It would have taken Cacky only an instant to release the bowstring, and Wayne would be hurt bad or dead. She was close enough not to miss.

I climbed down through the rocks and onto the clay hill and approached Cacky from the side so she could see me clearly without having to give up her position. I dropped down a little lower and edged along the slope toward the dry streambed. Clay crumbled under my feet and rolled. When I reached the bottom of the ravine, I angled up to a point between her and Wayne, but lower.

Then I sat down. The ground under me was warm from the

sun. I laid my bow on the dry clay.

"What the hell," Wayne said. "What're you doing?"

I didn't answer. Wayne knew his predicament. Such a situation was created by agreement: Wayne admitted the power of the weapon, and Cacky was determined to use it. Calling a bluff was tough. The only variable was how long Cacky could hold the recurve drawn.

The coyote was a thin one. Its head was away from me, but the shoulder, the broadest part, was barely as wide as the rump. There were marks in the clay higher up where the coyote had fallen, and Wayne's footprints coming down the slope. The coyote's blood oozed downhill and into the clay.

Cacky's face was hard-set, pretty, too, her lips tight. One eye was narrowed against the bowstring. She didn't look at me.

It struck me then what she was doing. "Why'd you kill it, Wayne?" I asked.

"What the hell is wrong with you?" Wayne said. He turned just enough to look at me.

"I want you to tell me."

"You know fucking *why*."

I smiled, though it wasn't a smile.

Wayne stared at me. "You're going to let her keep me here?"

"I don't see that I'm letting her do anything."

"Some kind of payment," Wayne said. "Is that it?"

"Are you going to tell me or not?"

I thought about payment. In a way it was a payment, though not in the way Wayne meant. And it was more than that. It was something I needed to know, too.

Wayne shifted his weight carefully from one foot to the other. He looked at Cacky. Her bow hand was shaking from holding the tension on the string.

"She isn't going to shoot me," Wayne said.

Then I picked up my bow, stood up, and fitted an arrow to the string. I drew and took aim at a spot of coyote's blood on Wayne's chest. "No, she isn't going to shoot you," I said, "but I might."

Cacky lowered her bow and let off on the string.

Wayne looked back at me.

"Drop your bow, Wayne," I said.

Wayne held his stance a few seconds, then let the bow slide from his hand along the string until the eccentric wheels at the end caught his fingertips. The bow spun across the clay and skidded to the bottom of the ravine.

"Now back up the hill."

He took a step backward. I raised my bow, following the spot of blood.

Wayne backed up another step.

I meant to say something more then, to Cacky more than to Wayne, something about the spirits of animals or love, but she wouldn't have understood. So I didn't say anything.

Wayne backed up the hill. When he was out of good range, when maybe he could have dodged my arrow, he turned and scrambled up into the rocks.

FOUR

That afternoon I took Cacky and Ruth and Jorge over to Monte Vista. Clouds had risen in the northwest and drove hard over the mountains. Rain slanted like gray curtains in front of the oncoming headlights of cars. I imagined the water collecting in the gullies and ravines, washing down the plateau over the sand, erasing tracks.

We rode in intermittent conversation, mostly Jorge trying to make me sound good to Cacky. He felt sorry for me. "He builds a fireplace like Michelangelo," Jorge said. "And foundations—shit, can he pour *concrete*."

"I'm hoping not to go on welfare this winter," I said.

"The man has ideas," Jorge said. "He *reads*."

The storm shifted south, and where we were the clouds broke apart. A new cool light flowed down over the fields of alfalfa and corn, though the highway was still slick with rain. The air was washed of smoke.

I left Jorge off a couple of blocks from the Valley Farmer where he was going to call his wife to come and get him. He kissed Ruth goodbye. Then I turned south on Washington Street toward the church.

We rode through a quiet neighborhood of white houses where the streets were puddled with water. Some of the sprinklers were still going on the lawns.

"What's wrong with you two?" Ruth said. "Can't you be polite and talk a little?"

"We're polite," Cacky said. "We're just tired."

"You aren't going to tell me what happened up there?"

"I already told you," Cacky said. "We didn't shoot an antelope."

Theirs was the only car in the parking lot at the church. Ruth got out and let Cacky and me be alone. I let the engine run.

There wasn't much to say. I suppose I thought making love ought to be love, at least a little, but I didn't know what Cacky thought. I told her I wanted to see her again, and she nodded, meaning neither yes nor no. "You should come out to the refuge and watch the cranes," she said.

I promised I would.

Then she kissed me quickly and got out. She passed in front of the Jeep's lone headlight still on from the rain and got into Ruth's Ford. Cacky waved to me, and then she and Ruth were gone out of the lot and around the corner. I turned off the engine of the Jeep and sat for a minute, looking at the gray sunlit façade of the church, wondering what existed and what didn't and what I was going to do in the long winter ahead.

THE MINE FROM NICARAGUA

Barkley Ravenel did not usually pay attention to things washed up on the beach in front of his house unless, for instance, it was a right whale or a dead sea turtle—something natural. Lately he considered the beach a thin landscape without motion or energy, a canvas devoid of any evidence of sea life. The birds, except for gulls and terns, had diminished markedly, and the shells which had formerly been profuse were now only a rim of tiny shards at the line of high tide.

That evening he was walking with Kate Pickering, a friend of his wife's, from Richmond, Virginia, who had been their houseguest for a week. Barkley claimed Kate had been on tour ever since she had lost her husband to intestinal cancer eight months ago. She had been traveling from one friend to another in the Carolinas, drinking their gin and talking about how much Creighton had suffered in the end.

"I'm going to say something terrible to her," Barkley had told Muriel in private when he changed into shorts for the beach. "If she mentions that nematode Creighton again, I'll let her have it right between the eyes."

"You will do no such thing."

"I swear I will. For once I'm going to lose my patience. It might behoove you to come with us and protect her."

"Kate's a sweet soul," Muriel said. "And I have this headache." She lay down on the apricot bedspread and put her forearm over her eyes. "Anyway, you take your walk every evening. What difference does it make whether Kate goes with you?"

"Because I'll have to be pleasant."

"Well," Muriel said, "Kate understands."

Kate might have understood, but Barkley didn't. Moving south had changed Muriel, and she confused him. He liked breakfast at seven, dinner at eight, just as they'd enjoyed it in Philadelphia for years, but she refused to cooperate. "What's the rush to get up?" she'd ask. "Are you going somewhere?" Or more often, "I won't be here for breakfast, Barkley. I'm playing tennis before it gets too hot."

And her manners had disintegrated. Muriel's going with Kate that evening was the merest act of politeness her friend might have expected, and, of course, it would have freed him for his solitary vigil over the demise of the sea. But he didn't argue with her. He stood over the bed for a moment and looked at Muriel's frizzy blond hair buried under her arm. How long had she been dying her hair that color, he wondered. Where had she bought the blue scarf around her neck or the gold bracelet on her wrist?

"We'll be back for supper at eight," was all he said.

It was a balmy evening. The beach stretched before them a good mile or more until it feathered away finally beyond the pier into a haze of gray and brown condominiums. This particular reach of sand on the south end of the island was more private than the northern part. A few live oaks and pines had been preserved here amidst the huge houses, and several rows of accreted sand dunes protected the houses from the water as well as from the riffraff who sunned themselves there on the beach. Still it was overbuilt. Houses opposed the sea on every lot, and the relics of *Homo horribilis* were inescapable: beer bottles, plastic milk containers, waterlogged boards. Barkley liked to imagine the day when a hurricane would sweep across the island from front to back and wash the evidence of man's arrogance—houses and all—to the headland.

Two older men in skimpy black briefs jogged along in front of the burnished calm of the outgoing tide. Nearby, a churlish woman packing her things stopped to admonish her child to bring to her the implements with which he was laying waste the sand sculptures of already departed children. A few people waded pensively in the shallow surf, staring blankly, Barkley thought, at their own destinies. One dreamer—hasn't he heard the news?—had rolled up his pantlegs to his knees and was casting a piece of bait into the murky waves.

Barkley had always thought of Kate as a woman contented with her time and place. She and Creighton had loved Richmond, the last undiscovered southern city, she said. When their children were grown, they had done the rounds of cocktail parties, oyster roasts, and polo games. She had been more retiring then, he remembered, in the tradition of southern women, and thinner, too, before she started consuming so much gin. She had dressed rather elegantly and simply, as if she aspired to the pages of *Southern Living*.

On this visit, however, she seemed more physical, more intimidating. The weight she'd gained was part of it, of course, but she dressed more garishly now in reds and greens. She was more outspoken, too. Sometimes, to his astonishment, she flat-out argued with Muriel. She debated the merits of onion in quiche, pine-scented spray for the bathrooms, and whether the new dishwasher Muriel had bought was as good as a Hotpoint.

Once Kate had even started in on him, and had he not been raised by parents who had served thirty-five years in the diplomatic service, he would have told her to go to hell. "Barkley," she'd said, "I don't like that shirt on you. You're too slender for stripes."

"I am?"

"You have a few good years left. You could still be an attractive man. Take heed what you wear."

"I'll remember your advice," he said. "And I'll speak to my buyer."

That was as close as he got to rudeness.

Barkley knew they would not be gone long that evening because the cocktail glass Kate had brought with her was nearly empty by the time they reached the first bend in the island. He was about to suggest a retreat to their porch when Buck Walsh appeared in front of them with his chocolate Lab, Westmoreland, on a leash. Barkley waved as a matter of habit because Buck never stopped to chat.

But that evening he did.

"Seen that thing down the beach?" he asked.

"Not yet," Barkley said.

"I'm going to get a wrench."

"What on earth for?" Kate asked. "What is it?"

"We don't know," Buck said. And off he went running.

"Who was that?" Kate wanted to know when Buck disappeared out of earshot over the dunes. "He's a hunk."

Barkley didn't see anything hunky about Buck Walsh, but if Kate found him so, maybe she would drink some of his gin. Buck did a daily grind with Westmoreland to the pier and back, lumbering along as if he too had four legs, the two in front too short to reach the ground. "Buck Walsh," Barkley said. "Nice guy. Retired military. Divorced."

"Where is the thing he was talking about?" Kate asked. "I don't see it." She held her bejeweled hand up to shade her eyes.

Just past the inward turn in the island they spotted a small knot of three or four people gathered around something in the sand. Barkley thought he recognized Alice Osborne, the cellist from Boston who spent the spring flower season there on the island, and Ned Menotti, the developer who owned an immense, three-story house behind the dunes. People said Alice was crazy, a euphemism which meant little to Barkley. If craziness produced the music Alice played, then insanity was a blessing. He had heard her in recital once in Philadelphia, and she had performed Beethoven and Haydn so perfectly that he still remembered, years later, how the air in the hall had seemed magical.

He angled away from the group, though, out toward the tidal pools left exposed by the receding sea. Even if Kate thought Buck Walsh was Schwarzenegger, Barkley wanted to avoid those people. He didn't like Menotti's glad-handing or the importunities of the man in the yellow trousers whom he strongly suspected was Marshall Cartwright. Marshall had been a college golf star and was always challenging Barkley to play for money.

But Kate called to him. "Don't you want to see what it is?"

"If it requires a wrench, it can't be too inspiring."

"Oh, come on," Kate said. "Don't be such a stump."

She started off decisively toward the group, as if she were going to demand surrender of someone. Her stride across the sand, her clenched fists, her red-and-white cotton dress flouncing on her hips: he could only follow her, as was his proper duty under the circumstances.

Barkley had retired at fifty from his own pharmaceutical manufacturing business in Philadelphia so he and Muriel could move south. She had felt claustrophobic in the city and was ill part of every year before they moved. "A little winter is good," Muriel had said, "but not too much. Don't you want to relax in your old age?"

"I haven't reached my old age," Barkley said.

"But you'll want to explore."

He had not wanted to explore, although he hadn't minded the idea of warmer weather, some golf, and Muriel's better health and mood. Pennsylvania's climate was little better than disease itself, and he had grown tired of gray days, acid rain, and the lack of a vista. Certainly they had enough money. That part had been simple.

What had surprised him, moving to the island, was how lonely he felt. Muriel had right away made friends and started playing tennis and bridge, and sometimes golf, though never with him. And she was stronger spiritually. Once, when he'd asked her to play golf, she'd simply said no. "You're a man. You're too good. And it's no fun to be beaten all the time."

"We'll handicap," he said.

"Don't you patronize me!" she said.

Or she would go shopping, leaving him alone for hours. She'd dress up in bright print blouses and slacks and lunch with her friends from the club, and afterward they'd tour the malls. Once when he heard her jangling her car keys, he'd asked her, "Where to today?"

"Belk's, Parisians, Macy's," she said. "Laverne wants to try the new mall across town, so I'll be late."

"Do you mind if I come along?"

"Oh, Barkley, you wouldn't enjoy it."

"I might."

"But what would you do? You're such a nickety-pick. You'd say this color wasn't right or that design wasn't perfect. You're a diddy-fuddy that way. Don't you trust me?"

"What does trust have to do with it?"

"And I don't spend that much."

"It isn't the money," he said.

"Then what?" She had paused almost defiantly in the white doorway to the garage.

"What do you get from it?" he asked.

She stared at him a moment and then gave a half-smile. "What did you get from all those years making chemicals?"

Kate reached the group first, though Barkley had raced to catch her in order to discuss the matter. It was Ned Menotti and, alas, Marshall Cartwright who were standing around a rather odd-looking object in the sand. One of the women was Alice Osborne. She was taller and older than Barkley remembered her from the night of the recital. She had seemed then small and vulnerable to the music—*camouflaged,* he had thought, by her instrument. Now, though, she wore shorts and a plain shirt and a dramatic turquoise scarf over her gray hair.

Ned put out a beefy hand as soon as Barkley and Kate walked up. "Barkley? Ned Menotti. We met once at the marina."

"I remember," Barkley said. He shook hands. "This is my wife's friend, Kate Pickering, from Richmond."

"I'm your friend, too," Kate said quickly.

Introductions went around, and Kate shook hands with both men and women.

Barkley nodded to Alice Osborne. "I've heard you perform," he said.

"Oh, where?"

"Philadelphia. It was several years ago now."

"Beethoven and Haydn," Alice said. "This is my former student, Lee Rodgers, who's playing one of the Beethoven concertos at Tanglewood this summer."

Alice motioned toward the other woman, who was younger, auburn-haired. She was dressed in pale blue slacks and wore a man's shirt untucked at the waist. She looked about forty, Barkley thought, and she was hardly tanned at all, which probably meant she never went outdoors, except when, as now, the sun slanted at a sharp angle from the headland and was not strong enough to harm the skin. She had blue eyes, rather eager, and a bow mouth lightly pinked.

"So what is it?" Kate said, pointing to the object in the sand.

"We don't know," Marshall said. "Fascinating, isn't it?"

Barkley shuddered. It must be utterly fascinating to interest such a dim-witted dolt as Marshall. But he had to agree it looked odd. It was black, cylindrical, made of—it was hard to say what. From end to end it was about five feet long, and its diameter was perhaps two feet, maybe less, approximately that of the husk of a palm tree washed up nearby on the beach. At the ends of the cylinder were two brass fixtures, patinaed green, and attached to a sturdy-looking plate.

"Buck went to get a wrench," Alice said. "The men are going to open it for us."

"Do you think it opens?" Kate asked.

"It will if we want it to," Ned Menotti said.

"I'd like the brass fittings for my flagpole," Marshall said. He gestured toward the empty pole in front of a massive blue house beyond the dunes.

The houses there were monstrosities with wraparound porches and decks, gabled like Ned Menotti's or topped like Marshall Cartwright's with a crow's nest high up for a panoramic view of the ocean. Alice Osborne lived in one of them, too, but Barkley couldn't remember which one, having never been there himself.

"Alice thinks it's filled with cocaine," Ned said.

"Marijuana, at least," Alice said. "It's got to be a smuggler's container."

"I think it's the bumper from a boat," Marshall said. "You know, one of those things they hang over the rail to keep the yacht from hitting the dock—a fender."

"Out of leather?" Kate asked.

"Is it leather?"

Barkley leaned over to touch the surface. It felt like hard leather or maybe rubber.

"The thing couldn't float, could it?" Kate asked.

"How would it get here," Barkley asked, "if it couldn't float?"

"Someone could have dumped it," Ned said. "Maybe a hospital wanted to get rid of an iron lung."

"You'd be surprised what can float," Marshall said. "Bonds, loans, all sorts of things. They make boats these days out of steel and concrete."

"So," Lee said, turning suddenly to Barkley, "what do you think it is?"

Barkley felt the heat rise immediately to his face. His mind went blank. It was the kind of moment he most detested—feeling he had to justify himself to others, to be knowledgeable about what he had no idea about, or witty, which was worse.

"Guess," Ned said. "I claim it's a wheel off a whale's roller skate. Buck thinks it's a roller for golf greens."

"Which reminds me, Barkley," Marshall said, "I've got a tee time Saturday, if you want to duke it out."

"No thanks," Barkley said. He circled the object again, tried to lift one end. It was very heavy, and he could barely move it. A drop of perspiration fell from his forehead. He stood up straight. "I think it's a mine from Nicaragua," he said, pronouncing the name of the country in rapid Spanish.

Ned slapped him on the back. "A mine. Ha-ha. That's very good. Very clever, Barkley. We'll all explode." Ned pinched Barkley's shoulder in the palm of his hand.

Just then Buck Walsh came trotting back up the beach like King Kong, carrying in one hand a socket wrench set and in the other a stack of plastic cups and a thermos. Westmoreland padded alongside. "I brought the wrench," he said, out of breath from running. "And I mixed some martinis."

"Be careful," Ned said. "Barkley thinks it's a mine."

Buck handed Ned the thermos.

Barkley knew Kate liked this turn of events, and he considered going on up the beach alone. He wasn't in the mood for Buck's martinis or Ned's histrionics or Marshall's vapid observations. Besides, he sensed Lee didn't like him, or at least wanted to put him on the spot. Lee was probably short for Leafy or Leeward.

But the beach was still splotched with people loading up their umbrellas and radios and coolers, and he had certainly spent enough hours wandering that wasteland. So he stood at the periphery as Ned poured the martinis.

Kate was served first, then Alice. Lee passed her cup on to Barkley. "I'm not a taker," she said. "I'm a giver."

Barkley gazed into the cup. "What?" he asked. "No olive?"

Lee's eyes were too blue, Barkley thought, and he didn't like the way they measured him so carefully. He didn't like, either, the way she had fastened her hair over on one side of her head with a barrette.

"Have you been to Nicaragua?" she said. She pronounced it the same way he had, though more gently.

"My parents were in the embassy there for ten years," he said. "I went to school in Managua."

"It's a brilliant country," Lee said.

"Somoza was in power when I was there," Barkley said. "But Managua seemed civilized."

"You think it's not civilized now?"

"There are desperadoes on both sides," Barkley said. "I still watch it, of course, but more in the sense of following the Phillies or the Red Sox."

"What a terrible thing to say!" Lee said.

"It's hard to get much information here," Barkley said. "The newspapers . . ."

But Lee had moved away. What he'd said wasn't exactly what he meant. He'd wanted to be impartial, and he felt he had in some way offended her. He'd been there so long ago, and he'd been so young, only a child. His memories about Nicaragua were of the gardens, the birds, the myriads of flowers, the wistful people. He remembered his mother rising early in the hazy heat and walking as if on smoke down the long hallway of the villa where they lived. His father was always remarkably calm, like a swimmer who, having just emerged from the pool, knew exactly where to extend his hand for a waiting towel. Meals were served punctually there, and the floors were made of glistening clean tile.

The Sandinistas had, for a while, taken the higher ground, but the U.S. policy had kept them on the run for years. It was hard to get reliable information anywhere. He supposed each side revised history to serve itself. He hadn't meant to disagree.

"I'll tell Muriel," Kate whispered to him.

Barkley broke from his reverie, surprised at the intrusion of Kate's voice. "Tell her what?"

"You're staring at that woman."

"I was minding my own business," Barkley said. He took a sip of his martini. "Look, why don't we get along home? It'll be dinnertime pretty soon."

"And miss the fun? Who is this Ned Menotti? I like the way he pours a martini."

Buck Walsh had squatted down at one end of the cylinder and had started fiddling with the various sizes of sockets, trying to see which one would fit the bolts. He found the right one, then paused to let Ned make a toast.

"To the mine from Nicaragua," Ned said, raising his cup.

They all gestured, even Barkley, and Buck turned the first bolt. It took some effort.

"I do hope it's cocaine," Alice said. "Then we'll have a real party."

"I hope it's money," said Marshall.

"You can't snort money," Ned said.

"You can try."

Barkley almost wanted it to be cocaine. He knew cocaine was an evil drug used primarily by professional athletes and rock musicians, but at that moment he would have tried some himself. He would have liked to escape the dreary present with something more potent and immediate than a martini.

"Is he in the Mafia?" Kate asked.

"Who?"

"Ned Menotti."

"He's a developer," Barkley said. "It's the same thing. He built Whispering Shores up the island—leveled everything and put in condos and ninety holes of golf. He's done shopping malls, too, including the Georges Pompidou Annex in town." Barkley paused, seeing that Kate was barely listening. "I'll tell Creighton," he said.

Kate stared at him in astonishment.

"I'm sorry," Barkley said. "Really."

"You bastard," Kate said. Then her expression transformed from shock to an eerie delight. Her whole face brightened. "Go ahead," she said. "Tell Creighton. I wish I could tell him."

"I didn't mean it."

Kate looked away toward the ocean. "You know what? Creighton was a first-magnitude ass. He was one of those holier-than-thou Jimmy Carter types. He didn't drink. He didn't smoke. He didn't tell a joke. In all the time we were married, I never knew what Creighton thought was funny. Don't you think that's sad?"

"Muriel doesn't think anything's funny."

"Creighton probably got intestinal cancer from a broom up his rear end," Kate said. "I shouldn't have said that, but, God, Barkley, if you knew."

"Hey, Barkley," Ned called, "do you know what a mine looks like? Come over here."

Kate took Barkley's arm.

"The CIA does," Barkley said.

Buck had loosened the bolts and was twisting and pulling at the plate.

"I assume a mine wouldn't sink," Barkley said. "A ship would have to run aground to strike it. But wouldn't it have to be beneath the surface? Maybe the rings were used to tether it down."

A bird flew up from behind the dunes and landed near them

on the sand. It scurried a few yards, then stopped and gave a loud *whit,* as if in alert.

"It's a killdeer," Barkley said. "It's warning us."

"Wilson's plover," Lee Rodgers said. "One breast band. They nest here in the dunes."

Barkley had never heard of a Wilson's plover. This bird, now that he looked, was a little smaller than a killdeer. Westmoreland lunged at it, and the bird flew.

Buck whacked at the eye-ring of the mine with the wrench, but the plate didn't budge. A mine couldn't be too sensitive, either, Barkley thought. It couldn't blow up with the movement of the tides. He wondered what sort of trigger it would have, whether Buck's hammering could detonate it. He imagined a flash of light and an instantaneous noise. Shrapnel screamed outward into arms, legs, eyes, cheeks, into Lee Rodgers's auburn hair.

"Here, let me try," Ned said. He took the wrench back from Buck and straddled the cylinder to get a better angle to beat the thing into oblivion. But instead he threaded the wrench through the eye-ring and, using the handle as a lever, tried to break the seal. But even Ned couldn't do it.

"It must be screwed on from the inside," Buck said. "We'll have to cut it open somehow."

"I have a sharp knife at my house," Alice said. "Why don't we take it there? It's the closest place. We women will go ahead and fix food and drink."

Barkley shook his head. "Why don't we leave it until tomorrow? It's nearly time for dinner."

But the other men agreed with Alice and started to roll the cylinder toward the dunes.

"There's always one uncurious soul," Lee Rodgers said. "Kate, you can stay, can't you?"

Kate moved from Barkley's arm to Lee's, and the two women turned toward the row of big houses.

Barkley stepped backward toward the water. He was free of them, and the beach was empty now except for a few joggers heading back up toward the pier. The scene reminded him of a lovely old photograph, a tintype still and serene and fixed unalterably in the past.

Then he heard the Wilson's plover call again somewhere at the edge of the dunes. He scanned the grasses and the sea oats around whose stems the wind had woven tiny scallops. *Whit.* The bird ran out across the flats where the receding tide had left patterns of darker, heavier sand sculpted in wavelets. It was a robin-sized bird, brown and white, with a single black breast band. It stood erect for a moment, then folded its head under its wing.

Light was fading now behind the houses, but in the darkening, a glow spread like mist over the dunes and sea oats and out over the rising sea. Barkley felt a sudden pang of loneliness, and he made his way back across the barren sand toward Ned and Marshall and Buck, who were pushing the mine up and over the first tier of dunes.

Transporting the mine was a harder job than Barkley thought it would be with four grown men. It was heavy and, in the finer dry sand of the dunes, hard to turn over. It took them twenty minutes to wrestle it through three separate rows of dunes, and then they had to carry it through a thicket of freshwater reeds and wax myrtles.

When they got near the lawn, the women called to them and waved. They were bringing out trays of food and glasses to a table set with a white tablecloth and flowers.

The men brought the mine up onto the lawn. Marshall Cartwright sat down on it and wiped his forehead with a pink handkerchief. "You sure you don't want to play golf on Saturday, Barkley? Ten dollars a hole, and I'll give you a half a stroke."

"You're on," Barkley said.

Kate steadied herself with a hand on the table. She had been busy on a new batch of martinis, Barkley could tell, and she gave Ned a beatific smile. "So, did you boys hit it off?"

"Mission accomplished," Ned said, as if they had just stormed the beach. "Are you one of the island girls?"

"I could show you around," Kate said.

"Help yourselves to whatever you see," Alice said, waving her hand over the hors d'oeuvres. "And there are more martinis."

They all set upon the food as if they hadn't eaten in days. There was pâté, Saga blue cheese, carrot strips, cauliflower stalks, and a half dozen kinds of chips and dips. And two giant pitchers of martinis.

After the first rush, Kate took Barkley aside. "Well?" she asked.

"Well what?" He felt the martinis breaking in his head like tiny crystals.

"Did you talk about me?"

Barkley didn't understand why they should have.

"I've been helping you," Kate said. "She went to Julliard, studied with Alice for three years. She's here to practice for the Tanglewood engagement in two weeks. Alice says she's a real talent."

Barkley looked over at Lee, who was talking with Marshall Cartwright about his flagpole next door.

"Don't look," Kate said. She tugged on Barkley's arm. "She likes you, don't you see?"

Barkley didn't move. He couldn't bend a finger. His first thought was that he'd been unjustly accused of initiating a crime he'd never even thought of, at least not until that very moment. It wasn't proper. And his second thought was to telephone Muriel. *Whatever Kate might say to you is untrue,* he would tell her. *I'm here at Alice Osborne's. Come and get me.*

But he realized he would never call Muriel.

"Did he say anything?" Kate wanted to know.

"You mean Buck-the-Hunk or Ned-the-Sicilian?"

"Ned is cuter," Kate said. She stared past Barkley's shoulder. "It's all right for a woman to look. She's the one who has to say yes or no."

Muriel would already have started dinner. She'd have opened a bottle of white wine from which she sipped as she cooked, and she'd riffle through the catalogs from Land's End or L. L. Bean while the roast was in the oven. At seven she'd flip on "Wheel of Fortune," a curious program for her to watch, though she rarely missed an evening of the shrieks and groans. That was when he walked on the beach.

"What do you think, Barkley?" Ned asked. "Should we tackle the mine? I think we've done our stretching exercises."

"I think so," Barkley said. The crystals were still popping.

"The sharpest knife in the house is there on the table," Alice said. "Do we need more hors d'oeuvres?"

"We need a flashlight," Buck said.

"I have a penlight," said Marshall. He pulled a small light from his pocket.

"Let's do it," said Ned. "Those were Gary Gilmore's last words."

"Do we have enough martinis?" Kate asked. "This could take a while."

Lee picked up one of the pitchers and poured Kate's glass full. She offered the rest to Barkley, who held out his glass.

"You know birds?" he asked.

"I'm a musician," Lee said. She emptied the pitcher into his glass. "Every musician knows a little about birds." She lifted her eyes to his.

"I never knew Nicaragua," he said. "I remember the birds and the flowers and sitting in the garden."

"When it was civilized?" Lee asked.

"I was ten or eleven then."

"And now what do you do with your time?"

"I'm retired."

"I mean, what else?"

He had understood her exactly. Her words rushed at him from nowhere, and yet he might have been mistaken. He gazed past her to where the others were still grappling with the mine. Marshall was on his knees holding the penknife for Ned, who wielded the dirk. Ned had wedged the blade into the leather at an angle and was jiggling it furiously, as if he were slitting the throat of a wiry animal. Buck and Alice and Kate leaned toward the small light.

Barkley felt dizzy. He knew there was nothing in the cylinder. It was all a game played with a piece of refuse thrown up by the sea. But he couldn't think how to answer Lee, how to tell her what he felt. In the absence of words, he turned his gaze to the burgeoning dusk. The highest clouds still caught a faint glimmer of sun, and far up he thought he heard a nighthawk's buzzy call. He had not heard a nighthawk since he was a boy.

"I can almost see inside," Marshall said. "A little farther."

"It's got to be cocaine," Alice said.

"We're going to be blown to smithereens," Buck said. "Just wait."

Lee started across the lawn carrying the silver pitcher in her hand. She paused at the steps and looked back. The nighthawk called again from somewhere high in the dark air.

The beach was empty now. The dunes and sea oats had lost their color, and out on the sea the lights of shrimp boats shimmered over the gray waves. It was too soon to follow Lee into the house. He would be seen.

He waited a few minutes for the beach to darken.

Then he heard the cello. Lee had come out onto the deck

above the striped awning of the porch, and her music drifted out over the lawn, mingled with the voices and laughter of the others gathered around the mine. To escape the voices, Barkley moved back farther into the dunes. He reeled down into a swale, climbed a hill above the wide empty strand. Lights had come on in other houses—surely in his own not far down the beach, where Muriel would be waiting. But there was no hurry now to go home. Kate was a guest, after all, and had to be entertained.

Barkley smiled to himself. He had never felt so eager or so careless. Lee's music eddied on the breeze out to where he stood, the notes lilting or solemn, fading finally into the obscuring air. He imagined the notes as the songs of birds heard long ago in the gardens of Managua, notes which even now reached him through the intervening years and gave him pause. He imagined, too, the sea's long reach, churning up from its depth its new harvest of shells, while all around him in the dunes ornamented with sea oats were hundreds of sleeping plovers.

DISCOVERIES

Arliss, as usual, did not watch the scenery. She sat on the far side of the front seat writing in her journal while Jack drove the narrow two-lane toward Kremmling. The gorge of the Blue River was on her side, and above it the aspens in the cooler glens had already melted to yellow, but Arliss didn't pay any attention. Jack tried needling her by veering across the center stripe or by sliding the car dangerously close to the embankment, but Arliss was unfazed. Now and then she looked up, obviously thinking of something else, and then returned to her scribbling, teeth grabbing at her lower lip.

They were going fishing—or he was—and it pleased him to think of the stonefly hatch on the headwaters of the Elk River in the Zirkel Wilderness. Other troubles like cash flow, or his stepson, Sam, or the last, hastily done rendering at the office paled in comparison to trout fishing, though these other things were mixed into his reverie. He would have to do the drawings over when he got back. He wished solving Sam were so easy.

He loved Sam, and not just because Sam came in the deal with Arliss. He was a bright child, polite most of the time, and more curious than other children Jack knew. At twelve, he studied better than Jack ever had, and he was pretty in a girlish sort of way—long blond hair like Arliss's and dark eyes. The boy had never warmed to him, though. Jack had taken him skiing at Steamboat, helped him with his homework, and naturally would have brought him fishing that weekend, too, if Sam hadn't had to go to his father's. But nothing broke the ice. "Don't try so hard," Arliss had said. "Let him come to you."

He wished Sam had come fishing. Jack was not the greatest fisherman anymore than he was a great skier, but he had got proficient enough to enjoy the frustrations. He didn't mind the snags or getting cold and wet or losing a few big ones. He had discipline: that's what he told Sam.

He tried to get Sam to go to the park to kick the soccer ball while he practiced casting across the grass. "That's how you learn anything," he said to Sam. "Practice."

"Unless you're doing it wrong," Sam said.

At Kremmling they stopped for gas at a gnarled Texaco station at the junction of Colorado 9 and U.S. 40, and while Jack filled the tank, leaning on the butt of the Datsun, Arliss went inside to use the bathroom. He watched her long, fluid stride as she moved away, the purse slung over her shoulder. Her jeans were tight, and she wore a loose red-and-white striped soccer shirt, too bright for fishing. She looked like one of those Red Devil lures his father used when they'd fished for bass in Minnesota. That was before his father had started drinking so much. The drinking had changed everything, and his mother had ended up married to that bastard, Eddie North.

Jack smiled at the notion of a fish's snapping at Arliss. She looked good to him, too, certainly the best woman he'd ever known. He stopped pumping gas and honked the horn at her. She turned, and he waved to her.

Apparently she was still perturbed at him, though, because she didn't return the gesture. So what if he wanted to fish one weekend? Next time they'd go where she wanted. And anyway, after they'd argued about it, he'd agreed that if she spent two nights in the Zirkel, he'd sit for a day in the hot springs pool at Steamboat.

He paid for the gas with a credit card and sat on the dirty fender in the sun. Kremmling was a small, quiet place with a curbless main street and people who had stayed around all their lives. Summer and fall were idyllic: the sagebrush plateau and benches of aspens and the Blue River stocked with trout. He could have lived there, and it would have been good for Sam to test the elements. But for Arliss there was no college and probably not much of a county library. What would Arliss be like without work?

He got into the car and checked the map. They followed U.S. 40 all the way: thirty miles to the top of Rabbit Ears Pass, then twenty-five to Steamboat. North of Steamboat they cut off on a dirt road toward Seedhouse. What a name! He could have lived in Seedhouse, too.

He put the map above the visor on Arliss's side, then noticed her journal on the dash. Arliss's mind, if not her eyes, was always open, always moving. She recorded everything. Once she'd read to him her description of Canyonlands in Utah, where they'd g one a year ago. The rock formations were not of the natural world, she'd said, but rather were like pieces of sculpture in a museum. She had felt as detached as if she were in an air-conditioned room.

Jack had thought that silly, but he'd said nothing. To argue was pointless: she could feel however she wanted to. He'd been exhilarated himself. The wind had seared their faces at the rim of Dead Horse Point, and he remembered the startling red and gray cliffs, exposed slowly over the centuries, long before the rivers which carved the canyons had been named.

He picked up her journal and opened it to see whether he could find what she'd written about their trip to Frontier Days in Cheyenne. That had been a crazy time, with the town jammed with cowboys and horse trailers and tourists. Sam had liked the bull riding and calf roping at the rodeo, and Jack and Arliss had drunk too much in the crowded bars. The pages had only a few dates on them, and he skimmed a line or two here and there. She had such tiny, meticulous handwriting that Jack had always teased her it was a code. Of course he was familiar with it, even if he couldn't make out certain words. 'Very' looked like 'wavy,' and some words had to be deciphered by context. He paused to read on a random page to get a sense of time, whether to go forward or backward.

I imagine RG's doing to me what Jack does, can even sense his skin against mine, the touch of his finger. Would he if I asked him? Could I ask?

Jack glanced up and saw Arliss inside the Texaco buying an orange soda. Her red-and-white blouse wavered through the glass. She was smiling at something the man said, a brilliant smile.

Jack snapped the journal closed and put it back on the dash. Heat was already in his face when Arliss breezed out of the open doorway and into the sunlight, swinging her purse as though nothing had happened.

He pretended to delve into the glove compartment, and when she opened the door on her side, he looked up to the visor. "Oh, here it is," he said, pulling the map down. He leaned back into the driver's seat.

"That man in there was funny," Arliss said.

Jack folded the map open in his lap and started the engine. Ahead of him the asphalt was a black sheet in front of red brick, and he gunned the car into the street. Then he noticed the faraway clouds banking in over Rabbit Ears Pass. As soon as they'd swerved onto the highway, he felt her gaze.

"What's wrong with you?" she asked.

"Nothing."

"What is it this time?"

"Look at those fucking clouds," he said. "If it's raining here, it'll be raining in the Zirkel, and the streams will be mud." He took a breath and tried to calm himself. Then he asked, "What did the man say that was so funny?"

All the way up the pass she seemed content to drink her orange soda and stare out the window. When he could see her eyes, her gaze seemed to range past the road, beyond even the rocky slope and the spruce forest which gave way higher up to clouds. Or was he imagining? What did she really see? Who was RG? He ran through a mental list of the people they knew—his friends first, the couples they socialized with, her friends at the university. He couldn't remember the names of all the professors and graduate students, but of course it could have been someone else, some stranger she had met at lunch or on a bus coming home. *Would he if I asked?* Jack wondered whether she had.

He couldn't admit he'd read her journal or he'd have confronted her right then. Once when she was deciding whether to marry him, she'd asked whether he would ever read her mail. Certainly not, he'd said. Privacy was the foundation of a relationship. Even if you shared a life with someone else, you needed a certain space of your own.

"To grow in," she said.

"Yes," he said. "To grow in."

He had liked the idea of her not knowing everything about him. He had never told her how frightened he was at work when he submitted a rendering for a house, or how lonely he often was before he'd met her.

The road climbed several hairpin turns, and the mist oozed right from the heavy timber beside the road. Jack leaned in close to the windshield to watch for the headlights of oncoming cars. He was all concentration now.

Toward the top of the pass—he thought it was the top, judging from the odometer—the road leveled out and trees diminished because of the altitude. Frost had already killed the grass in the high meadows, and the dead yellow was draped in an eerie gray. What else had she written in the journal? Was what he had read the account of a fantasy? A dream? If it were a dream, when had it occurred?

He braked suddenly when, in the lane they were in, the red rear lights of a truck loomed up from the mist. The car skidded, but Jack caught it, slowed, and followed the red lights around a bend.

"I'm sorry about the fishing," Arliss said.

He was surprised by her voice: how could she even speak to him? But her tone was as natural as ever, even kind.

"Screw the fishing," he said.

Why should she be silent? That was absurd. She didn't know he'd read anything, and anyway, what did the words mean to her? That was the important thing. She'd probably been in a mood months ago and had forgotten by now what she'd written.

The journal was still on the dash. Black cover, maroon binding. She usually kept the journal in her purse, which she carried everywhere. He wished she'd taken the journal with her to the bathroom.

On the downslope it began to sleet, but the driving was easier because they had come out of the clouds. Jack geared down for the steep grade and used the brake sparingly, winding along the flank of the mountain. For a few miles he followed the truck, and when the sleet turned to rain, he passed. To the west, the clouds were a lighter gray, etched with light; to the north it was still dark.

"Steamboat," Jack said, pointing across the valley toward the chunks of a distant town. "Why don't we spend the night there instead of hiking? It's another eighty miles to the trailhead, and look at the weather."

It was only forty miles, not eighty, and usually by evening storms in the mountains cleared away. And even if it rained every afternoon for a month, the wilderness could absorb the water. The rain would fall into spongy tundra or onto spruce slopes thick with undergrowth or onto the grassy glades of aspen filled with skunk cabbage and cow parsnips. The streams might rise, but the water would stay clear. But he knew Arliss would trust his knowledge.

"I thought you wanted to get up there," Arliss said.

He shrugged. He had looked forward to time on the river. He liked the deep pools and the reflections of the sky and the rhythm of the white water. Bubbles popped on the surface where the river flowed over the rocks, and insects were suspended in the sunlight like tiny helicopters over the eddies. He had always thought of skiing or fishing as pure time. But it would not be pure time now.

They had last made love Wednesday night, two nights before. She'd been willing, and he'd lasted a long time for her pleasure. Afterward they'd held each other before drifting into sleep. Had she been thinking then of someone else? She had twitched in her sleep, and he'd smiled at her childish expression illuminated by lamplight from the street. And all the time making love she'd been lying.

She'd always claimed she was honest. "Jack, I've never told you a lie. Why do you lie to me?"

"What do you mean, lie to you?"

"I can feel it."

He had lied to her a few times, but they were small lies about the distance to the Zirkel trailhead or about money lost in a card game. Or they were innocent lies, like when he'd had a few beers with Hank Carey, whom Arliss didn't like. Why get her started on *that*? Maybe he'd flirted a few times with women on the street, and he'd had opportunities when Arliss didn't go skiing with him, but he'd never lied about loving her.

Everyone had fantasies. He sometimes imagined making love with Arliss's friend Kathleen, and he had reveries about Catherine Deneuve and Kim Basinger. Everyone had such ideas, especially about Kathleen. He smiled at that. He dreamed, too, and could not control his dreams. Sometimes there was another woman, and he would feel the pleasure and moan.

Arliss woke him in a fury. "What were you doing?" she asked.

"I wasn't doing anything," he said. "I'm right here in bed with you."

If he'd thought about it, he'd have assumed Arliss had such notions, too. She probably dreamed about Robert de Niro and William Hurt. But there was a difference between thinking something and writing it down. Thoughts were harmless spirits—ethereal, transient, and essentially meaningless—while words were solid. Words had intent and the drift of truth.

TWO

The motel room in Steamboat was within walking distance of the hot springs pool. When they were unloading the car, the clouds had already started to break up in the northwest, and the new sun slanted in with a knifelike light.

"I don't understand why you wanted to stop," she said. "I thought this fishing was all that mattered to you."

Jack lifted out the backpacks from the cargo hatch and carried them inside. When he came out again, he said, "What do you care if I change my mind?"

"I'd rather have my time at the end," she said.

He walked past her with the suitcase.

The room was large and sterile, with gold-painted lamps beside the bed and pastel green walls. A strained silence spread around them after Jack closed the door. He lay down on the hard bed and watched Arliss unpack her travel case.

Finally he got up. "I think I'll take a shower," he said, though he barely directed the words to anyone.

He closed the door and undressed in the bathroom. Under the hot water he felt no better. Steam billowed into the small space, but the slag on his body did not melt in the heat. He turned the water to cold and let the dross harden on his skin. So maybe he was not the best lover of all time, but he tried to make her feel something. He wasn't the hump-and-run type. And she didn't complain. "You know me," was the way she complimented him. He thought that meant he did something right.

He turned off the water and dried himself briskly. He was clean but not clean.

He emerged from the bathroom with the steam, a towel around his waist.

"How was it?" Arliss asked. She was lying on the bed, still in her jeans and her red-and-white shirt, writing in her book.

"Wonderful," he said. "You should try it."

"Since we're here, I'm going to the hot springs."

"Now?" He tried to joke with her and pulled the towel from around his waist. "I thought we'd sleep a while."

He lay down naked beside her and peeked casually at what she was writing. All he saw was the word 'never' before she tilted the journal away.

"Why can't I read?"

She was coquettish about it. "Because you can't."

He settled his wet head on her shoulder and touched the swell of her shirt.

"It's only four o'clock," she said, taking his hand away and putting it on his bare hip. She rolled over to sitting. "I'm going to the pool."

Never: the extreme case. Was it something he never did? Never said? Not *ever*? He told her he loved her often enough, perhaps too often. Was it something he never felt?

She stood up and started to change into her bathing suit, peeling down one jean leg, then the other. He wondered who else had seen this little act. She turned her back and pulled her shirt from the bottom over her head. Then, looking at herself in the mirror, she tied up her hair in back.

She was beautiful with her hair up, he thought. She had a long, delicate neck, and wisps of blond hair fell across her skin. With her hair up, her eyes seemed larger in proportion to the rest of her face.

"What are you watching?" she asked, meeting his eyes in the mirror.

"You."

He wondered whether she went to motel rooms like this one or to an apartment somewhere. Her class schedule gave her free hours. Did she meet him at an arranged hour, or whenever she could get away?

"I take it you don't want to swim," she said.

She slipped off her underwear, and he studied the flare of her hips, the drawn waist, the curve of her spine as she bent over. She could have been a dancer as easily as an assistant professor of English. Her body was lithe, her movements graceful as a crane's.

She put on her suit and tied the thin halter behind her back. He had never thought about the suit before—it was a two-piece, green and black, not so small as some he'd seen, but revealing enough. When he had believed she was unreceptive to stares, he'd not minded that other men admired her.

"I guess I'll go," he said. "I wouldn't sleep without you anyway."

The new ski area above town was in bright sunshine. The mountain looked as though a huge lawn mower had cut swaths through the dark timber. Over the slope the motionless chairs of the ski lift hung suspended from a thin wire.

Jack knew Steamboat better in winter when it was cold and snow was piled on the street corners. Everyone wore colorful sweaters and jackets then, mukluks and ski boots and stretch pants. He had brought Sam a few times, but Sam hadn't liked skiing or the cold, or maybe he hadn't liked skiing with Jack. He'd liked the pool, though. The hot springs steamed like a geyser, and Sam had shot the waterslide a hundred times, shouting and laughing through the mist.

Now, in the rain-cooled afternoon, only a thin ribbon of vapor rose above the pool's wooden fence. Jack and Arliss walked apart on the sidewalk, Arliss's purse between them like a ticking bomb. She had looped the bag over her shoulder and rested her forearm across the mouth. Was the journal even there? He had last seen it on the bureau when she was putting her shirt back on.

At the gate Arliss paused to find her wallet.

"I don't think I'll go in," Jack said. "Maybe I'll walk around town."

"Oh, come on, Jack." Arliss gave him a nudge, a familiar urging. "I'll pay."

The frightening part was that she acted the same. Thinking he was blind, she treated him as she always did. She might stay with him for a few weeks, months, maybe for Sam's sake, but caring for him less and less. If she were honest, would she tell him if there were something he should know? Or, would she tell him she was sick, if she thought she would get well? One thing was certain: he was not blind now.

She paid for her ticket and started into the tunnel toward the pool.

"All right," he said, "I'll come."

There were three pools—one for the water slide, one very hot pool for soaking, and one large pool for swimming. While Arliss changed again, Jack stood on the apron and watched the swimmers doing laps. Some of them slid through the water so effortlessly, as if on oil, while the beginners churned and splashed. He wondered whether practice really helped: would the thrashers ever become smooth?

Arliss came up behind him and gave him a small push. "Watch out!"

He recoiled from the edge. "Jesus!"

She laughed and caught him. "Will you watch my things?" She pointed to a bench where her jeans and the Red Devil shirt were folded neatly across her purse.

She tested the water in the hot pool, sitting in profile at the edge, her shoulders hunched forward, her weight resting on her hands. When her legs were acclimated, she slid further until she stood waist deep. "It's so hot," she said. She leaned against the side and immersed herself slowly until he could see only her face and neck. She closed her eyes.

He sat on the bench, trying to think of a pretext to look in her purse. If they'd been on a longer trip, he might have asked her for her address book to write a postcard. Money. He had brought his own wallet, though she'd paid for him. He glanced toward Arliss, whose eyes were still closed.

He jostled the jeans and shirt from the top of her purse. It wasn't zipped all the way, but he couldn't see into it either. He looked around to check whether anyone else was watching him. The water slide crowd was mostly screaming children and adults acting like children, and the people in the hot pool were oblivious. He unzipped the flap a little. Gum, he thought. He was looking for a stick of gum.

The journal was there, tucked down along the side. He felt its sturdy back against the leather. Maybe he could steal it, and she'd think she'd misplaced it. She was always losing her keys. But if he read it, he'd have to confront her. Or he could take it to the men's room, bringing her clothes and her purse for safekeeping.

He gauged her smile. Was she luxuriating in the water or dreaming of RG, or maybe of their friend Ed Heitmann, whom she'd always liked. Jack could barely sit still. He wanted to get away from the journal. He wanted a drink.

He smiled grimly. At the same time he was miserable not

knowing the truth, he realized he derived a perverse pleasure in what had happened. He didn't want to know more, but he had to. And for the last three hours, Arliss had taken on an intense aura of mystery.

On impulse he pulled the journal from her purse. He couldn't help himself. He had no plan except to read as much as he could before she caught him. If it made a difference to her (he knew it would), they could have it out right there in front of the people in the pool.

He leafed through the pages toward the back to find out what she'd written last. Never *what*? He glanced up at Arliss, but her eyes were still closed.

> *Driving through the mountains on the way to fishing. Jack is uneasy, silent, closing me out. Or am I closing him out? I'd rather stay at home than go on these excursions. He wants so much his own way. He's selfish and brittle and weak. Maybe what D says is true: he'll never be different.*
>
> *Same day. We have a motel room! Jack is sweet, but there must be a reason. He never does anything without a plan. Maybe he wants to look up some woman he knows here. I can't and won't think of that when I have my own. . . .*

He could not make out the next word. The writing went on further down the page, but he looked up into the sun, confused and ashamed and angry. Arliss's expression in the hot water pool was blissful.

He put the journal back, closed up the purse, and piled the clothes on top of it.

He sat a minute longer, trying to feel the warmth of the sun on his face, but all he perceived was light shining through his eyelids like slivers of ice. Reds and oranges danced in the interior darkness, and he felt dizzy. Even on his bare arms, goosebumps prickled, and he rubbed his arms hard with his hands to get his skin warm.

Arliss spoke to him, and he opened his eyes without understanding what she said. He stood up. "I'm going to get a newspaper," he told her. "Can you watch your own things?"

That night they lay curved in arcs, Arliss behind him under the covers. She rubbed his back lightly, but he didn't respond. Selfish and brittle and weak. Selfish maybe, yes. He wanted to go fishing and skiing, and he argued and sometimes went over her objections. But she was always invited to go; he didn't want to go without her. He wasn't deceptive. And there were many times he did what she wanted. He went to poetry readings or to movies withMeryl Streep in them. She liked department parties, but not his office picnics, and she refused to go with him. Wasn't that selfish in the same way?

Brittle and weak: were those the same? Brittle as a dry twig or as a pane of glass? A twig snapped; a pane of glass shattered. He did get hurt easily. When someone promised to call and didn't, or when he was left off a party list, he felt let down. And he took it personally when his supervisor didn't like a rendering. He was brittle maybe, but not weak. How could she call him weak? His father had been a drunk, and his stepfather had beaten him, and despite all of it, Jack had worked his way through college and architecture school. How was that weak? Sometimes he brooded about his job because the pay was low. And they had moved from one apartment to another because he never felt at home. But he had persevered with Sam. And he loved her. Was it weak to love someone?

D was her friend Diane, but they also knew two Davids. Which of them would say he would never change? Never? And there was Dob Milligan, who lived in Aurora, who used to quote Colette and Laurence Durrell, whom Arliss liked.

Arliss tapped his back.

"What?"

"Why don't you want to make love to me now when you wanted to before?"

He couldn't bring himself to turn toward her. The desire he had felt, certainly the teasing and the warmth, had deserted him, and her ministrations did not bring the usual urge. She had lied to him, if not in words, then in omission. He couldn't make love to her. And yet if he didn't, she would write about that, too. God knew what she would write about that.

He wanted to tell her he knew no other women in Steamboat. Where had she got that notion? From Sam? Last winter at breakfast one morning, he and Sam had run into the wife of a friend who was out of town. But that had been coincidence. Could Sam have said anything about that to Arliss out of the blue?

He turned over and put his arms around her and kissed her, but his mind went spinning into other questions and vague answers and more questions until he had lost the thread of what he had meant to think of, which was what Arliss felt now. She saw through his ruse of holding her. He couldn't stir her passion simply by putting his body against hers. He kissed her further, across her neck and breasts, and slid his hand along the flare of her hip.

But she went cold.

"Now what?" he asked. "I thought you wanted to."

"Don't."

He paused, kissed her again.

"I want to talk," she said, pushing him away. She groped for the lamp beside the bed.

"Don't turn on the light."

She didn't, and he lay on his side, fearful of what was next. How many journals did she have? He couldn't remember—six, seven, a hundred? He imagined page after page, thousands of pages, documenting every tiny episode of their life together, every argument, every reaction, every loud word, every nuance of emotion. He would always be the unfeeling one, the guilty one, the perpetrator. That was the pernicious part: she could make him over in any way she wanted to, as if her version of him were immutable and correct. How did he defend himself against that?

Arliss got up in the dark and went to the bathroom, and he stared at the white line around the door. The toilet flushed; water started in the sink. He softened his heart. The journals might be mere effusions, impatience boiled over rather than indictment. She needed an outlet. What was the harm in that? She could write what she wished to and did not have to measure the truth. Probably she didn't read them once they'd been written, and so against whom did he have to defend himself?

But didn't what she wrote seem truthful to her? Why would she put down such words if they didn't reflect her feelings? And once she'd written them, the words had their effect on what she felt from then on. Density and mass altered inertia. A deer's tracks told where the deer had been and when and the direction it was going. Or was the journal more like a whale's footprint on the sea?

She opened the bathroom door, and the shadow cast by her naked body moved across him like the moon's eclipsing earth. She did not turn off the bathroom light, but rather came forward from the bright rectangle until she was near the bed. He turned away from her.

"Jack, you have to tell me what's wrong." Her voice was gentle. She sat down on the bed beside him. "Please."

She tried to pull him over to face her, but he was heavy.

Finally he turned toward her on his own initiative and stared at her for a moment, the tears rising slowly in his body like a spring seeping to the surface.

THREE

The Middle Fork of the Elk River ran beside the county road to Seedhouse, though the stream was not always visible through the thick brush, or when the road followed easier terrain. The road could not deviate much from the river valley, particularly higher up. The river was always there around the bend or beyond a slight rise in the land. The Middle Fork was fast, and not blue from the reflection of the sky—though the sky that morning was a deep blue—but rather green and golden brown from the aspens and birches along the bank and black from the shadow of the cliff. Where it plunged over rocks and fallen logs, the water was ruffled like lace.

Jack had seen a few good pools beneath the banks, but he had continued to drive, thinking the farther they got up toward the Zirkel Wilderness, the better the fishing would be. But there would be no peace.

The night before had been a nightmare. He had not been able to tell Arliss what was wrong, though she had begged him to. Finally she had become intransigent, too. He was to blame for her anger; he accepted that. Her bitterness had nowhere to resound, which made her more resentful, and all he could think of was her writing furiously in her tiny script how he had become devious and artful.

Was it sickness to want to know a truth which would hurt him? He'd lain on the bed after Arliss had gone to sleep, and he remembered the day his mother had taken him into the backyard one afternoon in Minneapolis and had held his hand so tightly it hurt. "Your father's gone," she said.

"Gone where? When's he coming back?"

"Never," she said.

His mother had held him close, and he had cried, and afterward he had assumed his father, because he had died so suddenly, had been sick in a way he was not able to comprehend. He was never able to attach a name to the sickness, until his stepfather moved in. Eddie North had beaten him and hit his mother, too, and one night during a rage, he'd heard his stepfather say,

"Is that what you want me to do, too? Kill myself?"

When Jack was old enough, he went to the police. There were photographs of his father's old Pontiac parked on a country road, with the piece of a malleable plastic hose attached from the exhaust pipe and run through the back window.

Arliss was breathing slowly, and he had got up, careful not to wake her. He had sat by the window, watching the traffic moving ghostlike along the highway. An electric transformer hummed nearby, and above him a half-moon drifted above the sparse clouds. It would have been beautiful, he thought, if they had been up in the Zirkel.

"How far do you want to go up?" Arliss asked. She had been quiet for miles, as if guarded now and wary of him.

"I don't know."

"What was the moon last night?"

"The moon?"

"Doesn't the moon have to do with how the fish bite? You sat up so late. I thought maybe you'd seen the moon."

"It was half."

He wished the road did not end at the trailhead. He wanted to keep driving right on through the aspen glades and past the beaver dams and up into the dark timber. He would gun the engine up the rocky scree and roll past the high lakes to the top of Zirkel Peak, where he could see out across the mountains to Wyoming. His doubts would seem inconsequential. It was ludicrous to worry whether Arliss loved him or not. What did it matter if her love was imperfect? No thoughts or feelings were ever pure. Love was replete with inconsistencies, with vagaries of lust and fantasy and the desire for free rein. No one had ever loved another human being purely and completely.

And yet he aspired to that pure love. He wanted her with him. He wanted to love her without thinking of her friend Kathleen or of Catherine Deneuve. He wanted her to believe he was strong.

Or did he only care about not being deceived?

He stopped at a vacant turnout in the road where picnickers and fishermen had worn a path through the sage meadow and over a small knoll toward the river. He knew the river was there: he could hear its rill through the aspens and the scattered brush.

"You're going to fish here?"

"Yes."

"I thought you wanted to hike up where no one went."

He got out of the car without answering. The sun had just cleared the rim of the canyon, and its light flowed over through the trees on the ridge. The smell of wet sage rose up, heavy on the air. Across the river gorge two deer skirted an outcropping of granite. Arliss did not look. She was watching him.

He opened the rear hatch, slid his fly rod from its metal case, and began to fit the sections together. The rest of his gear—flies, leaders, assorted small implements for repair—were already arranged in his canvas vest which he had laid out, along with his bone-handled knife, on the backseat.

"You sure you don't want to try?" he asked, threading the green flyline through the eyelets of the rod.

"No, thanks."

"I've got a spinning rod."

"I'll just read," she said, "or write a little."

He stopped at the last eyelet and looked at her closely. An eerie sensation, sudden as the snap of a bone, made him start to shake. "Write what?"

"Just a few lines," she said casually. "Maybe a story. Are we going to have lunch, too?"

He was still trembling when he pulled the line taut to the reel. What did she mean a story? A life story? A piece of fiction? She would not be making up a story lying on the bed in a motel room or riding in a car. He tried to recall what he'd read, but could only remember his name was in it.

He pulled on his waders and fastened them over his shoulders. Then he tucked his arms into his vest.

"You can go ahead if you're ready," she said. She was getting out the bread, mayonnaise, and ham from the cooler.

Oh, he loved her all right, but what did that matter if she did not love him? He watched the way her eyes moved as she made the sandwiches, the ambiance of her mouth. She knew he was looking at her. He felt at that moment as if he could kill her—she seemed so much in control.

She offered him a chocolate bar before she closed the cooler and put it into the car. He shook his head.

"Will my purse be safe in the car?" she asked. She paused beside the open door, got out her journal, and then slid it back into her purse. "Maybe I'll just read," she said. She found her book and laid the purse in under the seat.

• • •

From the rim of the knoll, the path led at an angle downstream to a stretch of smooth water. The canyon leveled out for a quarter of a mile before it curved again and the river disappeared into a line of willows. But he turned upstream along a narrow game trail. They climbed fallen logs and broke through the thickets near the river.

The river was faster in the upper canyon, and there were fewer deep pools. The trout would be smaller in the fast water, and fishing would be more difficult with the spruce overhanging the narrower stream. At a bend where the boulders along the bank were accessible, Arliss stopped and checked the angle of the sun. "This is fine for me," she said.

"I'm going up," Jack said. "But I can fish from here on."

Arliss settled in, and Jack waded into the fast water. He liked the weight of the current against his legs, the sharpness of the light and air. He tied on a leader and, keeping an eye on Arliss, pretended to tie on a fly.

Then he rolled the line into an eddy, followed it in the rush of the stream. Arliss was reading, her knees tucked under her chin, her arms wrapped around her long legs. He snapped another cast up the current and worked his way upriver through the welter of logs and boulders.

When he was out of sight, he waded to the bank and followed the game trail farther up. Around another bend, he took off his vest and braced his rod against a tree. He climbed the hill quickly, pulling himself up the steep slope by holding onto roots.

The waders were heavy and awkward, but he ran across the sage plateau. The car was farther than he expected, down a long gradual incline. Sweat poured under his arms and inside the airless boots. He'd gone back for his fishing knife: that was what he'd tell Arliss.

The journal was in the car where she'd left it.

Would he laugh at himself? Was he foolish to think she'd been unfaithful? And what if she had been? Would he forgive her? That was a terrible thought: how much pain would forgiveness require? He would think of her betrayal all the time and wonder whether it would happen again. She would know he was thinking of it.

He felt the heat in his face, the sweat cooling on his forehead in the thin air. He got the fishing knife he'd left in the back seat of the car, then took the journal and walked back along the trail to the rim of the canyon.

The sun had moved higher, and in the riffles where the stream bent downriver, there was a brilliant flash without color or depth, as if the light had its source not in the sun, but in the river itself. He was in no hurry now. He sat on a rock at the lip of the canyon, where the trail descended, knowing he could not read, knowing he had to read. He ran his hand along the hard spine, closed his eyes.

He didn't hear Arliss until she was right beside him. "Jack? What are you doing?"

He opened his eyes. The sun was sharp against her smooth cheek. The daypack with the sandwiches in it and her jacket were slung over her shoulder.

"I thought you were fishing," she said.

The river was an unmoving, hot light. He wanted to throw the journal into that white light, to have it explode like a star. But there were other journals, he knew, other evidence he would feel compelled to discover, more things he didn't want to know. He lifted his hand, and without its weight, the written-on pages expanded in the air.

"You've come for this," he said. He handed her the journal and got up and went to retrieve his vest and his fly rod, which he had left upstream.

ABSENCES

You forget what it's like to walk across traffic. You don't remember the color of the curtains in the living room, if there were curtains in the living room, or the sound of a soft voice. You can't go to the refrigerator for a beer or turn up the heat or put on Cannonball or telephone a woman you liked in the bar. The trees have no bottoms, and you can't take a crap behind a solid door. You get used to those things, adjust to them, stop thinking. But the worst is something you can never stop thinking about. When one thing is out of place, when something starts to slide and the tension stretches the air, there's nothing you can do but sit tight and wait.

It's nearly free time, seven-thirty, but something hurts. Across the tier and down the rows there's an undercurrent, a strain that's like the clouds' tightening on this hot summer evening. Arrangements are usually made in advance, but this time there was no warning. If there's a search, for instance, everyone hides his weapon in a shop or in the hollow pipe of a bed leg or behind an air duct. Or if a screw is nailed for bringing in porn, you can live for a while until someone else fills the gap. But porn is one thing and pills something different. They give you the pills to calm you down, a steady flow from the hospital, or maybe from a screw if you want something heavier, or from another inmate who has a connection. It's all known, a part of the plan, just like putting scabs on one block or sending a pixie to appease a trouble-maker who wants meat.

But when they cut the power without warning, look out.

Whitcomb stands across from me, sixty feet away. My cell matches his, and I can see into his life the way he sees into mine. Whitcomb's life is not fun to watch. He has the same desk, the same bed, the same coverless john. He's smart, but a loner, doing time for kicking his wife to death in a drunken stupor. He didn't mean to, but he was crazy. Is crazy. He fidgets, screams, some-times has visions. Last year he threw a homemade cocktail in the dining room with the vague notion of getting out. The screws were the first to run because they're targets, and the alarm went off. A couple of scores were evened: Danny Piña was stabbed with the shard of a plastic plate, and Booker Conrad, who on the outside raped an eleven-year-old girl, got slugged senseless. Other than that, nothing really happened. In all the running and yelling, Whitcomb just stood there, and he ended up with nine months in the Plant. That was when they started him on the pills.

James C. Enoch is making out fine, reading a sci-fi thriller. He's below Whitcomb on the next tier, a little left. Maybe he had advance word and he bought a stash. There are preferences. So maybe he will sell to Whitcomb, and Whitcomb will be all right. Maybe not.

Nothing means anything to me. I'm the nonobserver. All the rules. Do what they say. No ripples. I've done three years of a five-to-seven cheap shot, so I get along. When something happens I turn my back so no one catches me looking. I haven't seen any-thing. If someone asks a favor, fine. I kept the peek for Bollinger in the cell beside me because he had lots of friends. And he paid me plenty to stand on the rail and watch for screws and listen to the moans. Lovers and ex-lovers. It didn't affect me one way or the other when Garland short-circuited Bollinger's cell door and torched him.

I don't like it when the routine gets broken. The screws are holding us longer than usual for free time, and I'm ready to go paint. Education, reading for the blind, Christian Action—all for parole—chess and TV, painting, and woodworking. Stay busy. Whitcomb paces around his cell. I can see how much he needs it.

On the left side of me, opposite where Bollinger was, Iron Balls is talking to himself loud and clear about nothing. I don't listen to the nonsense anymore, don't even hear it. He's like a radio announcer in the background. The story is that six years ago he tried to go out in a heavy fog and got to the top of the wall. He had sneaked across twenty yards of asphalt, hooked the top of the wall with a handmade grapple, and scaled twenty feet. He was just straddling the electric fence when a tower guard threw the switch. Iron Balls: the juice scorched his scrotum and threw him over the wall for a few seconds of freedom.

Someone yells, "Open the fucking doors!" and a chant starts up. The noise of voices and the clattering of cans on bars rises until the block is bedlam, and a screw gets on the loudspeaker and cools it off with the threat of no free time at all. But the tension is still there when the men quiet down.

Why does the warden cut off the pills? It doesn't matter to me. I've stayed away from whatever might make me vulnerable, whatever might give me more time. Maybe he wants to show a state senator that the department needs more money. Or the screws once in a while want some action, a chance to break heads. Or the sadistic side: they want to make some of us suffer, to make deals, to harass, to show how much power they have, if they want to use it. Maybe it's a way of beating the natural cycle and getting the upper hand in the violence, so they're prepared for it. After the storm, things will be calm again.

The doors slide open electronically. There's a shout about nothing, almost a furor, and everyone goes out. I get to the bottom of the stairs and wait in line for my pass. Whitcomb is behind me, a slight man with a shy smile, dark red hair, a young-looking thirty. If you saw him in a park, you'd never think he had it in him to kill his wife. He looks at me, and I read his question before he asks it, so I turn away.

"Henschel," he says, calling me.

I nod and say hello. Sometimes he goes with me to art. Before the pills he went to basketball. Once in a while he tried chapel. Nothing helps him, and he never sticks with anything long enough to get good. Tonight he says he's going to the hospital.

"I need help," he says.

"I haven't got a button or a dime," I tell him. I try to take any hint of sympathy from my voice.

Along the line there is con talk: cheers teers meers beers. The screw, Dolan, looks up and pretends to understand. Someone wants coffee is all.

Booker Conrad walks by on his way to play checkers, and Whitcomb grabs him. He hangs on close, terrorizing Conrad, and asking him for a hit. They dance a few steps.

"Cut it," Dolan shouts.

But Whitcomb holds on like an exhausted fighter.

"He doesn't have anything," I tell Whitcomb.

Whitcomb stares at me and lets go.

Dolan gets up and measures Whitcomb, but I stand between them. Other men pressure Dolan to get the line moving. Whitcomb takes my interference—just standing there—as a sign of aid, and leans closer. "Listen, down in avocation you'll see Muhammad."

"He's in woodworking," I say, "if he goes."

"So it's across the hall. You can get over there."

We move up in the line, and Dolan has my pass ready. He hands it over, and I go through, but he stops Whitcomb.

"Not tonight, hot stuff," Dolan says lightly. "You stay in the block where we can watch you."

I don't even turn to see Whitcomb's face, and I blot out the argument that follows, Whitcomb's pleading voice. I walk up the corridor, take a right, descend the steps to the cellar, and it's as if I never heard of Whitcomb.

What a studio for painting. A low ceiling, ducts and pipes all over, a couple of sixty-watt light bulbs. The studio was the afterthought of a riot. Give the men more options at night. Tonight is particularly stifling in the cellar, airless and hot. But I can live through anything. If I were serious about my work, it might be different: I might complain. But I don't pretend to have talent. My sense of proportion is awkward and my eye for colors is exaggerated. My reds are too bright, blues too brilliant. I have no idea of perspective. At first I came here to get away, but I've grown to like the rumbling of the heating ducts, the clicking of the expanding metal, the shaking of the gym floor overhead as the men run through their half-court game. I've given up painting now for design, simple arrangements which can be measured with a compass, a protractor, and a straight-edge.

Fair. No one said anything about fair. I get left alone while Whitcomb gets hassled. Fresno Gagliardi gets raped because he doesn't know enough to cover his ass. That's a joke. Sad, but true. Iron Balls belongs on the Ranch, not here. You have to deal with things as they are.

I give my pass to the screw in the cellar hall between the studio and woodworking, and go in and get out my apron, pencils, and set up the drawing board. Like anything, the more I practice, the more complex things become. I silk-screened for a while, but when the materials got more expensive, I slid back to something easier.

Muhammad saunters past in the hall, smiling as usual. He's up, a friendly john with the pity of a cobra. Seeing him makes me uneasy, as if it's not safe to be in the cellar with him on a night like this. I think of Whitcomb and James C. Enoch, but the thought itself makes me erase it. It's none of my business.

For twenty minutes I hold onto this absence. The room grows hotter, and I sense those clouds which I can't see moving toward me. I can't think. The design I've started, a hexagon repeated three times with varying shades of red, suddenly means nothing.

Finally I get up and put my drawing tools away. I cash my pass, claiming I don't feel well, and head back to the block.

At first glance everything seems calm. The games of dominoes and betting are underway. Ordway and Julio Cruz are playing chess. The television is blaring, and several men lounge on metal folding chairs, staring at Loni Anderson in some garish comedy. No one laughs.

"You back?" Dolan asks.

I don't ask him what it looks like. "Where's Whitcomb?" I say.

Dolan points toward the corner where Whitcomb is walking away from James C. Enoch. For a moment I'm relieved, thinking Whitcomb has solved his problem, and I pause and give Dolan a chance to chat.

"You know something, Henschel?"

I crack a smile. "Never."

"You're a smart one, aren't you?"

I nod. "Very smart," I tell him. "But not tonight. I have a headache."

I start toward the stairs and Whitcomb sees me. He reaches me before I get to the stairway. "You see Muhammad?" he asks, almost without a breath, as though he's been running.

I shake my head. His eyes are pinwheels, screaming at me.

"What about James C.?"

"He says no."

"No?"

"He has it, but won't sell."

I don't ask the reason. Either he has customers he's promised, or he's waiting for men like Whitcomb to get more desperate so he can jack the price. But I'm not the one in trouble, so why do I feel anything? Whitcomb is not worth the worry.

Yet I feel that edge, just for a moment, long enough for me to recognize that it's the same helplessness I felt on the outside: that something ought to be *done,* had to be done, that I was watching myself waste away like a piece of sand sculpture in rain.

But the feeling doesn't last. "I'm sorry," I tell Whitcomb.

Whitcomb turns away abruptly, and I climb the stairs and walk along the tier railing toward my cell. Iron Balls sits with his head in his hands, still gabbling to himself, clutching his hair as if he's going to pull it out. He looks up at me as I pass.

The cell is open, but I pause at the rail and gaze over into the block. James C. Enoch is kibitzing for Julio Cruz at the chess game near the wall, and Ordway complains. Cruz moves. There is some joke.

This clean place, safe from the outside, is taut, as if this one moment were suspended from a weak thread. I feel each second is about to happen, that time is freezing slowly, and I am trapped beneath the ice.

Whitcomb moves nonchalantly toward the chess game—another figure in blue denim, wiry, red hair against the beige wall. A few others may have followed Whitcomb, too, but if they have, they are not watching him now. Dolan is talking idly with another screw. I know I should do something, yell, call out, something, but I can't. I should look away, so as not to be a witness, but instead I hold tight to the rail, even lean forward a little. Whitcomb nears the game and takes a piece of pipe from under his shirt. With only a slight hesitation to make certain of his grip, he raises the pipe over his head and takes two long strides. Enoch turns, but too late, and Whitcomb smashes the pipe into the side of Enoch's head.

Enoch crashes through the chess game and pieces go flying. Cruz topples over backward in his chair. Ordway jumps away. James C. Enoch raises himself on his hands and knees, his face already bloody, too bright, and he crawls unsteadily for a few feet as though searching for something on the floor. No one looks or tries to help. Whitcomb moves forward and starts scratching through Enoch's pockets.

Then all at once there is running and screaming. Two men grab Dolan, while others wedge the desk into the doorway so the door can't be closed from Control. The other screw runs into the hall, and the siren goes off. Dolan tries to get away, but someone hits him with a metal folding chair. The next block erupts, too.

James C. Enoch has collapsed on the floor. Whitcomb stands a few feet away against the wall, calmer now, knowing he will be okay.

I turn and go into my cell. From beneath the mattress I take out a file I have shaved into a knife in case I have an enemy I don't know about who, in this frenzy, might come for me. Tomorrow pills will be available again at the hospital. Maybe there will be a day's lock-up to cool things off, but the routine will start up smoothly a couple of days after that. I take a deep breath and lie down on my bed and wait.

A COUNTRY OF MY
OWN MAKING

The red Ford pickup ran the straight asphalt of U.S. 50 along the flood water of Tomichi Creek, and from where I was, high in the upper meadow by the weir, the sun flashed intermittently from its windshield. For an instant the explosion of light blinded me, leaving my vision blurred, the way a gust of wind might ripple the reflection in a calm pool. I had no reason to expect the driver was Angie Warren, though she must have known I was back in the valley. There are preternatural moments when time stands cold and still as stone, and other moments when it evaporates like false rain or like a story one has read but can't remember. I watched the red truck carve a line through the backdrop of gray sage hills and fluttery light green aspens and pass out of sight behind one of the knolls. Poised with my shovel at the ditch, dressed in my mother's old plaid shirt and her black rubber boots, I felt as if I had never left the valley, that the intervening eight years had vanished like the red truck. I was gazing out at the same highway, at the same meadows of timothy and alfalfa, at the identical patches of rapidly melting snow which lingered in the shady depressions of the ridge. A mountain bluebird—perhaps the same one—shimmered like an azure butterfly above the new grass.

But the truck emerged from behind the hill in predictable sequence, and when it slowed and turned onto the county gravel along the barbed wire fence at the edge of the lower meadow, I was not surprised. I returned to the ditch work, braced my body on the bank, and sliced the shovel into the earth. The bank did not need shoring up so much as the ditch needed cleaning, for over the years willows had grown up along its length and the channel had silted in. I lifted a heavy clump of wet earth and grass and tamped it into a gap through which water was flowing.

The melt was uncommonly high for so late in the spring. Snow had stayed long into April and now, down the length of the valley, the broad curves of Tomichi Creek looked like the surface of a lake—glistening, dancing in the slight breeze and sunlight like quicksilver in the mind's eye. Yet though there was high water, there had been no rain. The roads were dry, and dust trailed behind the pickup which had turned into my gravel drive.

I spaded more earth into the leaks, pretending not to notice Angie waiting in the cab for the dust to settle.

Three weeks before, I had been living in Casper, Wyoming, which was where Henry Carris came to tell me my father had died. I hadn't been long in Casper—only two months—but already I knew the hills above the river, the barren prairie east of town, the highway west toward Riverton. It was a depressed city because of the oil bust, a city I liked for its empty houses and blank stores.

I was surprised when Henry appeared at my efficiency apartment. He was a balding man who always wore a yellow Stetson a little askew. His face was kindly and soft looking, though he had worked the weather of his ranch all his life. "I'm sorry to be the one," he said. "Someone had to come."

"How did you find me?" I asked.

"Oh, well, Casper isn't a very big town." He gave a shrug.

"I've been gone a while."

He nodded. "It's the first place I looked," he said. "I don't know. I guess I had you figured right."

Before Casper I had lived in Cheyenne and Denver and Colorado Springs, each time moving north a little toward the cold. I wanted to make my migration slow and solitary, to wash out the traces of my life in each place I lived. In Denver I'd sold toys; in Cheyenne I'd spooned out vegetables in a cafeteria line; in Casper I was a maid in a motel. I had no expectations in these jobs, no ambitions beyond the regular hours and the money. I had chosen to live in silence.

But there was always someone who remembered your face, someone for whom you did a favor or to whom you seemed lonely—some clue which lingered after you like a scent. "Was it the old woman who sells newspapers?" I asked Henry. "Or the man who waves to me every morning from his window? The bus driver?"

"It was your mother," Henry said. "Rest her soul."

I was at the sink, running the water, waiting for the hot to siphon through the pipes, while Angie paced the linoleum floor in and out of the sunlight which slanted through the filmy curtains. "I called earlier," she said. "I called yesterday and let the phone ring a long time, and the day before that, too."

"I was outside," I said.

"At night?" She stopped and looked at me. "And Henry said you didn't even know your father was sick."

"No."

"Didn't you ever call?"

The water came hot and, filling the kettle, I lingered at the window. The laundry I'd done that morning—red and yellow and blue clothes fluttering on the line—looked stark and incongruous against the sunburned barn and the old tractor at the edge of the yard. I didn't answer Angie. I turned the stove on and set the kettle on the burner.

"And he said you didn't want a funeral or anything."

"That's right."

"There was one for your mother," Angie said. "What about the rest of us? What about your father's friends?"

The illogic and the earnestness of her voice made me smile briefly. To think that others wanted to pay their respects to my father was a notion that struck me as insufficient and shallow, but Angie had always been one to believe in appearances.

I measured instant coffee from the jar into two cups and kept an eye on the kettle.

"It was Del who insisted we look for you. Did Henry tell you that?"

I shook my head, and Angie stopped again.

"You don't know anything, do you? You don't know about Del and me. Of course you don't. Henry kept his mouth shut."

"He said I was going to inherit the property," I said. "That's about all. He said he'd been taking care of things since my father died."

"Well, Jesus," Angie said. She sat down in a chair at the kitchen table and put her hands out flat, palms down. "Me and Del got divorced three years ago. He found me in a motel over on the west side with Teddy Platte. Wasn't Teddy an old flame of yours?"

"Long ago."

"It wasn't Del's fault really. I was restless. Things went on, especially in the Wagon Wheel where I been working. Del didn't have much patience with that kind of thing. He's working in the mine now over in Jeffersonville."

"Del is?"

"It's real good money."

The water boiled hard, and I poured two cups full.

It was hard to imagine Del as a miner. Even in grade school he'd loved the outdoors—fishing, hunting, cattle, weather. When my father was sick in bed, Del helped my mother mend fences and doctor the cows. He loved to ride up into the high country looking for strays. Sometimes I went along on my pinto pony, and we'd climb the steep gullies, circle the aspen benches, and go on up higher into the Engelmann spruce which was good habitat for deer and grouse. Once in the white-skinned quakies we found a cow which had calved. Her hind legs had been paralyzed from the birth and she couldn't stand. She'd drag herself a few yards and collapse. But she'd managed to lick her calf so it hadn't suffocated. Del took the calf down over his saddle and brought the cow food. Every day after school he rode up three-quarters of an hour with oats and hay until the cow finally died.

"I always liked Del," I said.

"So did I." Angie smiled and blew across the rim of her coffee cup. "I always liked men in general."

Angie had been the pretty one when we were younger. She and I were friends because we lived at the end of the bus line—the first to be picked up in the morning and the last to get off in the afternoon. We waited together at the row of mailboxes on the highway, watching the sun's first breath tarnish the hills. Angie never talked about homework or assignments. She spoke of ordinary things: what someone else had said, how people looked, who liked whom. Her body filled out long before mine, and she drew puerile snickers and stares from the boys on the bus and in the hallways at school. She wore her hair in cascading, lacquered curls which smelled vaguely of roses, and I used to wonder why she made herself such a spectacle. What did she hope to gain dying her hair blond and wearing makeup and perfume?

Once when we were riding home and Angie was talking about Del, I reached over and touched her frosted curls, stroking the brittle teases she had constructed so carefully. She stopped in midsentence and smiled at me, as if accepting this gesture as an intimacy which could not be defined in words. *Didn't I know?* she seemed to ask. And I understood then and afterward that even as friends we were antagonists, even as confidantes we were enemies.

But we were older now. Angie's hair was still bleached, but no longer stiff and sprayed. She still had the same graceful movements, but the lines at the corners of her mouth were more vivid than her body. Sitting at the table, she seemed to me like a ludicrous aging doll.

She talked to me. She turned her cup round and round on the table, held it poised in the air, looked wistfully around the kitchen. She recounted her life—hours in a motel room in Moab, Utah, days and nights in the Wagon Wheel, arguments with lovers. It was a life not unusual, a slow dissimilation not unlike my own, but with different details.

When she got up to go, the sun was already sliding into the west. She gave me a hug and asked me to visit her at the Wagon Wheel. Then she held me by the shoulders. "Did you ever find your mother's stories?"

"I wanted to settle in first," I said, "to see whether I could manage."

"Of course you can manage."

I gave her a brief smile.

"I'm sorry about your father," she said, and she turned away.

As a girl I was often frightened in the night by the darkness in my room. I woke and wished for the cool moon, the breeze beyond the window, the rolling sage-scented hills. But it was not merely the darkness which troubled me. The room lacked movement, air. And sometimes, then, through the frame of the wooden house, I heard my mother's clicking typewriter, like an insect's language I could not fathom—bursts of static trailed by long pauses, as if she were responding to heat or barometric pressure. I would creep from my room, past my father's open door through which came the noises of his anguished sleep. I descended the stairs and, so as not to risk the door's creaking, climbed through the open window onto the front porch. Stars pelted the sky, and the sweet-grass breeze cooled my forehead. I edged around the corner of the house to the window in the vestibule alcove where my mother sat hunched over a yellow page rolled into her typewriter. Her face was illuminated by a single shaded lamp, and she stared at the yellow sheet with such a ferocious glare that seeing her gave concrete and sensory rationale to my fear. Her dark hair was damp at her temples, her fingers poised like talons over the keyboard. But for minutes she would do nothing. What was she thinking? What did she know? What were these stories about?

Then suddenly she looked up. She looked directly at the window, though not through it, seeing perhaps in the nearness of the glass her own likeness, yet not herself, not me. She seemed to me then brilliantly alive, as if what tormented her a moment before also gave her pleasure now, and I thought: I do not know this woman. *I do not know my own mother!* And all I would ever know of her was the face she chose at any particular moment to show me.

My father had died nearly two weeks before Henry Carris came to find me. He had been in and out of the hospital for weeks, then for several days during the last siege, at the mercy of those who would prolong the functioning of his cells. And then he died. Del and Angie made no progress finding me until Del ran into Henry.

Henry had been thinking about me, he said. The lawyer, Wesley Pape, had asked where I was.

But it was not me Henry was thinking of. It was my mother. He had loved my mother for years, and I think she loved him, too, though she never spoke his name. So much was hidden from me then. When Henry, with his wife Anita, visited my family, they would all sit on the porch drinking beer and talking. My mother had a way of speaking that was like music. Her physical appearance was stern, and she always wore work clothes or plain cotton dresses. Her hair was coiled at the nape of her neck. But when she talked, the lilting cadence of her voice was as astonishing as finding a sapphire on the sidewalk, as if the words borne on her soft voice leapt directly to the imagination. Henry listened intently to everything she said. I remember one night sitting on the steps listening to her tell stories of her girlhood in Casper, how Henry asked her questions about the plains and the riverbed where she played, about the school she had gone to there, as if he were trying to discover the makings of the person she was then. And I listened, too, hearing beneath her words the shrouded meanings of a landscape and the surreptitious wandering of her heart.

In my father's absence when he was sick, Henry had kept an eye on the ranch, grazing the cattle in the high country, which in spring was lush with grass. The sick ones he hauled by truck to his own feedlot to doctor. It was almost as easy to look after twenty sick cattle as a dozen. But he didn't have the manpower to do more on the land than ride the fences and, now and then, to look in on the house.

So the ditches had been untended and the meadows flooded, and when I came back, rending myself from my anonymous life in Casper, I had no one to help me. A hay meadow was like a single plant: it could be killed by heat or by drought or drowned by too much water. What little grew in too much water wasn't worth cutting, and if a season were wasted and no hay put up, the winter was expensive. Cattle had to be fed or sold, and either choice made under duress was a bad one. It was costly to buy feed, and forced selling was a sure way to lose in a cattle market whose prices were fickle as the wind.

Of course I inquired about part-time labor, but construction in town, Henry said, had absorbed every available man. "You wouldn't know the place if you drove through," he said. "There are office buildings and new houses everywhere. There ain't no one going to dig ditches."

So every morning I put on my mother's black rubber irrigating boots and her gray gloves with the palms worn smooth by the handle of a hay rake or by the steering wheel of the tractor, and I worked on the ditches. I diverted water from one field to another while I repaired one section. I cut and sprayed the willows, removed silt, shored up holes that muskrats had riddled through the banks. Every day my muscles cried from lifting and shoveling, and my hands blistered despite the gloves. My thin, bare arms below my shirtsleeves were burned by the sun; my eyes ached from the sun glancing off water and wet mud.

This had been my mother's life for fifty years, and I stopped often, out of breath, to rest my eyes against the blue sky. It was like homesickness how well I knew the path of the sun, how each day I felt the arc ride higher into the north, how the clear morning gave way to clouds in the afternoon. A curtain of rain appeared every afternoon over the far peaks: a storm which seemed to gain strength as the day progressed, but which never reached me.

In the evening the clouds dissipated in the cooler air. It was dusk when I went to bed. I lay on the bed my mother slept in, conscious of the light's ebbing outside the window, aware of the strange images which whirled through my mind like clouds— fantasies, cirrus pictures, scudding scenes of childhood that invaded my thoughts unbidden. I assumed my exhaustion spawned these musings which formed themselves from nowhere and blew heedlessly across the blank terrain. I remembered, for example, how one night, fresh with fear, I knocked on my parents' bedroom door and listened to their whispering voices: "It's Becky," my mother said. And my father answered, "Don't get up. She has to learn."

And my mother could not disobey him. I slumped against the cold door, shivering, my face pressed to the wood. My mother coughed, and though I needed to hold her, I understood her signal. We were together against him, always, both of us awake in the darkness.

And I remembered spying on them when they collected the bales of hay from the fields, how I hid behind the bales and peered out, hating my father for the work my mother had to do. She drove the tractor, wearing a red handkerchief over her nose to keep the dust and pollen from her sinuses, while my father walked behind and lifted the bales onto the flatbed trailer. I ran from bale to bale, pretending to shoot him with a stick, sliding to safety each time behind an imaginary bunker, until one by one the bales disappeared from the field and I had nowhere to hide.

These were fragments of my dusk dreams. It was always to my mother I gravitated, to her who fueled the deeper dreams which haunted me in the black hours of sleep.

One Saturday I walked up into the high country above the meadows. The moraine was brittle soil, capable of growing only sage and mesquite and rabbit brush, but on up another thousand feet the aspens and spruce gave good cover to blue grouse.

Grouse were elusive birds, cyclical in their populations from year to year, silent. When they were alerted to danger, they froze, and if someone came too close, they exploded in frenzied flight. But that morning there were no grouse. I climbed up through the trees and sat high up on a granite outcropping from which I could see the ranch below and the valley stretched out between the foothills. The highway followed the straight line above the creek, down through the miles of willows, toward the chunks of the distant town.

Clouds drifted from the west and banked in behind the mountains—that was the pattern in spring. But the days would erode gradually into pure blue summer.

That morning I had searched for my mother's stories. The house had felt right to me again, the rhythms of my day more secure. I had become used to the cool silent mornings, the midday sun, the slow slide from evening into night, which were my mother's daily encounters. I looked through boxes in the attic, the logical place, and found only tax receipts, cattle records, checkbooks from the last twenty years, letters from aunts and uncles. In the closets I found some letters my father had written my mother when he was in the military, rambling accounts of Valdosta, Georgia, and the countryside around Fort Ord, California—seldom anything gentle. But I found not a single sheet of yellow paper, not one manuscript or jotting in my mother's hand that might have been called a world invented. Were there no stories? Had I conjured them from her sorrowful face, from the nights of ebb and flow of the typewriter keys, from the sweetness of her voice? Or had they been destroyed? My father's demands for attention had already consumed her physical life. Had he taken from her as well, after she died, her only real existence besides me?

Someone pulled into the driveway far below me and steered a dilapidated Volkswagen into the yard. When that someone emerged, his face was hidden by a cowboy hat, but as he walked to the house, the stride was apparent, the way he rocked each step forward onto the toes of his boots. It was Del Kinney.

How ironic that he was the one to call me home when, long ago, he had given me the impetus to leave. He knocked on the back door, and when no one answered, he shielded his eyes to the window glass and peered inside. He might have seen my coffee cups unwashed on the counter, the greasy pan on the stove, the spray of buttercups on the table. Though the door was unlocked, he didn't try it. A gust of wind caught his hat, and he chased it across the short porch and down into the yard. When he caught it, he stood for a moment, hat in hand, his red hair lifting in the breeze, and gazed up into the hills as if he knew I was there.

But by then I had ducked out of sight.

In high school Del and I had been friends, not lovers. We liked the same things. Sometimes, when I was checking the ditches as part of my chores, I used to stop by the main weir at a pond where he fished, and one evening I saw his truck there and pulled in. I expected to see him at the edge of the pond, arcing his line out over the smooth surface, settling the fly on the sheen of reflected clouds. But he was up above the pond in a brace of thick willows. He signaled for me to come over.

He had discovered a water snake in the grass. The snake had caught a small brookie. "He got it sideways," Del said. "I heard the fish slapping water."

The snake had dragged the trout out into the air and was not the least concerned about us. When the fish was weak enough, the snake released its grip little by little to maneuver it around to be ingested head first. The fish still wriggled, even when it was halfway down into the snake's mouth.

We watched this small spectacle until it was nearly dark, and then we sat together by the pond, letting the dusk sift over us. It was as though the scene we had witnessed had pressed us into some new world where death had its place. We might have stayed in that silence forever. We might have agreed to the seasons, to the aging of our own bodies, to the endless measuring of water into and out of the pond. But suddenly the air came alive with the sound of ducks' wingbeats—greenwings and cinnamons spilling through the dark. They swirled and diverged above us, and once our presence was assimilated, slid onto the glassy water.

This was the time to say yes to him, to embrace in words what we knew of ourselves. But Del did not ask, and I was too shy, and the moment passed beyond us. When the night chill came on, when the moon rose, we made our way back up to the gravel road with nothing said, nothing changed.

Del left no note for me that morning. He had taken a piece of paper from his wallet and tapped his jeans pocket for a pencil, but when I climbed down after he left, there was nothing in the door. What would he have said to me? That he was sorry about my father's death? That he wanted to see me? Perhaps he had thought better of giving himself away. He had carried out whatever intention he had to a certain point, but when he was actually there, where I lived, he must have known his coming had made no difference. I could imagine he preferred his act to be a solitary event without consequence, as harmless as that night years ago at the pond when I loved him.

And it would have been true: no matter what his motive was for coming, it would have fallen silent as a tree in the forest, except that I had seen him.

My father used to come into my room in the middle of the night when I was sleeping. He pulled the covers from me gently, and after a while I would wake to the chilly room. I'd feel the cold air and search for the covers and see him there.

"You were having a dream," he'd say, or "You were calling out."

But I did not remember dreaming or calling out.

Sometimes I woke to the touch of his hand on my shoulder or my back.

"I was just watching you," he'd say.

And sometimes I woke as if I sensed he was there. The black room lay around me, and though I thought someone was in the room, I was too ashamed to call out, too afraid to investigate the darkness at the foot of my bed where I felt my father breathing his own shame.

I went into town to the lawyer's office on Monday to sign some documents which had to be filed with the probate court. These were the final dispositions of my father's estate, including the house and the land, though it was not his only legacy to me. "Mere formalities," Wesley Pape said. But for me there was always memory.

Afterward I decided to stop by the Wagon Wheel to say hello to Angie. The Wagon Wheel was the kind of bar I imagined existed in every town, a place off-limits to me—dark, filled with men drinking and playing pool. Once in the broad daylight of my girlhood I remembered seeing a man stagger from that bar, eyes slitted from the sun, to urinate in the street.

That afternoon was chilly and the room was dark and warm. There was a jukebox, a pool table, a mahogany bar at which a few men sat on stools. Behind the bar a mirror reflected the liquor bottles and the wagon wheel light fixtures that hung low over the tables. Dozens of dollar bills were taped to the wall at the end of the bar, each with a signature on it, as if the patron had been enshrined by his money.

Angie insisted I have a drink. "It's a celebration," she said. "You have to respect being rich."

She fixed two old-fashioneds and set one in front of me on the bar. She held the other up as a toast. "I'm not supposed to drink on the job, but everyone knows me. If the owner wants to fire me, he can. Here's to your safe return."

We drank.

"So what are you going to do with all that land?" she asked.

"I'm thinking of selling."

Angie drank another swallow and smiled. "Have you seen what's happened to town?"

"I'm not in town."

"Ferguson's Soda Fountain is Ferguson's Drug Center. Safeway's building a new store. Widemann's Lumber is booming. There are houses going up along the bluffs and in Springer Canyon. And condos. In a year or two, the town will be spread out to you."

"Like a disease."

Angie shrugged. "You might as well make some money from it."

She took another drink, and I sampled mine. What did I care what happened to the town? I had lived in places far worse. I drank again.

Angie mixed two more old-fashioneds and slid another to me. People filtered in. Then she was busy for a while, setting up Coors and Budweiser for the crowd just off work. She took orders with a minimum of fuss, smiled, flirted a little, laughed. I envied the way she could make three or four people at once feel as if she were paying attention to them.

I finished my second drink, and Angie refilled it.

A man slid onto the stool beside me and looked at the three toothpicks I had lined up on the bar. "You been here a while," he said. He was a construction worker and smelled of cedar.

"A while."

"Angie'll chalk them up for you." He smiled cheerfully.

I felt my old inclination to harden, to shrivel like a leaf curled up by a frigid wind, but I resolved to resist the instinct. The man hadn't meant anything. He was just someone who had sat down. "I'm really not much of a drinker," I said.

A pool game started up at the back of the bar, and the jukebox, silent until then, rolled out a country-and-western song which came disembodied from behind a knot of people in the corner. Voices rose around me like wind chimes clanging metal on metal.

"You look kind of familiar," the man said. "My name's Teddy Platte."

I didn't answer. I drank my third old-fashioned quickly to make a break, but I began to feel a heaviness in the air, the pleasant distancing of sounds and light that one might experience on a boat at night, floating on a river through the heart of a nameless city. But I was not in a nameless city. I was in a bar called the Wagon Wheel in a town I grew up near, in a crowd of people, some of whom I used to know.

Even so, I was about to get up and leave and had spun my stool a quarter turn away from Teddy Platte toward the exit when I saw Del. He was standing in a wedge of sunlight as someone threw open the door behind him. He was sweaty and dirty, and a line of grit crossed his forehead where his hat had been. His red hair was usually the first thing one noticed, but he had a way of standing which was just as distinctive, like someone slightly off balance, leaning forward, unable to stop a spring into midair.

But Del didn't spring. He searched the crowd, and I had the eerie sensation he was looking for me. Heat rushed to my face. The room whirled. He gazed past Angie right at me.

Then his gaze slid across me, too. It was a moment as brief as a thin cloud's passing in front of the sun. No one would have noticed a shadow. He pushed his way forward into the crowd, apparently having seen someone he knew over by the jukebox.

"What did you say your name was?" Teddy Platte asked.

I smiled at him and lowered my eyes.

The road wavered before me like a moving reel of film. It was dark, and my father's old truck floated across the pavement as if through space. The headlights beamed out into the willows along Tomichi Creek and the high water shone like muted diamonds in the moonlight. It was not late—perhaps nine o'clock— but I had been drinking old-fashioneds in the Wagon Wheel all that time. Angie's fault. Teddy Platte's fault. Buying drinks for me, talking. Telling everyone I was back. Angie up on the bar announcing it. I couldn't get away.

Teddy was nothing like I remembered him. He was losing his hair. He told jokes. He told one about a truck driver who saw a naked woman, but now I can't remember it. I saw Del's face, too, swimming from the crowd, past the bar, as if avoiding me, though he knew I was there. He went out the door to wherever men go when they leave a bar, and I felt free, not as if chains had been loosed from me—nothing so simple—but the way a woman feels when she grasps looks do not matter anymore. Del was not the person he was; he couldn't have been. Nothing could be as it was before.

I passed the Lancasters' ranch and saw ahead the brilliantly illuminated feed pens at the Carrises', as if out of the night there emerged some new spectre. I had an odd sensation of stillness, the motor's stopping, the truck's sliding, though I was holding it straight on the road. I remembered one time when my father had gone elk hunting, and I had gotten up early, overjoyed at the quiet in the house. I went to my mother's room where she was putting up her hair. The sun fell through the dust motes in the room, striking a portion of the unmade bed. She sat at her mirror, now and then smiling up at me in the glass. Her hair was long and fine and dark, grown out nearly to her waist. Her sturdy arm swept the brush through it as if there were no resistance in the brushing. Several times she paused and pulled her hair over her shoulder and gazed at herself in the glass.

"Why don't you wear your hair that way?" I asked.

"I couldn't," she said.

I did not see why. She looked at me in the mirror with a wistful glance, tilted her head back so that her hair hung straight down over the back of the chair in the sunlight. I remembered her expression then, how her eyes stared upward at me as if in supplication, how beautiful she was, and how sorrowful she must have been all her life for having to transform herself from the woman she was that moment into the woman she had to become for my father.

The glistening arc lights of the Carrises' feed pens swirled past me like dust, and the whiff of manure—that savage, acrid smell—wakened me for a minute, filled the tight space of the truck cab. I rolled down the window, and by the time I'd escaped the lights, the smell was gone, cleansed from the cab by the scent of sage.

The road smoothed out a mile or so after the Carrises', where new asphalt had been laid. I slowed to let the calm take hold, and the truck glided. The hills were shadows beyond the reach of the headlights, but I knew that road: I knew the bends and the swales and the hills. It was a country of my own making, and there were stories there, tales I had already dreamed, new worlds I intended to make of the passing of the seasons. In the far distance—miles away still—the solitary light of my own house appeared beyond the low hills, disappeared, appeared again, trembling, it seemed, in the clean air, like a comet moving away from me even as I rushed toward it along the highway through the dark air.

YELLOW FLOWERS

Sharrie and I had lived in a suburb of Boston for fourteen years. She was a computer programmer in Cambridge, and I worked downtown as a marketing consultant. But how could that have prepared us for what happened? The general pulsing of our careers, evenings with the children's homework, weekend TV, an occasional ski trip to Vermont, or an afternoon on the Cape had taken their toll on us. Though we spoke often about the commute and the long winters and the deteriorating neighborhood, we weren't about to do anything different or go anywhere else. We would have persisted in this holding pattern, too, if it hadn't been for Davis.

Davis was in third grade then, Alicia in sixth, about to go to junior high. Alicia was well-mannered, calm, a reader. We received the kind of reports from her teachers that made parents think they were doing something right. She was sweet, if absentminded. She forgot where she'd left her jacket or whether she'd had breakfast that morning, but nothing bothered her. Davis might tease her, play tricks on her, assault her with commando forces, but she would turn away as if his words and pranks were of no avail against what she possessed.

Davis was an insightful boy, blessed or cursed with too much energy. He'd always searched for edges—kicked the soccer ball in his room upstairs until we had to take it away from him, pestered Alicia mercilessly (she was unfazed by it, but it drove Sharrie crazy), hammered nails into boards in my workshop in the cellar until he had blisters. At school he spent part of every day in the hall outside Mrs. Coolidge's door for talking, poking, passing notes, or talking back. We lectured him, threatened to take away his allowance, grounded him twice.

It was spring—this was 1988—when Davis made the first of his peregrinations. He had been in the corridor where Mrs. Coolidge had sent him, and he sneaked away for two hours before he returned to class. It worried us, naturally, when the principal called and told us.

That evening Sharrie, rather than I, talked to Davis. "Where did you go?" she asked calmly, trying not to be threatening.

"Nowhere much," Davis said.

"And what did you do?"

"Nothing much."

"Did you go alone?"

Davis nodded, but in a way that implied he had to think of an answer.

The school counselor spoke to him, too, but couldn't determine why Davis had left school. "He says he likes Mrs. Coolidge," the counselor said. "It's a minor infraction. It's happened before at this school. He isn't belligerent about anything."

"Of course he isn't," Sharrie said.

"On the other hand," the counselor said, "he doesn't explain himself. It's something to concern ourselves with."

And it was. Davis disappeared the next week at recess.

As most parents would have, we at first attributed his truancy to others. He'd been misled. Nothing Davis instigated, no idea of his, could have prompted this behavior. Sharrie spoke to the principal at length. But no other child had been absent either day without a verifiable excuse. "Can't you watch him then?" she asked.

The principal promised to do what he could. He asked Mrs. Coolidge not to send Davis to the hall. She should keep an eye on him. But, of course, there were several hundred students at the school. As the principal said, parents had to be responsible for their own children's whereabouts.

We monitored him at home, too, but there was no difference we could detect before and after. He was animated; he tortured Alicia. He wasn't withdrawn or secretive. Nothing was amiss in his room—no unaccounted for money, no Walkman or candy or video he might have stolen. He was eight: he had the usual toys and games and sports equipment, the complement of comic books and knickknacks and models of boats and fighter planes on his shelves. He had put up posters of the mountains of Wyoming and Colorado on the walls.

We waited. Nothing happened for several weeks. We relaxed. Then on a Tuesday after school Davis disappeared again.

Alicia called me at work. She was in tears. "I couldn't find him," she said. "He didn't meet me at the door."

"Are you sure you were at the right door? Sometimes you forget things."

"Daddy, he's *gone*."

I wasn't used to Alicia's panic. "All right," I said, "I'll be right home."

When I got there, having fought through traffic, Davis was in his room. "Where were you?" I asked. "You were supposed to meet your sister. Where'd you go?"

"Nowhere," he said.

I spanked him hard. "Don't you ever do this again," I told him. "Alicia was scared to death."

The next day he was gone from the middle of the morning recess until after lunch.

We couldn't imagine he was doing drugs. He had no money. The counselor didn't think so, either (there had been one case of a sixth grader's using marijuana), but he recommended testing, maybe private therapy. We had Davis checked thoroughly. The physician assured us Davis had no symptoms of sickness or signs of substance abuse. We called a child psychiatrist who, in two visits with Davis, found no dysfunctional behavior. "Normal" was how he phrased his diagnosis.

"It's not normal for an eight-year-old to disappear for no reason," Sharrie said.

The doctor shrugged. "He's exploring. He's very smart and articulate."

"But he could tell us where he goes," I said.

"He could, but he doesn't," the doctor said. "It's a little unusual, but I wouldn't press him on it. In the meantime, I see no reason to continue the visits unless some clear pattern emerges."

Sharrie wasn't mollified. She talked to Davis. She begged him not to wander. It wasn't safe for a boy his age, even with friends, to be gone like that. There were people in the world who might harm him, dangers he didn't know about—kidnappers, child molesters, automobiles careening through intersections. She got specific. She was worried he wasn't dressed warmly enough. Someone might beat him up. She thought of a hundred things and warned Davis of them.

The obvious thing was that Davis needed supervision. Sharrie had stayed home with each of the children during the two months of her maternity leaves from work, but after that the children had been in day-care or in school. For most of those early years, after Alicia was in school and Davis was in Montessori, one of us was able to get off work by mid-afternoon to collect Davis and be home when Alicia got there. Then when Davis started first grade, Alicia was old enough to babysit. She was so serene, we thought she could manage a few hours a day watching Davis. This had worked for more than two years.

Alicia, in fact, coped so well with Davis in the afternoons that Sharrie finally committed more time to programming for Webb Delaney, Inc. She'd been rewarded with two promotions, which led to more responsibility and even longer hours. With the cushion of her increased salary, and with the extra hours Alicia freed up, I felt able to break from the consulting firm I worked for and start my own service—advising retailers on marketing strategies. Some of my longer hours were at home, but as clients materialized and developed (basically I was paid to have their common sense for them), I had to be on the road more often to Connecticut and New York.

That was how life progressed: events interwove, consequences ensued. We weren't blind to the notion that Davis was rebelling against our deserting him for our work. He wanted attention. Yet it wasn't easy for either Sharrie or me to cut back. Careers have an on-going current. You're in them and have to swim, and sometimes you get a fair distance from shore. Besides, we didn't know whether Davis's behavior was a phase. That he was rebelling was pure conjecture, not to be dismissed, but not to be given total credence. We were worried, anxious, caught.

We were coming up against summer then. It was mid-April, still cold in New England, but with June not far ahead. School would be out. What then? We had a series of activities planned for the children, but no matter what we'd thought of—camps, day-care, tennis and sailing lessons—or which grandmother might take the children for a week or two, we couldn't let Davis do anything if he were going to disappear.

What we did, finally, was to hire someone to watch him. I don't mean a nurse or a sitter. My idea (I convinced Sharrie this was sound) was not to prevent him from going—keeping him in the house wouldn't tell us anything. We wanted to protect him and at the same time to gather information. We wanted to know where he went and what he did. If we could find out his reasons for being gone, maybe we could provide answers. That's what I thought we wanted: answers.

We agreed a woman would be better for this task than a man. A woman could move unnoticed at the edge of the playground or along the sidewalk, and she'd be less intimidating if Davis should be aware of her. We interviewed several investigators and liked one named Doreen Massey. When we met her one morning in the restaurant, she was sitting near the door, and neither Sharrie nor I noticed her. She was short, overweight, maybe forty-five or so, with short brown hair—not the sort to call attention to herself, not a woman from the pages of a magazine.

"Usually I follow men suspected of having affairs," Doreen told us when she found out the assignment.

"We hope that isn't the issue," I said.

Doreen smiled. "Is he hyperactive?"

Sharrie was indignant. "No, he's not."

"What about school? How does he do?"

"Fair to better-than-average," I said.

"Why?" Doreen asked. "You people seem intelligent." She held up her hand at Sharrie. "I'm only trying to learn about who I'm watching."

"We're hard-working anyway," I said, "if not smart."

"We try to make him study," Sharrie said. "He's more interested in other things."

"Like what?"

"Sports. I don't know."

"How's the sister do? What's her name?"

"Alicia," Sharrie said. "She's an honor student."

"You have photographs?"

Sharrie took several from her purse, some from the beach, some from Christmas, and Doreen studied them. "Cute," she said, "if eight-year-olds can be cute."

"They can be," Sharrie said.

"Does he ride a bicycle?"

"Yes, but not to school. We don't live that far away."

"If I'm hired," Doreen said, "I'd like to visit the scene of the crimes."

We drove to the school in Doreen's car, cramped in a red Chevette. Sharrie gave directions. I'd never noticed before there were no trees on the playground—swings and jungle gyms and basketball goals, but no trees. The playground was part cement, part gravel. Worn places marked where bases had been put for whatever games they played—kickball, T-ball, baseball. Doreen parked and made notes and sketches of the schoolyard—the gates in the fenced playground, the shape of the building, the entrances and exits.

When she was done with that, we followed the route Alicia and Davis took home. Doreen, though, was more interested in the route he took to go elsewhere, so we circled back and showed her the terrain around the school. Immediately adjacent to the school on the north were woods, not that thick. Houses were visible through the trees just starting to leaf out. Along the south, in front of the school, was a U-drive and the street with the usual caution lights and crosswalks. Row houses lined the opposite side and behind them the land dipped down toward Taylor Pond. At the nearest intersection toward town was a Friendly's Ice Cream, and to the right down the hill was a bridge over the creek that fed Taylor Pond, then a strip of businesses including several car dealers, a McDonald's, and a Kentucky Fried Chicken. To the left from the Friendly's was the town center where buildings were closer together and businesses spread out like a bruise into the welter of streets and houses.

We cruised this area, and Sharrie in front pointed out the landmarks—the old churches, the house where Otis Welch had lived, the site of the first sawmill in the United States.

"How long until recess?" Doreen asked finally. "I'd like to go back and see what Davis looks like in person."

We drove back to the school and waited. Davis was one of the first out of the building. He had on a blue sweater with white reindeer on it, and he ran in crazy circles as if he were glad to be out in the cooler air. When the other children came out, a soccer game started. Davis was good. He scored two goals while we were watching.

"Every morning call me," Doreen said. "Tell me what he's eaten. Let me know what he's got on—shirt and jacket."

"What he's eaten?" Sharrie asked.

"Diet," Doreen said. "Don't you believe you are what you eat?"

We informed the principal Doreen Massey was watching Davis. If she wanted information, he had our permission to give her whatever she needed. And we called Doreen every morning after Davis left the house. He ate good breakfasts—eggs, cereal, waffles. Nothing happened for days.

"He's a good athlete," Doreen said during her nightly report. "He's always on the winning side." Or, "I can see he'd be a handful. Jesus Christ."

There was a lull. Then on a Thursday toward the end of April, Davis slipped away. Doreen didn't see him.

"He came out for the lunch forty minutes ago," she said over her car phone. "I watched him play some T-ball with his friends. Then he went inside. He must have gone out through another door."

"Is he in school now?" I asked. I looked at my watch. It was 12:20.

"That's how I know he's missing," Doreen said. "He's not in class."

I thought of everything at once—saw Davis in town, at the pond, up at the Friendly's. "Was he alone? I guess you don't know that either."

"Like I said, I didn't see him," Doreen said. "What do you want me to do?"

I sighed and cleared my head. "Wait there. See if you spot him coming back. I'll go home in case he shows up there."

I canceled my interview with a client and, before I left, called Sharrie. She was furious. "What are we paying that woman for?" she asked. "My God, where is he?"

"Take it easy," I said. "Doreen can't see through buildings."

"Well, damn you, Ted. I won't take it easy."

"I'm going home," I told her. "I'll call you back when Davis comes home."

Davis showed up with Alicia after school. He seemed surprised to see me. "What are you doing here, Dad?"

"I took the afternoon off to work on a project."

"Then what are you sitting around for?"

"I'm getting to it," I said. "Anything happen at school?"

"Nothing much."

"He skipped out," Alicia said. "That's something."

"How do you know?" Davis asked.

"Jenny's sister told me."

Jenny was Davis's sometime girlfriend. I looked at Davis. "Did you leave school?" I asked. "Where did you go?"

"Nowhere," Davis said.

"You must have gone somewhere."

Davis stared at me with an expression that stopped me cold—not anger or rebellion, but right at the edge of hurt. I was glad when he let me go. "You want to pitch some baseballs, Dad?" he asked.

I called Sharrie and then pitched some baseballs with Davis in the backyard. I didn't mention his being gone from school.

Sharrie talked about how similar what Davis was doing was to a disease. When he'd go off, it was like a relapse, she said, a slide backward from his otherwise normal self. She speculated he might be a split personality. One minute he was Davis, boisterous athlete, the next someone else more devious, more desperate. Or maybe he was dreaming when he disappeared. That was another theory of hers. The psychiatrist couldn't know if he were dreaming.

None of this helped very much.

Doreen was frustrated, too. "A man, if he wanted a woman, would be easy to trace," she said, "but this. . . . He's so quirky. I can't promise anything."

The next week, May fourth, Doreen watched Davis follow a group of boys across to the ice cream truck, slide around back, and walk between two houses in the direction of the pond. He was wearing the red plaid shirt he'd gone to school in that morning.

At the time Doreen was in her car at the far end of the playground. That's what she told us that evening. She'd crossed the street and ducked under a clothesline at the side of one of the row houses. She'd startled an older woman gardening in her backyard, but hurried to the fence where she surveyed the pond and the unmoving yellow reeds along its border. Nothing. Davis wasn't there.

"At first I thought he was Houdini," she said. "Vanished into thin air. I said to myself this was the kind of thing Stephen King writes about. You know, total bullshit."

"He wasn't there?" Sharrie said.

"No one just vanishes," Doreen said. "Maybe he was hunkering down somewhere. Maybe he was hiding. But no one vanishes, even Houdini."

"But Davis did."

"In a way," Doreen said. "But this time I knew where to look for him." She paused on the line. "You know those houses across the street? They're all built on an old railroad bed." She stopped again as if that explained something. "In the old days they built tunnels so you could walk from one side to the other without going over the tracks. There's a tunnel a little way down from the school."

"That's where he goes?" I asked.

"That must be where he goes," Doreen said. "After recess I went down there. The tunnel cuts through the woods, and there's a path pretty well hidden that runs past the teachers' parking lot and comes out behind the cars and gets on that trail. From there he can go either toward the pond or toward town."

"But you said he wasn't at the pond," I said. "Maybe you should station yourself one place or the other, town maybe, where the path comes out."

"All right," Doreen said, "now we're getting somewhere."

We had kept records of when Davis had been truant. There were seven episodes, the longest of which was three hours after a morning recess. The shortest we knew of was after lunch when he'd missed one period of arithmetic. We couldn't determine reasons: tests in school, weather, day of the week—nothing formed a pattern. So far as we could tell, Davis hadn't harmed himself.

At home, if anything, he had calmed down a little. He concentrated better on his schoolwork, and though I wouldn't have called his application diligent, it was more consistent than before. He was more cheerful, too, and neater. He sometimes offered to help with chores that piled up during the week—gathering dirty clothes, raking the grass, sweeping the walk and the steps.

"Maybe it's best to let him wander," I told Sharrie one night after Davis had put the dinner dishes in the dishwasher.

"We can't," she said.

"I was being facetious."

"He's still mean to Alicia."

"It's not meanness," I said. "It's the duty of the younger brother."

"It's not a joke, Ted."

With the weather's warming, we suspected Davis might take off more frequently. I tried to relax about it, though always the possibility was there that if he left, some accident would befall him. Yet what more could we do than we'd done? I wanted to stay calm, but Sharrie couldn't rest. After each night of a day when nothing had happened, she wound herself more tightly, knowing the chances were greater tomorrow. She read, put the book aside, picked it up again. Sometimes she would go outdoors to smoke, which she hadn't done in ten years. Sometimes she went to bed early, tried to sleep, then got up and ate sherbet and went for a walk.

Doreen, too, said she felt something in the lengthening days, or maybe in the cold spring. "It's seasonal," she said. "And you don't have to tell me what he eats. I know you're good people."

It was May sixteenth, one of those New England spring days that isn't so warm as it appears. Leaves were already out in full force, flowers bloomed, but a breeze swept off the cold sea to well inland. Davis left for school. Sharrie called Doreen. I remember that because I'd heard her say Davis had on a jean jacket and a tan T-shirt underneath. I drove the same route that morning I always took to my office.

Some days at work I was conscious of when Davis had recess or lunch—10:15 A.M. or 11:40—and I would think of him out on the treeless playground playing catch or climbing on the jungle gym. I'd imagine him laughing with friends, throwing orange peels, or racing down the soccer field to take a pass from a teammate. Then in the midst of the revery, I'd wonder whether he'd wandered off. I'd see him in a record store or in the arcade, in a coin store looking at buffalo nickels. Or maybe he was sitting by the pond turning up mud in the swatch of reeds to find out about all the life that must have been there in the wet earth.

Around 10:30 that morning Doreen called. Davis had just

come up the hill from the woods behind the stores. I knew where she meant—the alley that ran for a block along the wood's edge to the YMCA on the corner. She wasn't sure whether to follow in her car, which was parked behind the shoe store, or whether to go on foot.

I buzzed my secretary to get Sharrie on the conference call and then came back on the line. "Does he seem nervous?" I asked Doreen.

"No. He doesn't know I'm here, if that's what you mean. But he's looking around. He's walking along the backs of the stores."

"What's his expression?"

I heard Doreen start her car, the tinny sound of the Chevette.

"Maybe you should go on foot," I said.

She put the car into gear. "I will as soon as I see where he's headed."

As she drove, she kept up a running commentary. "He's stopped at the back of Aldo's Market looking at the boxes. He's looking at the fire escape that goes up to the apartment on the second floor."

Sharrie came on the line. "Hello, Ted?"

"Now he's moving on," Doreen said. "He's found a tennis ball and is throwing it into the air and catching it. He's chucked it into the woods. He's looking into the woods. I can't tell what he sees. It's just leaves."

"Where is he?" Sharrie asked.

"In the alley," I said.

"Now he's walking again," Doreen said. "He's getting close to the Y. I'm going to pull in there and leave the car."

Doreen parked the car and said goodbye and hung up, all in a few seconds. Sharrie and I were left with each other on the line.

We were silent a moment. Then Sharrie said, "I want to see what he looks like."

"Let's let Doreen handle it," I said.

"I can't sit here," Sharrie said. "I'm going."

I didn't like the idea, but if Sharrie was going, I was too. "I'll pick you up," I told her. "Be out on the sidewalk at the station."

I left immediately. I raced down Storrow Drive, across the bridge at Harvard, up Fresh Pond Parkway. Sharrie was waiting on the curb opposite the subway station, and when she stepped down someone honked at her.

It was another ten minutes at least to the place where Doreen had parked her car. We found it in the lot at the Y. "Now what?" I asked Sharrie, pulling up behind the red Chevette.

"Let's make one pass through downtown," she said.

I turned the corner at the Y, went stop-and-go down the street. The trees along the sidewalk were not so far along as those in the woods, but they lent a subtle color to the brick storefronts. Most of the shops were small ones—single proprietorships holding out against the malls. Three blocks down at the end of the business district was the gray stone Presbyterian Church with its blue slate pyramid steeple which defined the horizon.

To our surprise we spotted Doreen standing under the awning of the delicatessen. We waved to her, but she didn't see us, and I slipped around the corner and parked. I looked at Sharrie. She seemed haggard, as if all the weeks of worrying had come to her face at that moment. "Oh, Ted," she said, "what if he isn't Davis anymore?"

"He will be," I said.

We got out and went arm in arm around the corner. We approached the delicatessen as though we were going to have lunch there and gazed into the window where salami, wurst, and cheese were displayed beside the menu.

"He's in the flower shop," Doreen said. She didn't look at us.

Sharrie turned around. "Has he been in there the whole time?"

"What are you doing here?" Doreen said. "What if he sees you?"

"He's our son," Sharrie said coldly.

Doreen shrugged. We went into the delicatessen, and Sharrie took up a post at the plate glass window. I ordered a ham and swiss on wheat bread to keep the deli owner happy, then joined Sharrie by the glass. Almost as soon as I'd taken a breath, Davis came out of the flower shop carrying a bouquet of yellow flowers.

He didn't look across the street. He turned to his left and walked up the sidewalk holding the bouquet—carnations or, maybe, chrysanthemums—about shoulder high, like a gift. He had a distinctive stride, bent forward at the waist, up on the balls of his feet. He had on high-top sneakers and no jacket against the breeze. The cold sun streamed over his bare arms.

"Where's he going with the flowers?" Sharrie asked, almost in a whisper, as if she were talking to herself.

"I don't know," I said. "Maybe he has a girlfriend after all."

"Ted, don't."

"Maybe he's befriended an invalid."

Davis passed the men's store, a tobacconist's, the copy place. He waited for a pedestrian light at the intersection. When he crossed and cleared the Gulf station on the corner, Doreen left the awning of the delicatessen and followed him. Davis didn't look back.

Beyond the Gulf station was a sporting goods store, a vacant lot, a dilapidated house for sale, zoned commercial, then another couple of shops at the edge of town—a small grocery store and a gift shop. We watched him pass these buildings, the yellow flowers more vivid than he. He disappeared behind the trees along the sidewalk, reappeared farther along. It was fascinating and frightening to watch him—his other life, his secret. Yet I had then a sense of unease about what we were doing, as if Sharrie and I were violating some unspoken vow more powerful than any order a superior might issue or any law a government could pass. Maybe Sharrie felt it, too. Or maybe she was torn by seeing Davis slide away from her. Where was he going with the flowers? After the gift shop were houses, the gray stone church, and more houses.

"Sandwich," the deli man said.

I went to the counter and paid. I heard the bell chime on the door, thought someone else had come in, turned in time to see Sharrie running past the window. I called to her, but she couldn't hear me. I left the sandwich on the counter.

By the time I got outside, Sharrie was across the street, dodging people on the sidewalk. I wanted to call again, but it was pointless—the traffic, the cold wind, the distance between us. She was walking quickly, trying to keep pace with Davis.

I glanced down the sidewalk to where Doreen was ignorant of what was going on. She was still watching Davis who, by then, had reached the hedge along the sidewalk in front of the church. Sharrie couldn't have seen him at that moment. A gasoline truck was pulling out of the Gulf station and blocked her view up the sidewalk. She had to wait until the truck rolled forward into traffic.

When it did, what confronted her? I can't say. Perhaps, not used to hurrying like that, she saw only a blackness which scared her. Or she could have seen the yellow flowers Davis held so high above his head. Or was the sidewalk empty, Davis vanished again?

Davis had turned down the walkway to the church. Whatever Sharrie saw or didn't see, she began to run and to yell out Davis's name. She wasn't following him anymore to see where he went. She wanted *him*.

"No," I said. But a whisper so far away didn't make her stop.

I ran down the sidewalk on my side of the street, opposite Sharrie and a little behind her. I sprinted past Doreen, who had reached a point in front of the Otis Welch house where the sidewalk turned from cement to brick. Sharrie was in front of the gift shop when Davis heard her voice.

Turning at the sound, Davis saw me. I was right across the street. I was too far away to see his face clearly, but I imagined it— stunned, drawn, his wide eyes full of hurt and sorrow. The flowers fell from upright above his head to a slanted position at his waist.

Then Sharrie came around the corner of the hedge between Davis and me. She stopped. Davis turned abruptly, pulled open the heavy door of the church, and went inside.

For a long time after that I felt an eerie grief. Davis was not much different. I noticed only a few subtle things, but these changes pained me more than Sharrie's endless discussions about what we should do next for Davis. Sharrie wanted him to go to counseling; she held Davis and hugged him; she wanted to talk about him every night before we went to sleep. But in my mind, Davis was all right. He was perhaps more silent than before, though there was no evidence for that conclusion. It was true he wouldn't talk about what had happened. We learned from the florist that he had bought flowers there several times. She didn't know where he went with them, but he headed in the same direction down the sidewalk. The pastor told us he had found yellow flowers on one of the pews.

One afternoon on my way home from an errand, I stopped and went into the church. I hadn't been inside a church for some long time, since just after college and then only for a wedding. I pulled the heavy door open, astonished that Davis could manage it alone, and stepped inside. My first thought was of the quiet—not just the lack of voices or the absence of music, but the stillness of the air. The smell of the air was silence. I stood in the back of the church for several minutes, gazing around at the empty pews, the carved pulpit, the huge round stained glass window above the altar. I tried to imagine how Davis had felt in the time he had spent there, what he'd thought, what had led him to come there. But my own attributions only made me realize how shadowy and unfathomable even my own child was to me.

That June I sold my consulting service for much less than it was worth. School had ended, and I wanted to be home. I took the children to the beach. We went to the aquarium in Boston and to several Red Sox games. They had riding lessons at the Audubon Farm. Sharrie wanted to know what I planned to do beyond the summer—clearly we couldn't afford our life if I didn't work. But I couldn't answer her. I considered buying a restaurant in the town center. That would have suited me well enough. I thought of moving the family out west where there was clean air and mountains. Davis had always liked the mountains.

In the fall Alicia started junior high school. Her grades suffered for a time, whether out of sympathy for Davis, I couldn't tell. Sometimes she cried out in her sleep, but when Sharrie or I went to her, she'd be wide awake as if nothing had happened. Davis was in the fourth grade at the same school he'd been to before. He had a new teacher, Mrs. Kennedy, who was more patient with him than Mrs. Coolidge had been, and he wasn't in so much trouble. His grades were a little better. At home he was about the same, though when he played with his soccer ball, it was always in the yard.

Sometimes those mornings after the children had gone, I was restless. I wasn't used to time on my hands. Often I walked over to Davis's school at recess and, from a distance, watched him on the playground. It wasn't like Doreen's watching him, not surveillance. Davis still played the same games with his friends, though I thought he was not so quick afoot in soccer as he'd been, or so strong when he hit a baseball. Perhaps this was my imagination. Now and then I'd see him pause in a game and stare into the woods or maybe at the clouds sliding across the early autumn sky. I know he wanted to disappear again. I felt that. Perhaps the risk was too great. It wasn't that he seemed so afraid as weary, if an eight-year-old can be weary. It was as though disappearing weren't worth the effort anymore. Someone would follow.

THE GARDEN OF ALEJANDRA RUIZ

It was April and beginning to warm up in the mountains. Snow melted from the deep basins, especially from the exposures facing south and, in shrinking, formed pictures on the slopes—a snow hawk, a pack of running coyotes, an antelope. Alejandra Ruiz knew these animals would disappear as the sun slid into its higher arc, so she told the neighbor children, who belonged to the woman Ernesto Saenz lived with. "That's an antelope," she said to them. "Can you see it?" She pointed to the mountain peaks and the children nodded. "That's a hawk," she said, "and a bear standing on two legs."

The children smiled. "We see them," they said.

But Alejandra Ruiz knew the mountains were too far away for them to make out what she meant to show them. It was too bad, she thought, because in a few days the antelope and the hawk would be gone, and the bear standing on two legs would be water in the rivulets and streams and in the river which was already brown and filling with the melt.

One afternoon on a day of fast clouds, with water tumbling into the gullies, Aleja Ruiz set out from her adobe house to prepare her garden. The best earth was above the river on a narrow plateau. Her mother had planted there, too, and with the same implements Aleja used. She had a hoe and a rake (whose handles had each been replaced by Ernesto Saenz, who had whittled the ends of two crooked junipers to fit tightly into the metal collars) and a small trowel Aleja had bought at the K-Mart in Española.

Aleja was not so old as she appeared. Each year she gathered wood for her fires, baked bread, raised chickens (from which she made egg money), hitchhiked into town for her groceries on the days when Ernesto, though he promised her a ride, could not get his truck started. She worked in her garden during the long dry season of summer. She had fine features, a skin tough from the weather, and sharp eyes. But she was prone to ailments. Her hip ached now and then, and sometimes her shoulder. She healed them by working.

From the plateau by the river, the dry land rose to the east in uneven hills of piñon and juniper laced with ridges of red sandstone and troughs of arroyos and eroded ravines. Higher up were the foothills and then the mountains, where the hawk and the running coyotes and the antelope disappeared day by day. These mountains were called the Sangre de Cristos for the color they bore in the evenings when sunlight flowed down red against the line of ascending shadow.

To the west was the river, which, even though brown with the melt, glittered with sunpebbles as it curved away downstream. Beyond the river was a paler terrain of plains and mesas—lower, dryer, hotter.

The crops for which Aleja was readying the soil were corn and squash and beans and potatoes, the usual ones for which she had culled the seeds the previous year and the same ones her mother had planted. Aleja bent over the hoe. Her hip bothered her, but if she held the hoe at a precise angle and leaned on it with just the right pressure, the pain dissipated. She was a slight woman, but work had given her stamina, and there was no hurry. There would be another frost before planting.

That afternoon, when they got home from school, the neighbor children came down the hill to watch Aleja Ruiz in her garden. Aleja spoke to them of the magpies and the scrub jays, of the eagles which circled in the sky above them, of the clouds which drove across the plains.

"Mama says it's going to rain," said Pattiann, the oldest child, though Aleja Ruiz never thought of them with the names their mother had given them.

"It's too cool to rain," said Aleja Ruiz.

"Maybe it will snow," said Ray, the little boy, the youngest.

"It's too warm to snow," said Aleja Ruiz. "The clouds are moving too fast. These are clouds between the seasons."

"What are you going to plant?" asked the middle girl, Elaine.

"I will plant what I always plant," Aleja Ruiz said, "which is corn and beans in the rows where the troughs will catch the rain. The beans will be on the outside where they will get the sun. And squash in the mounds at the ends of the rows. The potatoes will be over closest to the river because potatoes need the most water, and I won't have to carry the pails so far."

"What if the garden doesn't grow?" Ray asked.

"It will grow," Aleja Ruiz said.

"What if it never rains?" asked Elaine.

"It will rain a little, but not enough. When it doesn't rain, I will carry water from the river."

"What if the river goes dry?"

"The river won't go dry. It never has."

"But it might," Elaine said. "There is a chance, even if it's never happened before."

Aleja Ruiz admitted there was a possibility. "My mother never saw it dry," she said. "And neither have I."

The children stayed a few minutes longer, but they tired of watching the hoeing and went down the embankment to throw stones into the rising water.

On the second afternoon when Aleja Ruiz resumed her work in the garden, she had a pain in her arm. She stooped over the hoe, leaned on the juniper handle, scraped backwards, and loosened the dry earth. The day was partly cloudy and warm, and her shadow was fleeting along with the shadows of the clouds on the ground. She had finished three rows, each straight and tinged with the dark, moister earth beneath the surface. The rows were the length her mother had made them, and the same as last year.

When Aleja turned and began the fourth row, her shadow followed her on the same side, naturally, but it was altered because she backed up in a different direction. Her elbows in the shadow were more pronounced, her head slightly flatter in the kerchief she wore. Still, she looked as though she were doing over what she had already done.

Gradually her arms and shoulders stretched with the motion of the hoeing, and the pain left her arm. But she grew restless. Every few strokes she straightened up and gazed around at the mountains and the moving clouds and the sun, which, interspersed with the clouds, had already begun to coax the leaves from the willows along the river. She wondered whether this was a year when there would be no late frost.

Halfway down the row Aleja Ruiz struck a stone. The tick of the metal hoe blade on rock ran a shiver through her arms, up her shoulders, and across her back. She poked the stone, prodded it, clanked the metal on it again. The earth had been hoed and raked and planted so many times it was unusual to find a stone, though now and then, to her surprise, one worked its way to the surface.

She tucked a corner of the hoe against the sharp edge of the stone and pulled, but the blade slipped off. She gripped the juniper handle more tightly and positioned her body for better purchase. But again the metal gave way and the stone stayed in the ground.

Aleja scraped the earth away. The stone was not far beneath the surface, only a few inches, and she uncovered its rough outline. Of course, she had dug many stones before. Years ago, when she was too young for words, a rain had come in the spring when the river was full of snow hawks and antelope. The water had rushed from its banks and over the corrals her parents had kept, had sent sprawling the huge cottonwoods upriver. It had even risen above the plateau where her mother had planted the garden. She remembered they had been very poor that year, without corn and squash and beans—only stones to dig from the silt and carry away.

That had been long ago, and it was only a dim memory. The stones had all been returned to the river. Except here was a stone. Aleja got down on her knees and scratched it with her trowel. It wasn't sandstone or shale. Those would have crumbled with the abrasion. This one felt hard like granite. When she stabbed the stone, sparks flew from the blade of the trowel.

She uncovered more of it, found a good hold with her callused hands, pulled and pushed to loosen the stone. She couldn't move it. She dug a wider arc, deeper into the ground, and the stone expanded around the blade as if the trowel were making the stone larger.

Finally she stood up and went to find Ernesto Saenz.

She knew by the smoke coming from the tin pipe that he was

in his shed where, for his living, he fixed small motors—pumps, lawn mowers, weed trimmers, chain saws, anything that ran on gasoline, even outboard engines. He was a thick-set man, beer heavy and bean fat and glad for Maria Yglesias, who had consented to live with him.

Aleja Ruiz climbed the hill toward the blowing smoke. Ernesto Saenz was not always willing to help her. Sometimes he did and sometimes he didn't. Once he refused to fix her roof when the wind had bent a tin corner and the sun shone into her kitchen, but when her well froze and the pipes burst, he carried water for her every day from his shed and fixed the pipes when they thawed. So now she approached his shed unknowing.

She stepped into the doorway and peered into the darkness. It seemed like darkness compared to the sunlit air. Ernesto was hunched over an Evinrude outboard he had mounted on the back of a chair. Around him were five or six other motors, broken down and waiting, and along the walls were more he had not got to. "You're in my light, Alejandra Ruiz," he said without looking at her.

Aleja came inside, away from the door, into the cooler air. The room brightened. Juniper smoke from the leaky woodstove hovered under the roof. She smelled grease.

"What can I do for you?" Ernesto asked.

"There is a stone in my garden," Aleja said.

"There are stones in my garden, too," Ernesto said, peering into the engine. "And in my mother's garden in Chimayo."

"This stone is too heavy for me."

Ernesto went on tinkering, first with a screwdriver, then with a small wrench. "You're as strong as I am," he said. "Maybe stronger."

"You have tools," Aleja said.

Ernesto looked at her for the first time. "Take whatever you need."

She nodded and searched among the motors for what she wanted. She took a shovel with a factory-made handle and a long crowbar.

In the garden she dug around the stone, down deeper than the topsoil, where the earth turned to gravel and then to heavier clay. Several times she stopped and tried to pry the stone loose with the crowbar, but it would not come free.

● ● ●

It was nearly dark when she took the shovel and the crowbar up the hill to Ernesto Saenz's house. She paused now and then on the path to catch her breath and to look around her. Across the river the sunlight spread itself in lavender along the dark line of the mesas. But toward the mountains a deep blue sky settled and turned colder. A slight breeze drifted over the hills of Chimayo and through the junipers, and she knew the bear on two legs would stay at least until tomorrow.

She knocked on Ernesto's door, and Elaine answered. "It's Alejandra Ruiz," Elaine called into the house.

Aleja set the shovel and the crowbar against the door frame.

"Come in, Alejandra Ruiz," Maria called.

Aleja entered the house and pushed the door closed. The smell of beans and woodsmoke and chicken seized her. It was hot in the room. Maria and the children were eating chicken at the table from rectangular tinfoil plates, while Ernesto sat in the living room watching television with a bowl of beans in his lap.

"Would you like something to eat?" Maria asked. "I've cooked beans and venison stew for Ernesto because he won't eat Lean Cuisine."

"No, thank you," Aleja said from the doorway.

Ernesto was watching an Anglo program in Spanish, and he spooned stew and beans into his mouth and chewed. After a minute he looked at Aleja. "Were you successful?" he asked.

Aleja shook her head.

"It must be a big stone," Ernesto said.

"It is a big stone," Aleja said. For no reason she felt her jaw set tightly, the skin stretched tight across the bones around her eyes.

"What happened?" Maria asked.

"What is what?" Ernesto said. An advertisement came on TV, and he watched it more intently than the Anglo program. It showed a person's stomach acid being soothed by bubbles.

"What have you not done to help?" Maria asked.

"Her garden has a stone in it," Ernesto said. "My garden has stones. The gardens in Chimayo have stones. Alejandra Ruiz is the only one whose garden doesn't have stones." He turned to Alejandra again. "Where was this stone last year or the year before, when you were growing the best corn in the valley and the best squash?"

"It wasn't there," Aleja said.

Ernesto set his empty bowl on the floor, stood up, and got a bottle of beer from the propane refrigerator. "I see," he said. "Not there. It rose overnight in the ground."

"It appeared," Aleja said.

"Help Alejandra Ruiz with the stone," Maria said.

"It's dark," Ernesto said.

"I mean tomorrow."

Ernesto snapped the top from the beer bottle with his fingernail and looked at the children whose tinfoil plates were half-full. "All right," he said. "Tomorrow I will help."

On the usual morning in April, before the sun had gained momentum into the sky, Aleja Ruiz was slow to move about. Inside her house was cold. She would get up and start a fire, make her coffee in the automatic drip machine her sister had sent her from Albuquerque, watch from the window as the neighbor children set out along the dirt road toward the bus stop carrying their books and at the same time trying to get their hands warm in their pockets. But that morning she hadn't slept so soundly as she usually did. She had tossed in her narrow bed and had dreamed of voices soaring over her head like birds, calling to her as they glided away toward the mountains, disappearing one after another into the distance.

When she woke, Aleja felt her cold room was an unfamiliar place. She saw the stove, the automatic drip coffeemaker, and the same configuration of windows. But she got up immediately and went outside. Something was different.

Frost had patterned the ruts in her yard, glistened pink in crystals on the window panes. The dry stalks of weeds were layered in rime, as were the early buds on the apricot trees. Ernesto Saenz was coming down the path from his shed, pushing a wheelbarrow with tools in it. Aleja Ruiz met him at the edge of her yard where the path led down to the garden.

"I have to pick up parts in Española," Ernesto said. "And I promised a man his lawn mower by noon. I thought I would do this job early."

"Thank you, Ernesto Saenz. We've had a frost."

"It's cold," he said. "You can thank me when I get the stone rolled down the bank into the river."

"I will thank you then, too."

She followed him down the path. The early sun cast orange like an echo against the sandstone ridges, but it was still cold. Ernesto's tools—the shovel with the factory-made handle, two crowbars, a sledgehammer, and a wedge—rattled in the wheelbar-row as Ernesto steered it down the uneven terrain. They didn't speak. Aleja Ruiz held her bare hands under her armpits.

The frost was heavier in the garden. It lined the west-facing rows that Aleja had already hoed, and etched the rock in white. A pile of earth—topsoil, gravel, clay, pebbles—lay in the middle of the garden stubble.

Ernesto wheeled the tools to the spot and considered the job. After a time he said, "I advise you, Alejandra Ruiz, to cover this stone and plant around it."

"You don't think you can get it out?"

"I can get it out," he said. "But there will be a hole."

"I can fill the hole."

"Even so, planting around it would be easier. You'll have to bring in new soil."

"Nothing will grow over a stone," Aleja Ruiz said.

Ernesto looked at the sun, which was edging up from the mountains into the sky. He followed with his gaze a flock of crows flying from their roost, wherever it was, toward the dump at Chimayo. Then he measured Aleja Ruiz. "You're a stub-born woman, Alejandra Ruiz."

"No more stubborn than the crows which fly to the dump," she said. "No more than the bear standing on two legs on the mountain."

Ernesto tried the lever first. He brought a smooth, medium-sized stone from the river bank and set it at the edge of the trench. Then he lodged the crowbar as far under the big stone as he could—there was no part that was exactly *under*, but he settled the bar into a cleft. Then he inched backward into a crouch and pushed the lever down with all his weight. He grunted and pried. The stone stayed where it was.

He dug with the shovel. Sweat rose on his forehead, steamed into the cold air. He muttered. He swore. He thudded the earth with the blade of the shovel, lifted the heavy clay, showered the clods over the garden. When he got out of the trench to try the lever again, Aleja Ruiz climbed into the hole and went on digging. She lifted the shovelfuls of earth more carefully. The work warmed her. The stone moved outward from the shovel.

Ernesto pried with the crowbar. "Push from the side," he said. "We'll move it."

She put the shovel down and pushed. The stone did not move.

"If we can loosen it a little," Ernesto said, "then we'll have it."

They worked another half hour until Ernesto said he had to go to Española. "I have a business," he said. "I can't spend my whole day over a stone in the ground."

"Thank you for what you've done, Ernesto Saenz."

"Don't thank me," he said. Ernesto wiped his forehead on his shirt-sleeve and spat on the ground. "I did nothing."

Later that afternoon Aleja Ruiz stood in front of her house making bread to take up to Ernesto Saenz and Maria Yglesias to thank them for their efforts. She had sifted the flour, mixed in cinnamon for the children, kneaded the dough on a smooth flat stone under the still-bare branches of the apricot trees. She rolled the dough out, kneaded it again the way her mother had taught her. She made bread three times every week, had made thousands of loaves without questioning the task. She liked the smells and the differing lights of the weathers and the seasons, especially the afternoon light in spring and fall on the plateau and beyond, where the shadows danced across the river gorge.

But that afternoon she took no pleasure in the sunlight or in the sweet, warm breeze which slid down the arroyo into her yard. The making of bread was a chore and a sorrow. The shadows did not dance. All she could think of was the stone in her garden.

She had just set the loaves in a wedge of shade by the house to let them rise when she heard a motor churning the air, a motor not of a car which she would have recognized. This motor came too slowly around the barren hill beyond Ernesto Saenz's shed. With her hand she shaded her eyes from the sunglare. A tractor sputtered into view and came down the dirt lane toward the shed. Aleja recognized the driver as Raul Gadín, who was called El Pavo because with such a long neck he looked like a turkey.

Raul stopped at the shed, and Ernesto came out. The motor of the tractor softened. For a few minutes Raul and Ernesto spoke, and Ernesto pointed toward Aleja's house. Then Ernesto climbed up onto the fender of the tractor and the two men started down the hill toward where Aleja was watching.

Raul Gadín was a tall, wiry man, and he squinted all the time. He had a cherry orchard on the outskirts of Chimayo, and before the cherries came in, he hired himself out to cut alfalfa on the irrigated fields of the valley. He did other odd jobs, too, like cutting firewood or pulling stumps or, in winter, plowing driveways for the Anglos or rescuing cars from ditches. He made excuses before he started anything, but wherever there was a job for a tractor, the man to call was El Pavo.

Raul Gadín stopped the tractor at the edge of Aleja's yard. "He's doing this for nothing," Ernesto Saenz said. "I fixed his irrigation pump at the orchard, and Pavo owes me a favor."

"But why are you using the favor for me?" Aleja asked.

"Nothing is done yet," Ernesto said. "Do you want a ride?"

He helped Aleja up onto the fender, and Raul Gadín put the tractor into gear and drove down to the garden.

El Pavo stood near the stone and surveyed the terrain for the best position for the tractor. He squinted as if he were thinking very hard. "The problem is leverage," he said. "With a stump I could put the chain around and pull straight, but with this stone—you see how it is." He squinted again. "Or with a car there's a bumper to attach to."

The trench Ernesto and Aleja had dug was three feet deep and, from one side to the other, perhaps six feet across. The stone was dome-shaped, rough, pocked with dirt and gravel.

"It can't be that difficult," Ernesto said.

"I may not have enough chain," said Raul Gadín.

"This is a stone that wasn't here before," Ernesto said. "If we loosen it a little, we can dig it out."

Ernesto set about fixing the chain around the stone, while Raul steered the tractor into the position he decided was best. Ernesto looped the chain twice around the girth of the stone and attached the remainder double so the tractor could pull on two lengths of chain instead of one. Raul got down on his hands and knees and secured the chain to the ball hitch on the back of the tractor. Then he climbed up into the seat. He revved the engine and shifted into first. The chain creaked and tightened around the stone, bent over the lip of the trench. Nothing happened. The taut chain dug into the earth. Raul Gádin backed up, put the tractor into gear again, and tried to jerk the stone loose. The tractor surged in the air; the stone didn't move.

Raul turned off the engine and the motor wound down. "Block and tackle," he said, squinting at Aleja Ruiz. "That's what we'll need for this job."

Aleja Ruiz didn't know what this was.

"I have it in my truck," Raul Gadín said, turning to Ernesto.

"You'll have to drive me over."

Ernesto looked at his watch. "I got a chain saw to deliver," he said. "I thought you could do this in half an hour."

Raul Gadín shrugged. "We'll deliver the chain saw on the way."

"All right," Ernesto said. "Alejandra Ruiz, you stay here and make certain the stone doesn't go anywhere."

The two men climbed the hill on foot, leaving Alejandra Ruiz and the tractor and the stone in the garden. It seemed to Aleja the stone had grown larger since the morning, but she knew this was her imagination. The stone wasn't higher than the hills of gravel and topsoil around the trench, but it almost looked as if it were higher than the surrounding garden. It was an optical illusion, she knew, or the way the sun slanted in on the stone through the late afternoon clouds that were gathering over the plains.

She waited an hour, watching the snow figures in the mountains running and running and the sun begin to pink on the high peaks.

The men came back in two trucks. Raul Gadín had brought his own truck with all kinds of contraptions in the back of it Aleja Ruiz had never seen before. El Pavo, who always said he couldn't do a job, guaranteed the block and tackle would work, and he and Ernesto spent another long interval arranging the cables and the odd wooden apparatus. They hooked cables onto chains, wound the chains around the stone, fixed the chains to the tractor. When the time came to test what they'd done, Raul Gadín made the sign of the cross over himself. He started the engine of the tractor and let out the clutch slowly. The apparatus groaned and stretched and the engine of the tractor roared. Raul Gadín squinted back at the stone, which stayed in the ground.

During the night it rained. Alejandra Ruiz was jolted from her bed by lightning and thunder and the ratatat of rain on the tin roof of her house. Drips of water came through the seams of the tin sheets and splashed on the floor, but Aleja was too weary to get up. She sat in her bed and listened to the storm move across. Every so often lightning illuminated the grayish hills, the piñons and junipers, the rain itself, which fell hard across the dry earth. Then an instant later the land disappeared again and the night resumed as before.

The following morning, after the storm had passed and she

had spent a fitful night's sleep without dreams, Alejandra Ruiz woke to the shouts of people and the noise of cars. Usually she woke at first light, but that morning the sun was already over the mountains and was shining strongly into her doorway. Cars and trucks were parked up at Ernesto Saenz's shed and more were coming around the barren hill, sliding and splashing on the muddy road. Voices lifted from the shed and from the other side of Aleja's house where the path led down to the garden.

Aleja put on boots and a housecoat and went outside. The air was crisp and washed clean as it always was after a storm. Rain had fallen in the yard and over the river, but in the mountains it had snowed. The hawk and the running coyotes and the antelope were covered over.

Aleja joined the others on the path. Men had brought shovels and women had come with their children to work themselves and to watch the men. They all greeted Alejandra Ruiz cheerfully. "It's a fine morning," they said. "Hello, Alejandra Ruiz. We are glad to help you."

Fifteen or twenty people were already in the garden, gathered around the stone. Some of them Aleja recognized and some she didn't—Ernesto was there and Maria Yglesias's three children, and Raul Gadín, and a man called Vago, a strong man who wandered around the streets of Chimayo. Ernesto's brother was there, and Pedro Maestas, the butcher, and a man with a big mustache whom Aleja had seen before somewhere. Five or six of the men were in the trench digging. Raul Gadín, in an orange highway department vest, squinted from the seat of his tractor as he talked to Vago. Ernesto stood off to one side consulting with a thin man in white slacks and a yellow straw hat.

When Ernesto saw Aleja, he waved her over. "It's a beautiful morning after the storm, Alejandra Ruiz," he said.

"My roof leaked," Aleja said, "and now it's noisy."

"This is Señor Montoya, an engineer from Los Alamos," Ernesto said, holding the thin man's arm as though the man might escape. "He has owed me a favor since two summers ago, when I fixed his outboard motor out on the reservoir at Abiquiu."

"Many people owe you favors, Ernesto Saenz," Aleja said. "You will have none left for yourself."

The man took off his yellow hat and bowed to her. "I drove from Los Alamos this morning to be of service," he said.

Aleja avoided his glance and looked past him at the stone. The men had already uncovered more of it, three times as much as had been visible the evening before when Raul Gadín had tried to pull it loose with his tractor and the block and tackle. It was immense now. The stone was at least six feet across (the trench must have been ten) and five feet deep. Twenty men or fifty could never move such a stone. Ten tractors could not move it. And it had grown taller. She was sure of it. Maybe only an inch or two, but it was higher relative to the level of the garden than it had been the afternoon before. It was a stone getting bigger, she thought. Maybe only a corner of it was visible, a tiny part. Maybe it was big as a mountain, and if the stone were taken from her garden there would not be enough earth in Chimayo to fill the hole.

But she said nothing. Instead, what struck her was how beautiful the stone was, cleaned by the rain of the bits of dirt and gravel. Its shape was graceful, elegant. In the morning sunlight it shone whitish pink, and the mica in it glittered silver.

"Señor Montoya thinks it is necessary to use explosives," Ernesto Saenz was saying. "We will dig around the rock and prepare the terrain the way they do when they build a highway through the mountains. Senor Montoya has telephoned for the required permissions."

"Yes, Señora Ruiz," Señor Montoya said. "We will bore into the stone from the sides and sheath the explosives so that when they are detonated in the holes, the rock will fragment."

Aleja watched the children running around the trench laughing and shouting at one another. The men worked several minutes in the trench, then gave way to others. The women who had come had gathered on the hillside above the garden, where they were talking and passing around coffee from thermoses.

"It will not take long now," Ernesto said, smiling at Aleja.

"No, Señora," Señor Montoya said. "As soon as there is word on the cellular telephone . . ."

Aleja Ruiz nodded. "Stop," she said softly.

Señor Montoya stopped in mid-sentence. Ernesto stopped talking.

"Stop the men," said Aleja Ruiz.

"But we've just started," Ernesto said.

"Please."

Ernesto set his thumb and forefinger at the corners of his mouth and whistled loudly. The men paused in their work. They leaned on their shovels. Raul Gadín squinted at her, and the man

Vago stopped talking. The children stopped running and shouting.

"Thank you, Ernesto Saenz."

"We have done nothing yet," Ernesto said.

Aleja Ruiz raised her hands and waved the people away. She did not say anything. She gestured in the air, and everyone understood she meant for them to leave. One by one the men picked up their shovels and climbed from the trench. They moved away from the stone. Those that had not yet reached the garden turned back up the hill. The women left the slope carrying their coffee cups and thermoses. The children crept away quietly.

Even Señor Montoya bowed and backed away, and Ernesto Saenz turned from where he was and began to walk toward the path, following the others. The sun was warm and arced higher above the brown water of the river made fast by the night's rain. On that fresh morning, as the snow melted again from the mountains, Aleja Ruiz was left alone with the stone in her garden.

THE TARPON BET

Lee Allard narrowed his eyes against the white sun and watched the mangrove cover slide past as if on oil. Brian was stretched out in the bow seat with his hands cupped behind his head, braced upon nothing, his eyes closed. The boat floated idly toward the Gulf, and the late morning silence was as oppressive as the heat.

"Still thinking about it?" Lee asked.

"What's that?"

Lee, shirtless, a jagged scar at his ribs, worked intently on cleaning his .38 pistol. "She was a tease," he said.

"They all are," Brian said without raising his voice. "But she was a sure thing, too." He sat up and followed a blue heron's slow, methodical wingbeats against the green trees.

Lee smiled. He was thin and his fingers worked like wires. He spread oil on the square of cloth and threaded the cloth through the gun barrel. Now and then he squinted toward the bow. Brian's light beard had taken the sharp edge from his features, making hazy the outline of his cheek and jaw. His broad chest was tanned, and except for a slight tire, his heavy frame looked in good shape. "I've never known you to turn down a sure thing," Lee said.

"You could have given me more time."

"I see," Lee said. "I'm supposed to be patient." He pressed his lips together in what was not quite a smile. He had finished cleaning the gun and now he put four bullets into the cylinder and aimed at a flock of white ibis picking over a shallow pool on a mudflat a hundred yards away. With the crack of the pistol, the birds exploded like white paper in the wind. "I'm supposed to wait for you," Lee said calmly.

Brian jumped up when he heard the shot and then lay back down on the seat.

"What about Rosellen?" Lee asked.

"What about her?"

Lee shrugged. The ibis regrouped and headed upriver into the maze of creeks and the bay through which he and Brian had already come. He broke open the pistol and threw the empty shell into the water, then laid the gun under the stern seat. "What's a wife, right? Just shit."

"Tell me you wouldn't have done it," Brian said, turning his head. "If you'd had the chance with that woman, you'd have stayed for a week. Instead, though, we've got to hotfoot it down to Chokoloskee in a fucking sprint. Get an early start. You're jealous, you know that? Full of envy. A fucking early start so we can sit like this all morning getting our asses burned."

The boat curled in an eddy, turned broadside, and floated backward into the current. An osprey came over the trees and hovered against the pale sky. It started down, then rose and hovered again, as though deciding what to do. Finally it dived at an angle, striking the water hard. For a few seconds it struggled at the surface, then it took off slowly, weighted down by the fish in its talons.

"See that?" Lee asked. "We should be fishing now."

He took a rod from the bottom of the boat and wrestled a double-rigging from the tackle box. It was far enough downriver to expect something to happen. He opened the cooler and got out bait.

"How about a beer?" Brian said.

Lee took a beer from the melting ice and threw it into the bottom of the boat toward the bow. "Fuck you."

Brian grinned. "Jealous," he said.

Lee flipped back the open face of the reel and with a snap of his wrist sent the light monofilament spinning out toward the deep water behind them. He let the bait run with the current, now and then easing the rod forward. No snags. He could feel the bottom was smooth, scoured by tides and current, and he sat back wondering how the river bed would look if the sea tide never ran and the creek were completely empty. Salt water made a difference in what would grow, but he didn't know names of plants. Fish, slimy insects, plants would be on the bottom, maybe treasures.

The woman in the bar had been no big deal. She was a little on the heavy side to be dressed in halter and jeans. She had nice eyes though, eyes which made complex things seem very simple. Her brown hair was combed back, and her copper skin had looked like metal in the dim light.

Brian had the luck of the draw; he'd always had. Jesus, Lee remembered that night in the rain, the first night on leave from Fort Bragg when they had stopped in the liquor store in Fayetteville. That woman was better looking than the one last night, or maybe more willing. Divorced or separated. Lee couldn't remember that. But Brian had taken her along with the booze, and she'd stayed with them three days in a motel in Wilmington. Christ. Maybe Brian was right: he was envious. He would have cashed the woman the night before in the bar, if he'd had the chance. No, he wouldn't have.

Lorita was at home, maybe not missing him, but at home anyway. Small-boned, dark-skinned. He had brought her back from Thailand after the war in 1967. She had liked Loretta Lynn on the jukebox in the bar where she worked, so the GIs called her Lorita, the way she pronounced it. Brian had known her, too, but Lee had been the one she liked. No birth certificate, no court decree. Marrying her was enough. And now she was at home, lonely most of the time in Tampa. He never knew what was in her head. She was shy and rarely looked into his eyes. But she could be fierce, too. She was tiny, with barely a breastline and only a slight curve at her hips, but she took no shit from people like Brian.

When the fish hit, Lee was half asleep. His thoughts broke with the heavy tug on the line, and he jerked the rod back quickly. The boat rolled in the smooth water.

"I want to see you do that to a tarpon," Brian said.

Lee braced his foot against the side of the boat and lifted the rod. The fish was good-sized, he could tell that.

"Take it easy," Brian said. "You'll strangle him."

Sweat beaded quickly on Lee's forehead and on his bare shoulders. He felt anger rise to his eyes. Brian was right. He should let the fish run, let him tire, and then reel.

"Give him line," Brian said.

"Bastard says nothing all morning, then starts giving advice."

"You need advice."

Lee imagined the fish's struggle, the way it twisted against the pain of the hook, maybe darted into the swirling reeds at the edge of the current. There was the bite and the jerk of the hook through the mouth tissue, and then the unnatural motion of being pulled. To the fish, what had looked damn good was suddenly death.

Lee let him run. He gave twenty yards of line, then another ten, wishing he would run forever. But he kept the tension, making sure the fish was still there.

Brian stared at the smooth surface of the water. "You bringing him in?"

"What do you think? I'm tying my shoe?"

"Hold the rod farther back. Lower. Jesus, I want to see you with a goddamned tarpon. That's right. There."

Lee pulled and reeled, lifting the rod and then cranking as he let the rod back down toward the water. The weight of the fish was greater the closer it got to the boat, the more tired it got. Twenty yards out, the fish surfaced and then dived deep.

"Pompano," Brian said. "See the yellow?"

The pompano made a last run into the current, and Lee stood up and fumbled for the net. He held the long handle between his legs and let out more line.

"Want me to net him?" Brian asked.

"Fuck no."

Sweat coursed along the lines of Lee's face and fell in drops onto the canvas seat. He gazed intently at the shimmering surface of the river where the silver thread of the line disappeared into the murky water. He reeled strongly now, looking for yellow.

The pompano came up ten yards from the boat and was angling in on a run when the spectre of the shark rose from the depth of the tidewater. In immeasurable, eerie silence, the shark glided toward the yellow pompano, struck hard, then sank out of sight again. The line burned off the reel in Lee's hand. Then it snapped, leaving the morning quiet again, hot and humid, like the dead stop of breeze.

• • •

After the war Lee had taken Lorita home to Indianapolis. The friends he'd had there before the war were gone or too busy or were different from before. Even his parents, once the welcome home had worn off, began to wonder what he was going to do. No one gave him much credit.

"I'll find something," he said.

"What about her?"

"Lorita's fine."

He was not so sure. They endured one winter in Chicago, returned to Indianapolis, suffocated there through the summer. The war had been terrible, but the year back home made war seem clear-cut. At least he'd had a reason for going from day to day. He'd put a kind of physical stock in the war, and the training had turned his thin arms and legs hard. But home, where he'd at least hoped for a future to give Lorita, had no side to it, no angles, no obvious thing to do.

He'd had a letter then from Brian. "You remember him," Lee had said to Lorita. "He carried me through basic. When we were on patrol and I was scared, he was there. He wants us to come to Florida."

"Why this sonny want you in Florida?" Lorita asked.

"I don't *care* why," Lee said.

Brian had given him something to see ahead of him. During their tour they had shared a kind of closeness Lee hadn't known before, joking mostly. To ease the fear and the boredom, they had bet on everything. They bet dollar bills on who could throw a bayonet closer to a tent stake, whether the letter *A* would appear before the letter *E* in the next headline of *Stars and Stripes*. Brian wanted to bet fifty that Ho Chi Minh died before Lyndon Johnson. They bet on sports, women, cards, weather. Losing meant nothing so far from home.

The war had been a siege of silence, each side trying to lull the other to sleep. They had been warned to concentrate, but there was nothing to concentrate on. Day after day in the field they saw no one. The only sounds were the squawks of birds and the droning of insects.

Gradually Lee felt tired.

"You've got to keep alert," Brian said.

"Right."

"I'll bet a C-note I see a gook before you do."

"Deal."

Lee's fatigue was like a pall. He was tired of insects, officers' orders, rain, screw-ups, mildew. But he won the hundred. He had relaxed one hot afternoon, and a sniper's bullet had blown away the left half of his stomach.

In Tampa Brian had lined up a job for him in a machine shop. "I don't know anything about tool and die," Lee said.

"You have to see how things work out. The guy is a friend of mine." Brian winked at him. "Just show up every day and move along."

Brian always had some friend who owed him a favor, always had some angle. He would buy and resell a hot car, play a fixed race. Whatever it was, he knew where the influence lay, whom to ask, how to find out the weak spots. But from the beginning the job in the machine shop hadn't been right.

"You've got to make your presence felt," Brian said. "Tell them stories about the war. I'm putting in the good word for you up front."

"I'd just like something I can do right," Lee said. "Buy Lorita a few of the things I promised her."

"That piece of slant has you going," Brian said. "Relax."

"A few nice things is all."

Lorita was prettier in the American sense than in the Thai. The slightness of her figure did not bother him so much as the foreignness of her past. Even aside from the bar, he did not understand her gods and symbols. He did not understand how a person kept going when her sister had been blown up by a mine and her parents had disappeared and her village had been burned to the ground.

"How'd that piece of slant fall for you anyway?" Brian had asked once.

Lee smiled. "I had class."

"You and Marlon," Brian said. "But you had a ticket out of the country."

Lee had kept his mouth shut.

The job in the machine shop slipped away. For a couple of weeks Lee went on unemployment, and then he took work in a fast-food restaurant. He felt bad about Lorita. She accepted everything, but by the way she looked away from him, he suspected her life was changing. He quit the franchise to put together a deal to buy a gas station and garage. Brian knew someone who knew someone, but at the last minute, the bank reneged on the loan.

"Fuck 'em," Brian said. "I got friends. We'll get the money."

They were drinking beer in the Dew Drop Inn.

"I need *cash*," Brian said.

"Long-term or short?"

"Both."

"Christ, man, money's the least of your problems. If you want money, let's go play a couple of quinellas."

They had got drunk first and then had gone by Lee's apartment on the way to the track. Lorita was angry, first about the drinking, then about the racetrack. "You no go to dog," she said. "We have better place to give dollar away."

"Lighten up," Brian told her.

Lorita didn't smile. "Not for you, sonny. I not light up for you."

"We'll be back late," Lee said. "This man Brian does not lose."

Lee had learned long before to trust Brian's intuition. At the track Brian hit on three, four, and nine, and took in eight hundred dollars.

"This America," Brian mimicked. "Land of dream." He slapped Lee's half into his palm. "Show that to the piece of slant."

At the mouth of the river Lee started the motor and headed straight out into the Gulf to get around the shoals. A shirt draped over his shoulder kept off the burning sun. Scattered clouds crossed the sky in the pattern of a print dress, but they gave no shade. Without the canopy of mangroves, the sky was enormous, rising far beyond the gray sea.

Brian sat on the edge of the boat with a beer in his hand and the coastal chart across his knees. He looked from the paper to the shore and back again, estimating their position.

"We'll try the next river," he said.

Lee looked seaward. The water was etched in gray and yellow as it swelled around the boat. "Is that the Harney?"

"Yep."

"You found it?"

Brian placed his finger on the map, and Lee nodded. He looked over the top of his sunglasses. "All the same," he said, "you could spend a year in that jungle and never find your way out."

Brian sat forward and pulled a cigarette from a plastic box in his pocket. "What about putting something on the tarpon?"

"Like what?"

"Something interesting," Brian said.

Lee's hand vibrated on the wheel and he smiled grimly. He knew better than to bet Brian for something interesting. The last bet he'd won had cost him six months in the hospital. "We'll be lucky to get even one fish," Lee said.

"Wives," Brian said easily. "Rosellen and Lorita."

"No thanks."

Brian grinned but said nothing. He was letting the heat do the work.

"You'd tell Rosellen she owed me one on a tarpon bet?" Lee asked finally. He liked the idea of Brian's asking. Rosellen was tall, maybe five ten, with long red hair. She'd married Brian right out of high school and waited for him through the service. Longer than that. She was still waiting for him while he took his sweet time growing up.

Brian opened the cooler and got another beer. "I wasn't thinking of losing," he said.

"You're a shit," Lee said. In a way, though, he admired Brian's bravado. For Christ sake, the night before, Brian had sworn to the woman in the bar he wasn't married and had a whole week in front of him to spend his back pay.

"Red hair for a piece of slant," Brian needled. "I'd take that one if I were you."

Lee couldn't picture breaking the news to Lorita. "The only worthwhile bet I won from you I got shot," Lee said.

"That was to *see* Charlie," Brian said. "You never saw him, but I paid anyway."

Lee felt the rush of the shot, the stunned pain and then no pain. He'd never thought that he'd not actually seen the sniper.

"All right," Brian said, "forget the wives. Just cash. A C-note?"

Lee steered for a moment, concentrating on the shallows. Then he said, "Since when are you after Lorita?"

"A C-note," Brian said. "Straight bet. The wives are in the closet except as topics of the imagination. First tarpon. Each man helps the other land what he hooks."

Lee thought it was funny about the wives. Even if he lost, he'd like to see Brian try to collect. Then he thought of Rosellen. He sometimes dropped over to Brian's just to see Rosellen's long freckled legs.

"Why not?" Lee said aloud.

"A hundred, then?"

"Why not the wives? It's pure luck."

But as soon as he'd said it, he knew it wasn't luck. Maybe there was luck in hooking the tarpon, but after that it was skill. And Lee knew he could never explain it to Lorita.

"I was kidding," Brian said. "Really. I just wanted to see if you had the nerve."

"I have the nerve," Lee said. "But to be safe, I'd rather go for the C-note."

Brian smiled and his hazy jaw shimmered in the heat. Lee took a beer from the cooler, popped it open, and drank off a long swallow.

The sun rolled off the zenith and a breeze rose, but it did little to take the edge from the day's heat. Lee kept the boat well offshore until he spotted the entrance to the Harney River. Then he swept wide of any shoals and turned back toward the mangroves. The murky tide was in flood, already covering the flats, and he had to guess at the channel.

Once into the river, he cut the motor and let the boat drift on the incoming tide. The space around them was bordered again by the scalloped horizon of the trees.

They arranged their gear. The deep water reels had been overhauled in Tampa by a friend of Brian's, and Brian gave Lee the choice. Neither man spoke as he threaded the wire line through the eyes of the heavy rods.

Brian pulled the box of lures from the tackle box. "Flip for choice?" he asked.

"You choose," Lee said. "I got the reel."

"Maybe you'll hook another shark," Brian said. He took the gold lure and fastened it to the swivel at the end of the leader.

Lee finished his beer and started another. He took a silver spoon and fixed it on the line.

"You sure about the bet?"

Lee nodded. "Money will do me fine," he said. "You can't win all the time."

"So let's make it two C-notes," Brian said.

"Okay, two."

They agreed on rules. No hindrance of lines. If one of

them hooked something, the motor would be shut off. If they both hooked about the same time, the one who got his fish to the boat first got to land first.

When the gear was ready, Lee started the motor again and they trolled upriver. The tide was running against the current, and they settled on a speed. For a while they worked into the rhythm of the boat. Lee tried to relax, tried to think how it would have been if they'd bet on wives and he'd won Rosellen. But farther over, near the shore, a swarm of mullet and jackfish raked the surface like gunfire, and the idea of Rosellen was gone. The drone of the motor was the only sound except the slap of water against the bow. Lee took another beer.

After an hour, Brian relieved at the wheel.

Most of the birds had disappeared in the heat of the early afternoon. Dead marsh grass floated in on the high tide and covered the mudflats. Nothing moved. Lee could barely imagine the life systems: small creeks draining the jungle of mangroves, the huge freshwater flow that seeped hundreds of miles out of the Everglades. Crocs, manatees, deer, hundreds of species of birds, thousands of creatures in the water.

Lee thought of the chipped stucco rented house in Tampa where Lorita sat day after day. He had thought she'd like the warm weather, but after they'd come south, he'd realized it was not the weather that mattered. Indianapolis, Chicago, Tampa—all the same place. Maybe Lorita thought America was more than it was, or maybe that in America he would be more. Maybe Brian was right: all he had ever been was her ticket out. She couldn't have known what he'd be like in his own country.

Brian's rod wobbled in its holder, and he reached for it quickly, without jerking. The skin of a tarpon's mouth was tender as a baby's, and when it hit, it hit slowly. Brian lifted the rod and set it into the fitting in front of his chair.

Nothing. It had been only a pass, or maybe a false movement caused by debris in the water.

"Thought you had it?" Lee asked.

Brian grinned from the side of his mouth. "If it comes, it comes," he said. "They're after gold."

They trolled upriver nearly to Tarpon Bay, and then came around. Lee steered, standing for a long time with a beer in his hand. The tide had slacked. A single black frigatebird soared above them on the thermals.

Lee gazed into the thinning sky. He felt almost sick: fumes, sun, beer. He dug an old baseball cap from beneath the stern seat and put it on. He checked his watch: nearly four. Maybe neither of them would get anything, and tomorrow they'd be sensible. Two hundred dollars was too much. The wives might have been better.

The small creeks drained now into the lower river, and the sun drifted farther out into the Gulf. Lee managed the edge of the channel. When he finished his beer, he leaned down, bubbled the empty can full of saltwater, and let it sink. He opened another.

Then his rod moved. He sat down heavily and glanced at Brian, who did not look at him. He eased the rod back several times, testing, watching the smooth green of the mangroves' reflection in the water.

"Strike." He said the word almost calmly.

"Sure?"

He kept his two hands on the rod, felt his blood rush. "Got him."

He cut the motor.

"Anchor," he ordered, laughing suddenly. He gazed into the green glint of the water far beyond the boat.

The tarpon leaped from a calm backwater a hundred yards to starboard. Its silver belly was orange in the ebbing sunlight. Lee leaned forward, bracing his feet against the ridge of the boat. He pulled with two hands, tightening his back muscles and utilizing the strength in his legs. The tarpon splashed back, but the line stayed taut.

"Put in the anchor."

"Nothing in the rules about an anchor," Brian said. He didn't move, but his eyes shifted from the gentle swells near the boat to the shaking of Lee's rod.

"You like the bet now?" Lee asked.

"It's a long way between where that tarpon is now and where it has to get," Brian said. "A long way."

Lee pulled on the rod again. Sweat moved, rolled down his face. His shirt stuck to his back. Beer sweat. It would have been a hell of a lot easier to hold the fish if the boat weren't drifting.

He took the pistol from under the stern seat and laid it on his lap.

The tarpon jumped again, a good leap this time in the shadow closer to the shore. The silver looked gray against the darkening mangroves. What was on the bottom of these backwaters? Stumps, wrecks of boats, dead branches around which a fish could get tangled and tear free. He pulled the line even and without slack.

"You're a bastard," Lee said.

"A swell guy when you get to know me."

"But no bet now on Rosellen?" Lee reeled the crank with his thin arm. For a second he thought he'd lost the fish, but he got the pressure again. They kept drifting.

Brian laughed at him.

"I mean, if I'm so lousy, let's bet on the wives now."

"Hey," Brian said, "lighten up."

Lee felt the surge of beer. "Shit, you don't need Rosellen anyway. You got that woman back in the bar."

"Right."

"You got it going all different ways."

"Just a little something to do," Brian said, "in the off-season."

"And Lorita, too?" Lee picked up the pistol and held it in his right hand.

Brian didn't answer.

From where they were, the shadow of the mangroves extended farther upriver. They were nearing a curve where they would catch the sun straight from the Gulf.

The tarpon leaped again, arching into space, walking on its tail. Lee aimed quickly and squeezed off a shot before the fish fell back into the water.

Brian jumped at the noise. He stood in the bow and started reeling in his own empty line.

"Nothing in the rules about shooting the fish," Lee said. He lifted his rod, strained against the weight in the water. He'd missed the first time, but now he waited for the tarpon to rise again.

"You're fucking crazy," Brian said. "There'll be sharks."

"I'd like the anchor," Lee said.

Brian nodded, but before he could get up, the tarpon jumped. Lee fired again. A dull red hole flashed on the tapered silver. He fired again and hit it just behind the gills. The second shot pushed the fish over sideways. Lee reeled quickly. His arms ached, and he wiped the sweat from his face with the back of his hand. The dead weight came in more slowly.

The boat still drifted into the bed of the river, and the sun caught them flush, a huge red eye visible through the haze and the distant clouds on the horizon.

Lee loaded three more shells.

"Tell me about Lorita," he said. His own voice was eerie in the heat. "Tell me why I'm a ticket."

"It was a joke," Brian said.

"What kind of joke?"

"Kidding, that's all." Brian brought in the last of his line and laid his rod inside the boat.

"Tell me what good friends we are," Lee said.

Brian shaded his eyes with his hand. His skin was orange and sweaty. "Real good friends. You know that."

Lee stopped reeling. His arms were hurting, and the tarpon was not far now from the boat—maybe twenty yards. "And all I get is a lousy two hundred? No Rosellen?"

"You had your chance," Brian said. "For Christ's sake, take a joke."

"Good friends," Lee said. "Through all sorts of hard times." He stared at the tarpon, which rolled now in the current and caught for a moment on a shallow sandbar.

There were no sharks. Two gulls came from nowhere and alit and picked at the hole where the fish had been shot.

"Yes," Brian said. "We had hard times."

"Tell me how you got the idea about Lorita."

Brian's eyes shifted in the low sun.

"You suddenly have an idea about a piece of slant," Lee said. He lifted the pistol and aimed at arm's length at Brian's head.

"Hell, no."

"Tell me why I was supposed to come to Florida."

"You're crazy. I thought . . ." Brian did not finish. He sat down in the bow seat and squinted through the sun.

Lee lowered the pistol and smiled. The gulls distracted him. The first two had been joined by others, and the birds fought over a space at the tarpon's body which lay exposed on the mudflat. The boat had stopped moving and curled into the shallow, the tarpon as anchor. Lee cut the line and the boat floated free.

"Look, I thought it would work out," Brian said. "Really."

Lee raised the gun again. He wanted the motor running, wanted to feel the vibration to settle his nerves. He hated floating.

But he liked the quiet. The sun, even as it dropped over the rim of the Gulf, was quiet. Brian was a liar. He lied so casually and so often it made no difference what the lie was about. He won so frequently, too, it made no difference to him when he lost.

Oh, he liked the quiet. Lee liked the way the last sun turned the barrel of the pistol orange, the way it gilded Brian's face and arms. He had never seen Brian scared before.

Then an idea fixed in his mind. "There was no point in betting, was there? No point. You've already done it."

Brian stared at the pistol. The sun had ebbed, and the color went from his face. Lee gave a bitter half smile. True, he thought. His heart snapped at his temple. More gulls flew toward the mudflat which receded behind the boat. True, true, true. Lee watched the dark mangroves slide past as the boat floated toward the Gulf.

I HAD TO DO SOMETHING

It was the summer at the lake when Astrid walked around at all hours with the yellow snorkel in the mouth. She was two then, a recalcitrant, thick-set child, nearly ten pounds when she was born, with wispy brown curls and large eyes whose color we couldn't decipher—hazel, maybe. She said little, though she made her desires known: no one could pry the snorkel from her without her shrieking.

Larry was prosecuting a complicated SEC case and had stayed in New York, so I had to manage the children alone. Not that this would have been a great hardship under normal circumstances—I did it in the city. But that June in the Adirondacks the black flies had rallied much later than usual, and the lake water was freezing. And it rained. Even during patches of sun, you could feel the rain gathering, and for the whole month there wasn't a single day totally clear. Sometimes when the clouds banked so far down over the broad-backed hills, I was certain any second the lake would spill over into whatever was lower and disappear.

Larry's parents had bought the lodge in 1978 when it had ceased operation as a girls' camp, and they let us have it most of the summer. For the past ten years the place had been for me a saving grace. It wasn't just a respite from the city heat but, as well, an avoidance of summer parties on the Connecticut shore and a way to entertain the children. There were eighty acres heavily wooded with maples and white birch and a few pines which surrounded the screened-in cabins the girls had slept in. The defunct cookshed had bats under the eaves, but the pumphouse was clean, kept so by the caretaker, Rennie Joubert, who every summer started us off with a good pile of firewood.

Upstairs in the lodge were the sleeping quarters for senior girls, barren wooden rooms with names like The Belfry, Sardine Can, and Tombs. A narrow screened porch fronted the bedrooms on the lakeside, and that was where Larry and I had always slept, on a foam pad draped over two adjacent cots. From the porch at night we could hear water lapping on the rocks below, the rain in the birch leaves, and the calls of barred owls and loons. In the morning, the metallic flutelike ringing of thrushes was so close it seemed the birds had come to sing to us.

But being there alone with the children during the rain was difficult. Larry had always occupied George and Molly with fishing or canoe rides or hikes, and sometimes they all went to Saranac Lake to a movie or to shop for books and play miniature golf. Larry was more like himself at the lake, too, less like a man honed by his career.

That summer George turned seven. He thought he should be able to start fires in the fireplace or take the canoe out alone or hike up the bluff by himself. And it pained him beyond words that his older sister Molly couldn't keep the ping-pong ball in play so well as he could. But he was wonderful with Astrid. He coaxed her to eat when I couldn't, and he invented games that enthralled her— hide-in-the-bench, a toy machine that by magic turned one toy into another, and capture-the-lark, in which they chased after imaginary creatures just beyond reach in the air.

George had hooked Astrid on the snorkel. One day in our second week, he had braved the icy lake to look for bass among the rocks. He'd put on fins and mask and snorkel, and Astrid was fascinated. "What is that?" she asked.

"What is what, sweetheart?" I said.

"It," she said, pointing.

George dived suddenly into the cold water and came up with a shout. I explained to Astrid what he was doing—how the mask let him look for fish underwater, how the flippers enabled him to swim faster. The snorkel allowed him to breathe without lifting his head from the water.

"I want it," Astrid said.

A few minutes later, when George climbed shivering onto the dock, Astrid was waiting in a cloud of black flies. She took the snorkel from George's blue lips and put it into her mouth.

Larry came up for one long weekend in June. The sun hinted its existence briefly on Saturday afternoon, but the wind died, and the black flies were so bad we couldn't go out in the canoe. Then it drizzled. Larry had never been patient with the weather. In the city there were no insects and very little weather that made a difference. But in the mountains, of course, it was different.

Even from the natural world, Larry expected cooperation, if not perfection, and when he didn't get it, he was moody, sometimes surly. But that weekend he was sweet. He played ping-pong with George, checkers with Molly. He roughhoused, threw darts, taught the two older children to play casino.

He even read Astrid a story. They sat on the sofa in front of the fire, and Larry read a long, somber tale about the demise of the dinosaurs. An asteroid had struck the earth and wafted a fine cloud of dust in front of the sun. The plants died, and the herbivorous animals weakened, setting off a downward spiral of life for all creatures. Astrid loved the tale.

After the children were in bed, Larry drank vodka. He'd never been much of a drinker, and with each glass I studied his slide away from me. It was the only time we'd been free of the children the whole day.

"What's wrong, Larry?" I asked finally.

He sighed. "Work. Too much of it. This trial absorbs too many hours. Then I get up here and the weather's awful."

"Not Astrid?"

"What's wrong with Astrid besides that goddamned snorkel?"

I shrugged and didn't answer. When Astrid was born, Larry had been in Florida tending his ailing father, and when he first saw her a week after, he was shocked. George and Molly had each weighed around seven pounds, but Astrid was immense. He didn't want to hold her. And afterward he'd been guarded and aloof toward her, as if she were some threat.

That night when he came to bed, Larry stumbled in the dark

and fell onto the cot. He went right to sleep, but I stayed awake for a long time. I thought of all the nights we had slept on that porch, all the gentleness of the past that seemed at the moment to have faded like the lake in clouds. I listened to the mist coalesce and drop from the leaves, and once a bat, trapped inside the screened porch, scuttled low over my head.

The next day, despite the rain, Larry took a long walk alone up onto the bluff. In the evening he worked on legal documents by the fire, while I put the children to bed. Then he stayed up reading late.

The following morning, when Larry had to leave for New York, I woke early, threw on a robe, and went downstairs to put the kettle on. Then I went into the big room to make a fire. I looked forward to those few minutes before the children got up, when I could read in front of the fire or contemplate the lake and the terraced mountains.

But that morning there was no wood. Larry had burned it all the night before, and there was none on the porch, either, where it was supposed to be stacked. I walked outside: it was chilly. A gray sky hovered. Dew slid from the leaves, and a blue heron in ponderous flight crossed the dull sheen of the water. The lake was absolutely still, and the day loomed ahead of me—the children indoors again, the games and the squabbling, Larry's leaving—and I started weeping. I was helpless for it, the lack of air. I was water, limited by an invisible shoreline, and I was about to empty over into nothing.

Then I noticed Astrid in the doorway. She had the snorkel in her mouth, and her breathing was raspy going up and down the plastic tube. She had on a wet diaper, no pajamas. (Every morning she stripped off whatever she'd gone to bed in.) A welter of black-fly bites speckled her face and arms. She studied me without apparent sympathy or dismay. She didn't hug me. She stared at me a long time, then took the snorkel from her mouth, held it out to me, and said, "Breathe."

Larry came back to the lake on the weekend of the Fourth of July. I had expected him late Friday evening, but he arrived early afternoon when George and Molly were at a party. He was dressed in a plaid shirt and jeans and a hat I'd never seen—a jaunty canvas fishing hat with a green brim. He said the SEC trial had been postponed, and he was on his way to Newfoundland to go salmon fishing with another woman.

"What do you mean *Newfoundland?*"

"I've thought about it," he said. "It's what I want to do. I didn't want you to find out from someone else."

"That makes it right?"

"I know it puts you in a bad position," he said. "But I've made certain no one knows." He glanced around for Astrid before he went on. "Look, I don't want a divorce. I want adventure. I just want to do something new."

"It's not new, Larry. It's very old."

There wasn't a discussion—what about the years past? What about promises? He said the woman was waiting for him at the Grand Union in Au Sable Forks.

For several days after that I sat on the porch and watched the clouds flow across the lake. I tried to withhold judgment, to understand what I lacked. Larry wasn't a bad man. He worked too hard, never talked much about it, was too absorbed in politics and the stock market. He wasn't good at showing his feelings and he liked the social whirl, but those things weren't crimes. We had got along well through twelve years of marriage. What had I done to make him feel he needed someone else?

Then one cool morning when the clouds rose through the trees like smoke, Larry called long distance from Newfoundland. He wanted to know how I was.

"All right," I said.

"Fishing's pretty good," he said. He went on about the salmon.

I listened.

"How are the children doing?" he asked finally. "What did you tell them?"

"Nothing yet."

I paused. George was playing fetch with Astrid, caroming a tennis ball around the living room. Molly was reading in front of the blackened fireplace. Then I hung up the phone gently and unplugged the wire. I went upstairs and put on a wool sweater, the boots I hiked in, and an orange poncho, and thumped back downstairs.

"Where are you going?" George asked. He was holding the tennis ball just out of Astrid's reach.

"To cut wood."

"Can I use the chain saw?" he asked.

"No, you may not. But you can load and carry when the time comes."

"Aw, mom." George threw the ball; Astrid chased.

"What are you going to cut wood for?" Molly asked. She lowered her book and looked up with the dazed look that ten-year-olds have when they read.

"Because we need it," I said. "And I expect you to help."

Astrid recovered the ball and ran to George, huffing and puffing.

I went out to the shed. In other cool summers Larry had cut whatever extra wood we needed, sometimes with Rennie's help. I'd heard them talk about saws, axes, wedges. I'd been vaguely aware of their loading Rennie's truck and throwing the cut wood down the ravine behind the lodge, where they split it and stacked it on the porch. But I didn't know the first thing about how to do it myself.

There were two chain saws in the shed, and gasoline in five-gallon canisters, and an assortment of axes, wedges, and sledge-hammers. I hefted the larger saw, knew I could never hold it, then tried the lighter one. Better. I read the directions on the side.

George and Astrid came outside. "Why don't you call Mr. Joubert?" George asked. "He knows about this stuff."

"I don't want to."

The black flies and mosquitoes emerged from the silence around us. I added oil to the gasoline and filled the tank on the saw. I made certain there was oil in the reservoir. I choked the motor, pulled, got nothing, pulled again, and realized I hadn't turned the lever to ON.

"Jeez, mom," George said.

"You don't have to watch," I told him. I clicked the lever, pulled again, and got a sputter.

George flailed the air to keep the insects away, and when he saw I couldn't get the motor started, he retreated. But Astrid stayed. She stood a little away on the slope, still holding the yellow tennis ball, the snorkel askew in her mouth. Black flies swarmed around her ears and under her eyes. At first I thought she was, like George, judging my task, and as I yanked on the cord over and over, it took all my composure not to yell at her. But then I felt perhaps she was admiring what I was doing. Maybe in the wisdom

I ascribed to her, she understood how hard my day-to-day life was, even what had driven me to this. She saw I had to do something, even if it was wrong.

I reread the directions, choked the motor again, pulled mightily. The saw roared to life. I set it down and went over and brushed the black flies from Astrid's face. I hugged her and sent her back to the lodge.

I carried the saw in one hand and a gasoline canister and a hatchet in the other. I climbed up behind the last of the cabins along an old logging road to where Rennie hadn't cleared the windfall. Trees eight to twelve inches in diameter had been snapped off mid-trunk, the tops crusted with dead leaves. I imagined how this had happened—snow piled in the red-leafed branches in October and the freak wind's gusting with unaccountable force against the overweight. CRACK.

Black flies flew into my eyes, sought out the windless spaces behind my ears. I discovered when I revved the saw the exhaust kept them a little at bay. Gradually I got the hang of how to tilt the saw into the wood, how to bear down with my weight, rasping the chain back and forth. But it was still hard work. My shoulders and arms weren't very strong. I trimmed the branches with the hatchet, left the trunks and the larger limbs for another time, sawed what I could lift easily.

Some things just weren't solved by honesty. I didn't think of Larry with the other woman in Newfoundland. I thought of him with her in New York—all the feints, the subterfuges that must have begun long before the summer, all the murmurs and the words. I revved the saw full blast. "The bastard! The bastard!" I yelled over and over into the noise.

In three-quarters of an hour I had a good pile of wood.

Two days later Rennie Joubert showed up. By then, with the children's help, I'd already hauled the cut logs in the station wagon, unloaded them, and thrown them into the ravine. Now I was splitting them. I placed the wedge in the center ring of a log, tapped it with a claw hammer until it stuck, then stood away and raised the axe. I delivered the butt end to the wedge. The log didn't split.

"Works better with a sledgehammer," Rennie said. "You know, that's my job."

"No offense meant," I said.

"It's what the neighbors will think," Rennie said. "They told me you were out here sawing and chopping."

"Larry isn't here."

Rennie smiled a little, showing his gray teeth. I lifted the axe again, struck, and split the log.

Rennie picked up the two halves for me and stacked them on the pile on the porch. He rearranged a few pieces, then stood up straight and measured me with an odd expression. He knew I'd been alone all summer and that Larry hadn't been there on the Fourth of July. And he knew I was fond of him. He was a man I might have liked had I grown up in Au Sable Forks: wiry, bearded, blue-eyed, a man who could fix things.

He dropped his eyes from mine and reached out his hand. "Let me finish this," he said.

I turned my shoulder and kept a tight grip on the axe.

That night after the children were asleep, a storm swept through. Thunder pounded the hills, and lightning flashed beyond the windows. I was reading a book by the fire—an account by Anna Haviland, who had sailed the Drake Passage to Antarctica. A draught stirred the embers in the fireplace and fanned up the flames. Rain scattered like pebbles on the roof high above me. A few drops hissed into the fire.

Then the electricity went out. For a moment I was scared, but after a time I found it pleasant to have been rescued from ice floes and high seas by the darkness. I thought the power would come on again, but when it didn't and the fire burned down, I turned off the useless lamp and put the firescreen in place. Then I climbed the stairs, got undressed, and lay naked under the quilt on the cot on the sleeping porch.

Without any lights from the other houses, the lake and the mountains and the sky were the same black. Now and then lightning bathed the world in a ghostly white, but the darkness would fill again, deeper than before. The work of the past several days still burned in my neck and shoulders, in my arms, even in my fingers. I sensed through this pain how the larger muscles meshed with the tiniest ones, how one thing led to another, how unhappiness gathered into small failings of spirit. I was weary beyond words, but I didn't want to sleep.

The storm moved on. The rain eased. Then I was aware Astrid was at the foot of the bed. I could hear her breathing through the snorkel. She must have been wakened by the storm.

I sat up in the pitch black. "Come here, sweetheart," I said.

She crawled up onto the bed, and I took hold of her sturdy arm and pulled her toward me. She had taken off her clothes, so I made a place for her beside me under the quilt. I took the snorkel from her mouth, and she shivered in close.

"Your father and I are being divorced," I said, though I knew she didn't know what that meant. "We'll be all right, you and I. We'll be stronger at the broken place."

I took her hand and squeezed it, and she squeezed mine. The bat fluttered over us, a friend who knew the dark. Lightning flashed farther away and left in its wake the darkness and a soft drizzle which fell around us like music through the leaves.

INVISIBLE LIFE

I had over-prepared the event,
that much was ominous.
EZRA POUND
Villanelle: the psychological hour

My mother had little to add. She sat with her coffee after dinner and stared toward the plate glass window which faced the front yard. The porch light was on outside, and I could see the dead spring grass and the stark branches alive with buds in the warm and misted night air. At the same time, my mother's reflection shimmered in the dark window—shadowy, confused color mixed with details of the yard beyond. From her expression I couldn't tell whether she was gauging herself in the glass or merely thinking. She had been in fine health all her life, and she looked it. Her complexion was still smooth and her eyes clear. Her long hair was grayed but streaked with rich brown. Yet at that moment I thought she looked tired, as though the news Allison had given her had made her suddenly and irrevocably old.

Allison had gone upstairs to feed Livingston and to put Tricia to bed, and my mother had fallen into some dark memory, as she did sometimes when she came to visit and was reminded of my father. Finally she turned away from the window. "Is it really such a disaster?" she asked.

"Well, it's not divorce, if that's what you mean."

"I should think you'd be proud."

"There's nothing to be proud of yet," I said. "Anyway, if she wants graduate school, she could go to Penn in the city."

"But just the idea of history!" my mother said. She paused. "Perhaps she won't be admitted, is that what you mean? I suppose age is something they consider."

We were caught by loud, rapid footsteps upstairs. Hillary had slammed the bathroom door, and Allison yelled at her. The house seemed still for a moment, as it had often been lately—just a pause, barely noticeable, like a sigh between one word and another. Then Tricia appeared, modeling the new nightgown my mother had brought her.

"What was that about?" I asked.

"Hillary talked back," Tricia said. "She said she wasn't going to any party with Freeny Lewis."

"What's Livy doing?"

"Nothing, as usual."

"Did you sing him a song?"

"Mom wants me to go to bed."

Tricia whirled around so that the nightgown flowed away from her thin legs. At seven she was already gangly, thin as a rail, and sensitive. She read too much, if that were possible, and was so quiet we had been afraid that when Livingston was born she would disappear altogether.

I drew her toward me and hugged her. "You tell your mother I said you could sing him one song."

"Okay." She whirled away again. "Do you like it, Nanoo?"

"On you it shines," my mother said.

"Do I have to go to bed?"

"Yes," I said.

"Can I read?"

"Kiss your old Nanoo," I said. "One song. No reading."

Tricia climbed the stairs, pausing on each step as though to catch our secrets.

"Tell your mother we're talking about her," I called up.

We waited a little longer until Tricia had padded down the hall. A breeze blew across the yard, stirring branches and telephone wires, but the room was still. "It's not as though we were just starting out in life," I said.

My mother looked back toward the window. "You said she hasn't told any of her friends?"

"No, but she wanted to tell you."

"Why would she do that?"

I had no answer. Allison and my mother had never been particularly close, and while Allison was always cordial, I had felt in her a certain critical attitude about the way my parents lived their lives. Allison had always been reluctant to visit them in Bryn Mawr, for example, even when my father was alive.

"Perhaps to enlist your sympathy," I said finally.

"But you don't object to school."

"It's partly the timing," I said casually. "The children . . ."

"Children adapt."

"You know what I mean."

I stood up and went to the window. A dog passed through the edge of the light near the street, his legs clicking and his head down on some scent. "The kitchen was just remodeled four months ago because Allison thought we needed more space. And we got a station wagon last year, trading in Dad's good Buick. I agreed to do those things—now and then we have to accommodate others."

I turned when I caught movement in the glass. Allison was leaning against the jamb in the doorway.

"Go on," she said easily, without malice. She looked at me in a straightforward way. "Say what you think."

"It isn't the time to be liberated."

"Not the time for her or for you?" my mother asked.

Allison smiled briefly. She was not a beautiful woman—her mouth was too large and her skin sagged along her jaw and her curly hair was forever matted in sweat or flying out of some loose pin—but at that moment, as she moved into the center of the room, she looked so composed, so certain, that I felt a chill run across my shoulders.

"But I'm not trying to be liberated," she said, turning to my mother. "I'm trying to live my life."

The whole muddle had begun two weeks after Livingston was born, when Allison had announced she was applying to graduate schools at Stanford and Harvard. That had been in November, and

I had dismissed the idea out of hand. Given Allison's history, it was unlikely she truly wanted to study again after a fourteen-year hiatus, and even less likely she would leave a small infant. The doctor, of course, had warned both of us about postpartum depression. A woman's body restructured itself after pregnancy, and new hormones created havoc with the emotions. The additional burden of fatigue could overwhelm the unsuspecting. I assumed Allison's inspiration was in large measure a fantasy of escape.

But if anything, she seemed happier and more dutiful than ever. She carried on about Livy to friends, nursed him cautiously (though more privately), and spoke even to me about her guilt at feeling so much love for her son. The only difference, really, between her reactions to Hillary's and Tricia's births and to Livy's was that with Livy she seemed more intense.

In December she took the Graduate Record Examinations. She had been bright in college—Phi Beta Kappa from Mt. Holyoke, in fact—though she admitted her grades had been predicated more on her acute memory than on curiosity or ambition. She had said then, when we met, that she detested the deadlines and confining minutia of college life so much she could not even consider going on to an advanced degree. And in the twelve years of our marriage, I had never heard her voice a desire for a career.

"Just how do you propose to implement this dream?" I asked her one evening after the exams. I had prepared myself with a couple of Scotches.

"I will go to Palo Alto or Cambridge, and you will stay here."

"The logistics, I mean."

"We have enough money, don't we?"

"We are a family," I said rather harshly. "Perhaps not a glamorous family, maybe too serious on the whole, but steadfast and bright. Hillary vacillates between enthusiasm and silence, but she hasn't given us too much trouble. And Tricia has been mercilessly indulgent with Livy. She sings to him by the hour."

"Hillary and Tricia are in school," Allison said. "You may have to arrange Tricia's afternoons for recreation, but Hillary is old enough and would rather fend for herself. You can stay home with Livingston or hire someone to come in."

"Just like that?"

"I will think of you all the time."

"No emotion, though. You will go off, no muss or fuss, and never look back."

Allison turned away as though she did not want to think of it.

"You don't think Livy needs you?" I asked. "You don't think Tricia will miss you terribly?"

She turned around and her cheeks were wet with tears.

"We just can't get along without you," I said more softly.

"Certainly you can," she whispered. "What would you do if I died?"

Hypothetical questions have always irritated the hell out of me. I didn't know what I would do if she were to die, but she wasn't about to. I wouldn't know what to do if my law practice suddenly evaporated, or if Allison were miraculously beautiful, or if Hillary were taking cocaine. I only know what I do at the moment, in response to a real event or a real threat. And I began to consider Allison's scheme a threat.

My mother was no help. She seemed to side with Allison, not outwardly, but in subtle ways, as though she were the apologist for Allison's plan. "She has not confided in me," my mother said over the telephone one day. "I'm certain she has not told me anything she has not told you."

"But I know she's called you."

"Yes, that's different."

"Does she feel guilty? Do you sense that?"

"She wants me to know she still cares about you and the family."

"What else?"

"Nothing."

"What do you think? You must have some feel for it."

My mother paused on the line.

"What has changed in her?" I went on. "I can't think of anything except Livy's birth that might have been traumatic, and why would she react to that? She loves him. I mean, why, after all these years, does she want to go away to graduate school?"

"There's the obvious," my mother said slowly, "that for her, it's now or not at all."

"But she's never wanted a job or a career."

"Then she wants something else," my mother said quietly.

One Saturday in April we drove to Bryn Mawr at Allison's urging to wish my mother a happy birthday, her sixty-third. Hillary complained that she had promised friends she would jog with them, and when that excuse failed, that she had to do homework.

"Bring your homework with you," I said. "Your cousin Rob will be there to help you."

"That creep?" Hillary said. "He's another reason not to go."

"Can I play in the gazebo?" Tricia asked.

"You can ask Nanoo."

"Why don't you invite her here?" Hillary asked.

"Because your mother wants to go there."

"I thought Mom didn't like to go to Nanoo's."

"Apparently she's changed her mind."

"And Aunt Tillie always talks about Grandpa. It's dull and Mom hates it."

"It's not dull," Tricia said. "There's the gazebo and the woods."

"It's dull," Hillary said.

Allison came downstairs with Livy in one arm and a large package in the other. "Can you get the Port-a-crib?" she asked.

"What's that?" I asked, pointing to the package.

"A present."

"What present? I already got the bracelet you picked out for her."

"This is another one," Allison said blithely, and she breezed out the door.

The day was warm and sunny, and after lunch I took Tricia into the woods behind the house to explore with her the places I remembered from my own childhood. A dark stream ran through the woodland, and the leaves above us were yellow-green against the fast-moving clouds and blue sky. I pointed out, as my father had to me, the warblers darting among the oaks and maples. The stream swirled lazily over rocks and sodden logs, and for a while we sat on a boulder and watched the water flow.

"Did you know there are tiny creatures in that water?" I asked. "Animals that you can't see?"

Tricia lowered her face toward the pool beneath us. "Are there?"

My father had demonstrated the existence of the invisible teeming life by taking a sample of creek water and showing me slides under a microscope. I remembered the elaborate bulbous forms of protozoa and the bizarre, wriggling cilia which waved in the droplets of water.

"How do you suppose we could tell whether such creatures were there?" I asked.

Tricia continued to stare into the water. "By the fish," she said.

"The fish?"

"I can see fish, and the fish have to eat something smaller than they are, and those things must eat something smaller. . . ."

I nodded and laughed at what seemed so logical, and at myself for thinking I should believe only what I could see with my own eyes.

The birthday party went well enough. My divorced sister, Tillie-the-Hun, came over for dessert with her children, Rob and Virginia, and when my mother was ready to open her presents, we had to drag Hillary and Rob from the porch.

"What's in the big box?" my mother asked the smaller children. "Should I open it first or last?"

"Last," Tricia said. She liked surprises.

I expected Tillie to begin her neurotic, melancholic spiel about our father's absence, but she sat stoically with Allison on the sofa. My mother liked the housecoat Tillie gave her, and both Virginia and Tricia had made ceramic dishes in school. When she opened the bracelet, my mother uttered the appropriate words of joy and thanks.

Then she settled back in her flower-print chair amidst the explosion of colorful blue-and-white wrapping paper. The children crowded around the last big present which Allison had kept hidden from me.

To heighten the children's eagerness, my mother spoke in an exaggerated whisper as she slowly pulled the ribbon. "Now what do you suppose this could be? It's such a big package! What do you imagine is in it?"

"A stuffed animal," Virginia said, and she giggled. "No, you wouldn't get *that!*"

"What does Nanoo need?" Tricia asked.

I turned, feeling an uncomfortable sensation, and Allison was staring at me with a studied air, as though measuring me. Her eyes were relaxed, her mouth slack, in a half-expectant smile. I noticed for the first time that she had recently cut her hair, and though it was still unkempt, it no longer covered a childhood scar at her temple.

Inside the large box was a smaller one, also wrapped, and inside that, yet another. The children clapped and pressed closer. Inside the third box was an envelope, and my mother raised her eyes at the children and held it up with two fingers.

"An envelope?" Tricia asked.

"It's a ticket to Greece," Hillary guessed.

My mother slipped open the flap and before drawing out its contents, she paused and looked at Allison. In that simple moment there was a sigh in the room, as though my mother and Allison shared some silent pleasure. I knew too well, then, what was in the envelope, and I turned away.

The drive home to Haddonfield over the Schuylkill Expressway and the Walt Whitman Bridge was tedious, nerve-wrenching. Livingston cried half the way, and Allison sat in the back seat and fed him. I did not want to argue in front of the children, but when Tricia had lain down in the far back and Livy was asleep in the infant seat, I could restrain myself no longer.

"At least tell me why you would tell her before you would tell me."

"I told you both at the same time."

"But why not give me advance warning?"

"I knew she would be glad for me."

"And I'm made to look ridiculous."

"To whom? Tillie?" Allison smiled at the thought.

"I'm glad for you, too."

"Tom, I didn't mean to hurt you, but you aren't exactly sympathetic."

"Not exactly," I said. "I wish I could go back to school."

"Then go ahead."

I ran down a list of the responsibilities we had acquired together, in case they had escaped Allison's notice.

"You're driving forty," she said.

"I have to earn a living," I said. I looked in the rearview and saw the cars piling up behind me on the bridge.

"You're doing what you have to do," she said, "and I'm doing what I have to do."

Allison's acceptances to Stanford and Harvard made the situation quite different. The issue was no longer theoretical. For Allison it was no longer whether she would be able to go, but where she would go.

I still resisted with as many rational arguments as I could, but even my skills as a lawyer were no match for her determination. She weighed the merits of the two history departments, the climates, distances from home. She preferred palm trees to the harsh winters of Boston, but the determining factor was that Harvard was closer. I felt mildly appeased.

That summer we drove to Boston to scout a place for her to live. I had called ahead for a real estate agent to show us apartments—a place with large windows and bright walls was what Allison would like, and it should be close enough to walk to the Square.

"Who's going to live here?" Allison asked, standing in the middle of a sunny room overlooking the Charles.

"You are."

"I don't want it."

The real estate agent showed the children around while we talked it over.

"It's convenient. It's modern. There's good fire protection and adequate security. Think about . . ."

"I'm thinking about my mental health."

She refused to make a decision, and then the next weekend went back to Cambridge alone. When she returned home, she said she had found a place.

"How did you manage the children?" she asked.

"What's the place like?"

"Did Livingston take his bottle? Did he wake up at night?"

"Yes and yes."

"Were you able to get to work on Friday?"

"The children aren't in school," I said. "It wasn't too bad."

"You didn't call your mother for help?"

"You told me not to."

"Good. Well, the apartment is small. You won't approve, but I like it well enough."

She hurried up the stairs to see Livy.

The next week Allison went through the usual ritual of buying clothes for the girls for school. Hillary had grown three inches in one year, and none of her jeans and blouses fit. Tricia wanted to be a newly polished silver star.

"What about you, Mom?" Hillary asked before they left. "Do you get clothes?"

"She doesn't grow," Tricia said. "That must be awful."

"But I can keep longer the things I have," Allison said cheerfully.

"Aren't you worried at all?" Hillary asked.

"Yes, I'm worried."

"You can always come home if you don't like it," Tricia said.

"I'm worried it's the right thing," Allison said. She smiled and then added, "but I'll need your help."

"We'll be good," Tricia said.

"Not that so much. I know you'll be all right." Again she stopped, and her voice quieted. "But I want you to be new. Be new every single day."

We had a party for friends—the Saxes and the Gerards and the Hamiltons—and then the summer was over. The children started school, and we had an anxious two weeks before Allison actually went off to Cambridge.

I was cynical, suspicious, even jealous. I had perhaps been too supportive, too willing to let her try her experiment. Perhaps she had only meant to test me, to see whether I would comply or resist. Yes, I was sympathetic to her wanting to do something more than volunteer work and child care. But she had chosen that path herself. And I could not just shrug my shoulders the way Phil Sax had when his wife had started a dress shop and had an affair with a seller from New York. Nor could I be so analytical as Harry Gerard. "Economically you might be better off," he said. "And perhaps psychologically, too, in the long run."

I was not convinced. Allison had some other motive, I was certain, some demon as invisible as the protozoa in that dark stream behind my mother's house. But what could I do to learn what that was?

We drove two cars to Cambridge—the BMW, which I had jammed full of clothes and boxes, and the station wagon packed with furniture. Allison thought it better to leave the older children with the Gerards next door, and we brought Livingston.

The apartment was exactly what I feared. It was a one-bedroom place in an old converted clapboard house on one of the back streets of North Cambridge. We climbed to the second floor, turned on the timed light, and climbed to the third. The place was not even clean. The previous tenant had departed hurriedly, leaving newspapers and bottles in the pantry and grease in the oven.

• • •

The landlord had not fixed the light in the ancient refrigerator, and the windows above the kitchen sink were streaked with city grime. The whole place smelled of wax and acrid smoke.

We unloaded the furniture, and Allison went off in the station wagon to buy a bed. I carried in the boxes from the BMW, cleaned up as best I could, and began to assemble the metal book-case we had brought. I was sitting on the floor, swearing at screws and angle joints, when suddenly I turned and Allison was there. Sweat glinted from her forehead, and she looked terribly sad. I don't know how long she had stood there before I noticed her.

"I got the bed," she said.

"Are you all right?"

"I will be."

"I'll bring up the bed when I finish this."

She paused in the doorway and looked around the room, as if grasping the full measure of her choice. Finally she said, "Can I have the key to the BMW? I'll go get some Chinese food."

"I thought we'd go out. Sort of a celebration."

"There's too much to do," she answered slowly, "if you're going to go back. I'd rather you did."

I nodded and threw her the keys.

She took nearly an hour. I finished setting up the bookcase and went downstairs to get the bed. I opened the hatch of the station wagon, and I knew why she had looked so sad, why she was taking so long to get the food: she had bought a single bed.

In the first two years of our marriage, and before that, we had slept in a single bed, sometimes illicitly in dorm rooms, sometimes at friends' places, and even after we had bought the house in Haddonfield, while I was getting my law practice started. We had pressed together in the narrow space, holding each other in sleep, while the night unraveled beyond our walls.

Later our lives changed: we moved along in our world, with our children, new furnishings, new friends. Occasionally, long after we had acquired a big brass double bed, we found ourselves having to sleep on a sofa or, skiing in Vermont, in a friend's small guest room with a single bed. We laughed, wondering how we had gotten through years in a small bed when, then, twisted and cramped, we couldn't endure even one night.

Allison came back with the cartons of food, and I said nothing about the bed. The bookcase was against the wall beside her desk, and the bed was pushed into the corner near the lone window. We ate sitting on the floor, without speaking much, and later I drove home in the station wagon.

Hillary was either kind or mutinous, but overall she was helpful. Tricia had a toothache one morning, and I rushed her to the dentist. And Livingston's nurse walked out after a fight with her boyfriend, so I stayed home from work one day, then prevailed on Angie Hamilton to babysit until I found someone else to come in.

We survived. Livy cried at night, and I got up to comfort him, heat his bottle, and pat him back to sleep. With Allison gone, Hillary became slightly more responsible, certainly more independent, and Tricia more silent. Sometimes there were moments when the four of us sat around the table in uneasy truce, and I felt near tears and proud for having put in a day's work and got dinner on the table.

I missed Allison terribly. At first I called her often to complain about the small details I didn't know, and about the dilemmas that constantly recurred. Where were the winter sweaters? What was I supposed to do about the new drapes she had ordered? Did Tricia need shots? I told her how Livingston was faring, about Hillary's 98 in algebra, what Tricia was reading.

"It takes some time to adjust," Allison said.

"I don't want to adjust."

There was a moment's pause, and I felt we had nothing more to say. I was bitter. She was far away.

"Allison, listen to me . . ."

"No, I can't now. I love you, and I have to go."

The next time I called, two days later, her telephone had been disconnected. The telephone company couldn't give me a satisfactory answer, and the police refused to look for someone who was not officially missing. The history department kept no records of who attended classes and who did not.

I began to think perverse thoughts. Perhaps it had been Allison's intention all along to deceive me. She wanted adventure, to test herself with other men, and graduate school was a believable ruse. Why else had she given only vague reasons for her decision? And she knew, once her flight was underway, she could still choose whether to soar higher or to come home again.

Yet I didn't believe those things about her. Allison was not the kind of woman for whom such excitement was alluring. She would have been more tempted by a brazen fling than by a drawn-out subterfuge, and I could more easily have imagined her desire to see Europe or the Far East by herself than her desire to be with another man.

I wrestled with the issue of her privacy—whether, for the good of all of us, I had a right to know her intentions. I wanted to know the future of the family, whether I would have to begin the subtle explanations to Tricia and to Hillary. Were we going to stay married?

By the weekend I resolved to confront her: I would drive up unannounced and would not leave until I had answers.

"I want to see where Mom lives," Tricia said when I told her I was going.

"You can't, honey. There's no room to stay."

"Why are you taking Livingston?"

"Because I have to. I think your mother would want me to because he's changing so fast."

"Are you getting divorced?"

"Not that I know of."

I drove all afternoon, stopping once to change Livy and again to buy more milk at a Howard Johnson's. I prepared a self-righteous speech: "All the sacrifices, the willingness to give free rein . . . I'm sorry I was not the man you wanted. . . ." It sounded maudlin, impossible. "What do you think, Livy?" I asked.

I took a wrong turn at the traffic circle on Route 2 and ended up on Memorial Drive. Darkness was settling in, and with the sun behind me, the river looked icy, bleak against the far bank and the silhouetted skyline of Boston in the distance. I weaved through Harvard Square and west again on Massachusetts Avenue. When I found her house not far from Porter Square, Allison wasn't there. The BMW was parked out front, collecting soot and leaves, but her window was dark. I rang the bell anyway, but no one answered.

The door downstairs was open, so I took Livingston in and waited at the landing outside her door. I was not by nature a prying person, but in these circumstances when Allison herself was so secretive, I felt justified in trying to get into the apartment. When I couldn't jimmy the lock, I snooped under her door. There was a note there, just a corner visible.

Then the timed light went off, and Livy cried until I could find the switch.

A person with no telephone received notes. I tried to scrape the piece of paper from beneath the door, but my fingers were too thick and the penknife I had, too short. "Wait here," I said to Livy. "I'll get something from the car."

I raced down the stairs. In the car I searched through the jumble that had accumulated in the cargo space and found the cross-beam of an old kite.

Livingston screamed when the light went out again.

I tore the shreds of the kite away and was about to sprint back to the house when a woman turned the corner and came ahead. She was about Allison's height, but her hair was very short and she was quite thin. I hid the stick along my body.

"Tom?"

I stopped and turned back. "Is that you?"

"What are you doing here?"

"I came to see you. Hurry, Livy is crying."

I went in and turned on the light from below, and the wailing stopped. Allison took the stairs by twos. She snatched Livy from his seat and held him close, tight enough to smother him.

"I would have called," I said vaguely.

"Is anything wrong?"

Suddenly I felt crazy, stupid, as though, having believed a burglar was rummaging through the house, I had found only the family cat. "Nothing is wrong."

"Can you find the keys in my purse?" she asked. "What were you doing with that stick?"

I threw down the cross-beam of the kite and found the keys.

The notes—two of them—lay on the floor, and I picked them up and examined the handwriting. One was a woman's, the other a man's. Allison pushed past me, still hugging Livy.

"Did you bring diapers?" she asked, laying him on the bed.

I put the two notes on the table and went into the hallway to get the diapers. The apartment was bleak: nothing on the walls, the bed unmade, books and papers scattered across the desk and piled on the floor. In the small kitchen, a few dishes were stacked carelessly in the sink.

After she had changed Livy, Allison opened the notes. One was from a woman inviting her to a breakfast conference. The other, she said, was from a man who had found the sources she had wanted in Russian history.

That night, sleeping on the edge of the narrow bed, I understood less than ever.

• • •

By Thanksgiving little had changed. Allison came home for the holidays, and we went to my mother's house for dinner. Tillie had a thousand questions about how Allison was faring, how much she had to study, where she did her laundry. It was curious that Tillie seemed so interested until I realized how much Tillie and I were alike. Anything in the world outside that was not familiar to us was a subject of wonder.

"What do you *do* with history?" Tillie asked.

"You make it," Allison answered, perhaps too blithely.

"I mean, are there careers?"

"Teaching, government, politics. If you want, there are lots of fields which might use the intellectual discipline."

The children had gone out to play in the yard, and we sat at the table littered with empty glasses and plates and used napkins.

"Boston is a lovely city," my mother said. "Don't you ever get a free moment?"

Allison nodded. "I've been to the museum several times, and once to the symphony. But I'm afraid I've spent most of my time reading."

"The work must be quite hard," my mother said.

"Novels," Allison said. "I've never had such luxury."

I thought of her apartment, the unmade bed and the dirty dishes.

"What novels?" my mother asked.

"Particularly the Russians. I'm fascinated with the slant of fiction on history. Chekhov. Of course Dostoevsky, Kuprin . . ."

"Dostoevsky is so gloomy," Tillie said.

"But haunting," Allison said wistfully. "And I admire Tolstoy."

We went on to other topics, and as often happened when Tillie was there, the conversation drifted toward my father.

"He would have lived ten more years," Tillie said, "if he had kept on working."

"He had cancer of the colon," I said calmly, stating the facts as we all knew them. "His life would not have been pleasant."

"But he wouldn't have *had* the cancer."

I tried to soothe Tillie, who had begun to cry. Allison excused herself and went to the kitchen with some plates. I heard dishes clattering, and my mother got up to help.

Tillie had dwelled too long on our father's death. He had died two years after retiring from a lifelong career in the trust department of the City Bank of Philadelphia, and she saw no reason for him to die when he was on the brink of enjoying his life for the first time. I explained to her again that no logical connection existed between his retirement and his contracting cancer.

"We don't plan those things," I said, getting up to look out the window.

"But it's so unfair!"

I watched the children running across the lawn in their good clothes, the woods behind them. Their joy, in contrast to Tillie's tiresome sorrow, made me feel detached, suspended forever in the role of the one who comforted and provided. I was about to deliver my speech about fairness when a taxi pulled up outside the front door.

Allison came out from the kitchen. "I'm sorry," she said politely and without rancor. "I have to leave."

"Allison . . ."

"I have work to do," she said. "Your mother understands. Will you bring the children?"

She smiled at Tillie and went to the door, pausing a moment to look at me closely before she went out.

I considered taking a leave of absence from the firm. Allison needed help, and I thought the family's moving to Cambridge might be the answer. The children would have lived through the trauma, *adjusted,* as Allison might have said. We could have closed up the house or rented it. But for three years, maybe four? We were such a part of the town. The children had their friends. We knew the Saxes and the Gerards, the streets, the names of the shopkeepers. Allison and I had fought to save the sycamores along Kings' Highway, and the children's summer camp existed only because Harry Gerard and I canvassed the neighborhood for the cause.

Besides, I have never understood how people just pulled up stakes. How did they leave their homes and homelands and strike out into the void? The people I mean were not like the Portuguese or Columbus, or searchers for riches like Cortez, or dreamers of glory. They were people who had too little, who clung to a tiny speck of hope. They were cursed by their past and were willing to give up friends, family, and familiar surroundings, even their countries, for some tenuous vision of survival.

No, I wouldn't move. And so I waited.

Allison called the children every week from a pay telephone, and it made me anxious to think of her on some sidewalk or street corner, gazing into the reflection of herself in the glass case. I could hear the traffic beyond her, the horns of cars, voices.

Once I asked her, "Is someone waiting for you?"

"No."

"I can only do this if you tell the truth."

"No one is waiting," she said. "You can believe what you wish."

I did not know what to believe.

Christmas, I hoped, would be better. Allison insisted we go to my mother's again, this time for two days.

"Are you sure you want us?" I asked my mother on the telephone.

"Of course. Allison wrote me a letter saying she's looking forward to it."

"I hope she apologized," I said.

"She explained."

"I wish she would explain to me."

My mother hesitated. "But mostly she wrote about her studies and how much she likes what she is doing."

I nodded, though I knew my mother could not see me. "If only we all did."

The day we drove to my mother's, December twentieth, was gray and cold. Low clouds moved slowly across the Delaware River and, as we headed for Bryn Mawr, I sensed a new mood in Allison.

"At least Tillie won't be there," I said, as though my sister's presence had somehow been the catalyst for Allison's behavior.

Allison looked at me, that subtle glance, but I kept my eyes on the road. "It wasn't Tillie," she said.

"You know how she gets."

"I'm used to Tillie's problems."

Tricia put her head over the back of the seat and rested her chin on my shoulder. "Is it going to snow?" she asked.

"It's supposed to," I said.

"What happens to the little things in the creek when it freezes?"

"I don't know."

"Do they hibernate?"

"What do fish do?" I asked.

"Do you know, Mom?" Tricia asked.

Allison shook her head. "Know what?" Allison asked.

At my mother's we got settled in the various rooms. Livy was crawling and pulling himself up beside tables and chairs, so we cleared the low places of vases and glass figurines. Hillary disappeared into the attic, her place of refuge, while Tricia went out into the backyard to look into the barren woodland.

I started a fire in the grate, and Allison made hot buttered rum. We had a couple of these, and I joked about Allison's running away at Thanksgiving. "She won't do it again."

"I can't promise," she said, smiling.

"There's no need to promise anything," my mother said.

"Tillie should learn to manage herself," I went on. "I thought perhaps what she said . . ."

"It was Tolstoy," Allison said.

"Tolstoy?" Even my mother seemed surprised.

"I had been reading him—we were talking about it casually—reading about the way he lived, what he wrote. Dostoevsky, too. What energy they had! Tolstoy never stopped questioning his whole life. Did you know that when he was eighty-eight he tried to leave his wife?"

Neither my mother nor I could answer.

"He may have been terrible in some ways, but imagine living every day wondering whether you had done the right thing, whether you ought to go to some new place, whether you still loved your wife." Allison paused and drew a deep breath.

We were silent a moment, watching Livy pull himself up beside Allison on the sofa. She picked him up and set him on her lap.

Then Tricia came in from the veranda and shouted, "It's snowing! Look!"

Gray flakes swirled across the dark woodland and onto the bare yellow lawn. Hillary, having apparently noticed, too, rushed down the stairs.

"Will you come?" Tricia asked me.

"I'll watch."

I got up and stood by the window. Hillary and Tricia ran across the lawn, trying to catch snowflakes in their mouths.

I turned back toward the room. The fire ebbed, and the room seemed dark compared to the gray light outside.

My mother got up and put another piece of oak on the fire.

"Do you still remember what you felt when he died?" Allison asked.

My mother moved away from the fireplace and stood for a moment in the pale light, visibly moved by the question. She seemed to know Allison spoke to her.

"It's strange that I have forgotten him," she said. "He determined so much of my life, but . . . I don't mean that cruelly." Her voice trailed away.

"Do you miss him?" Allison asked.

The question shocked me—so tactless and direct—and yet, voiced as it was in the silence, with the low fire and the gray snowlight beyond the room, it did not seem so much an intrusion as a reaching out.

Livingston was still, and even the children outside had tired and ceased their yelling. My mother hesitated.

"I think of him carrying his case, as he called it, to the car, getting into the car, and driving to the station. I know that ritual is not uncommon—Tom probably does it, too—but I wondered sometimes what he thought as he went through these motions, whether he ever thought of me, whether he thought different things from day to day. He came home, kissed me, and never talked of his work, which took most of his conscious time. Did he care about it? Was there any satisfaction? Sometimes he would speak of the people he worked with or about some incident which happened on the train. But in a way he was like a man who never spoke about his dreams because he never dreamed."

My mother's soft voice ebbed, and I wanted to argue with her, but I could not bring myself to disagree. Words came to my lips and dissipated like wisps of children's breaths in the cold air outside.

"No, I don't miss him," my mother said. "I know that sounds ungrateful after all he did for me for so many years. I don't know what I mean exactly. I don't mean it as it sounds." She looked at Allison. "I knew everything about him, but at the same time, nothing. He always did what he thought he should do. He was that kind of man."

That night I got up with Tricia when she cried out in the darkness of the strange house. I held her and smoothed her hair. Hillary stirred in the next bed, but did not wake. When Tricia slept again, I went to look in on Livy, who had thrown off his blankets. I tucked him in and gazed at him. Even in sleep he did not look peaceful.

For a long time I stood at the window of my old room, looking toward the woods. As a child I used to imagine people roaming those woods at night, eyes sharp as owls', intent on some vague and nameless evil. Those men had nothing better to do than to creep through the darkness, and more than once I was certain I had seen a shadow lurking at the edge of the lawn. I would rush to my father's room, just short of screaming, and he would take me by the hand and lead me with a flashlight into the backyard.

"Now what do you think you saw?" he asked, shining the flashlight into the woods.

"Men who can find me in the dark."

"And do you see them now?"

"No."

"Then we shall all be able to sleep."

But the trees seemed closer now, as I stood and listened to Livy's even breathing. The rough, curved horizon was dark against the dim gray sky. Snow fell invisibly through the air, filling the woods, covering the lawn with gray.

In the morning I dressed warmly and put on my boots in the vestibule before anyone else was up.

"Where are you going?" Tricia asked, surprising me, barefooted, on the kitchen steps.

"For a walk."

"Can I come?"

"You may come after breakfast. Will you tell your mother where I've gone?"

"Why can't I come now?"

"There will be tracks in the snow," I said. "You can follow me later."

The snow had stopped, and low clouds hung along the flanks of the hills. I plodded straight across the white lawn and, near the gazebo, crossed the tracks of two deer. Beyond that, at the edge of the yard where the tall dead grass replaced the manicured lawn, I found the wingprints of quail.

A slight breeze stirred snow from the trees, and it trickled down through the branches onto my face. My footsteps crackled leaves under the snow, and once out of sight of the house, I paused and listened. Far away a truck's engine whined, spinning wheels, and when that stopped, the whole world was silent, and the gray trees and spiny limbs and the whiteness filled me. My father had often taken me here, even in winter, pointing out the small details—woodpeckers' holes or the tracks of mice. The stream swirled lazily over rocks and black logs, and I sat on a snowy boulder and watched the water flow. Not much had changed, except the trails had grown over and the water in the stream was low. I sat for a long time, watching the slow current curl among the rocks, wondering what did happen to the invisible creatures in the water, and waiting for Tricia to come to me.

ABOUT THE AUTHOR

Kent Nelson grew up in Colorado and is the author of two previous novels, *Cold Wind River* and *All Around Me Peaceful*, and a collection of short stories, *The Tennis Player*. His new novel, *Language in the Blood*, has just been released by Gibbs Smith, Publisher. Over seventy of his short stories have been published in magazines and literary journals. He has been awarded two NEA grants and an Ingram Merrill Fellowship, and has received many honors for his fiction, including a Pushcart prize, five PEN Syndicated Fiction selections, and the prestigious Emily Clark Balch Prize from *The Virginia Quarterly Review*. His work has twice been anthologized in *The Best American Short Stories*. He currently lives in New Hampshire with his wife and family.